CW00956249

On the Edge

On the Edge

Sebastian Beaumont

Millivres Books
Brighton

First published in 1991 by Millivres Books (Publishers)
33 Bristol Gardens, Brighton BN2 5JR, East Sussex, England

Copyright (C) Sebastian Beaumont 1991

ISBN 1 873741 00 6

Typeset by Hailsham Typesetting Services, 4-5 Wentworth House,
George Street, Hailsham, East Sussex BN27 1AD

Printed by Billing & Sons Ltd, Worcester

Distributed in the United Kingdom and in Western Europe by
Turnaround Distribution Co-Op Ltd, 27 Horsell Road, London N5 1XL

for Simon Lovat

ACKNOWLEDGEMENTS

To Lynda Del Sasso and Simon Lovat for their help with my manuscript, and to Peter Burton, my editor.

ONE

As I dashed to the house, cold rain chattering on the pavement, the air was full of wetness and decay. Dusk wallowed beneath a heavy sky. A taut line of pale mauve seared the horizon lighting the dark, yellow-edged clouds from below as they disgorged their January rain, under-bellies almost brushing the taller buildings of the city – York Minster, Clifford's Tower, All Saints. Micklegate Bar, whose luminous sandstone was already part dissolved by more than half a millenium of rain, seemed to rock in the fluctuating light like an autistic child. Gargoyles leered from the arch that straddled the insistent, cheerless traffic.

It was a time for peculiar deaths, or the discovery of improbable and painful secrets. I briefly imagined my mother comforting a grieving relative in the front room, or a bailiff standing at the door waiting to recover bad debts. But, breathless with premonition, I was unprepared to find the hallway bare.

The pigeon-grey wallpaper had faded so much over the years that darker squares and rectangles glared out from where the pictures had hung. With an involuntary gesture, I pressed my palm to one of these vacant squares. Here my favourite piece had been suspended from stiff wire and enclosed in a plain wooden frame. Now only a dusty ghost of it clung to the wall. The hall, like the museum where I worked, had always had an inviolable permanence about it, a sanctity. It had been a shrine to my father, to the the past.

'Mother!' I called.

Emily barked excitedly and chased after me as I went to hang my coat in the cloakroom. She pawed me without restraint, not understanding why I wouldn't give her my full attention.

'Mother, where are my father's paintings?'

1

She appeared from the back of the house, unconcerned. Her creased face, powdered like a dusted rum truffle, held no warmth.

'Ah,' she said, gleefully, 'the paintings!'

With a peculiar crab-like gesture she beckoned me towards the sitting room.

'There,' she breathed, 'all of them. I'm putting them up for sale.'

I held my breath as I stared at the stack of paintings leaning against the settee. They looked severed somehow, discarded.

'I had someone round from Bratt's today. Apparently it'll take months to set up an auction.'

She went back to the kitchen, leaving me in a cloying haze of Blue Grass – a scent she only wore on special occasions. I sat on the carpet and counted the pictures. There were thirty-four. Thirty-four paintings that constituted the tangible presence of my father. It was inconceivable that they could be picked from the walls like flesh from a carcass and sold to the highest bidder. Looking at the jostling frames made me feel as if I was suffocating and I suddenly had to get out.

Emily, responding to a low whistle, was eager for an impromptu walk. At least she was unaffected by the flushing-out of my father. She held her head high in the arrogant way that Dalmatians do, and haughtily allowed me to attach her retractable lead.

Outside, the rain had stopped though the gutter babbled towards the park. Emily quickly realised that I was upset and she walked passively beside me as far as the grass where, released from the lead, she sprinted away from me as though to disassociate herself from my mood, and began to nose around distant bushes. I saw her only as a pale movement in the gloom, dotting randomly here and there. My feelings were indistinct, shadowy, confused. I visualised the now-empty hall as a counterpart of myself, stripped bare inside, torn from the remains of my father.

The pictures were all I had. I didn't have any real memories to cling to. My father died just after my first birthday and now, aged nineteen, I had very little insight into this talented man, except for an intimate knowledge of every brush stroke, colour, shade, and nuance of his paintings.

Later, I sat with my mother at the heavy mahogany dining table eating a pale stew. We drank wine from a decanter that my mother filled from a wine box in the kitchen, and we ate off heavy antique china. I gazed distractedly at the walls. There had been seven of my father's paintings in the dining room. Now there were none. My mother absently tapped the table with her chipped, peach-painted fingernails.

'But why sell all of them?' I asked her.

'I couldn't bear to sell only a few,' she replied. 'It was all or nothing in the end. I should have sold them years ago, instead of scraping by with what little money I've got. And the other house is a joke. The surveyors say it's going to cost at least thirty-five thousand to put everything right.'

My mother was a landlady. She owned a large Regency house in Bernard Terrace that was split into five flats, and she used the rent that these generated to support an equally large house in the same terrace for just the two of us. Her tenants were constantly complaining of faulty guttering, leaks, rotting windows, bad wiring, crumbling plaster; and my mother was always complaining about being harassed. In the end they had gone to the council, who had sent someone round.

'And where am I going to find that sort of money unless I sell your father's paintings?'

'Move to a smaller house?' I suggested. 'Take out a mortgage.'

'I don't want any trouble or upheaval.'

I shrugged. I'd have been happy to live in a caravan if only I could be surrounded by my father's work.

'Anyway,' my mother said, 'I've never really liked them.'

I wasn't ready to hear this. I had always assumed that my mother felt the same way about the pictures as I did. That is to say, reverently, almost religiously attached to them. To even consider that anyone might dislike them

3

was a kind of blasphemy.

'And what about the sculpture?' I asked her. 'What are you going to do with that?'

'If you mean the little marble abstraction, I'm selling that too.'

'But it's mine! You gave it to me.'

'When? I don't remember.'

'You promised years ago, when I was a kid.'

'I'm sorry Peter, it's gone. They took it today to show to some man in Sheffield. He's going to value it.'

Value! I thought. Surely the value was incalculable and had nothing to do with money.

'My father is not merchandise!' I cried, 'and that statue was mine.'

My mother looked at me with her tired eyes.

'I've never said you could have it.'

I could always tell when she was lying because she was so bad at it, and it intrigued and annoyed me that she was lying about this. But instead of challenging her, I pointedly ignored her and went upstairs to bathe and change – to get ready to go out for the evening with my friend Martin.

My bedroom looked anonymous without the three silent works of art to give it meaning. It made me feel like a stranger there, an imposter unable to retrieve the real inhabitant. I crossed to the mantelpiece and stood looking at the empty space where the largest of the three paintings had hung. There was a long, dusty cobweb hanging from the dark nail and I brushed it away with a lover's touch. The nail wouldn't come out when I pulled at it – the head was jagged and rusty and I couldn't get a grip on it. Instead I placed my palm over it and pressed, gently at first, but then harder. The sharp pain brought tears to my eyes, tears that were appropriate in spite of this method of achieving them. They were a token of respect for my father's work.

When I took my hand away there was a thick drop of blood welling on the palm. I stared at it, thinking briefly how vibrantly red it was – how suitable for an artist's palette.

Later, I reclined in the shimmering heat of a deep bath, as hot as I could bear. I lay with eyes open in complete darkness and let the tight feelings of anger dissipate through my pores. In that blinded state I seemed to be sinking down, dissolving into a sensual buoyancy. There was something sexual about the feeling of heat and the pressing weight of water.

I imagined a man, a tall man, much taller than myself, wearing nothing but a towel round his waist. It was my father-brother-lover. And seeing as I had neither a father nor a brother, the sexual dynamics of this stranger were electrifying. He was my protector, my guide, my mischievous prankster – my brash internal voice – and in my fantasy I was ravished by this other-worldly emissary, lost in a breathless whirl of movement.

Afterwards, in a pulse of heat, I reached for the light chord and extinguished this fantasy in a wash of light. I lay back and watched the cum, suspended in tremulous threads through the water, attaching itself to the fine blond hairs on my legs, balls, navel.

I liked to walk to Martin's digs along the city walls, but they were always locked at dusk, and so I walked in their medieval shadow on the wet pavement of Nunnery Lane. The pale illuminated crenellations rose effortlessly in their permanence towards the orange-tinged sky. If only life were as stable, I thought, as I passed beneath the wall at Victoria Bar; if only there could be something in my life that was solid and lasting. But nothing, it seemed, was certain, nothing could be relied on. I'd relied on my father's paintings, without even realising my dependence, and now, walking through the clammy air, I felt suddenly alone.

Martin and I were going to a party, so I'd dressed carefully in faded but not yet ripped Levi 501's, crepe soled suede brogues and a thick denim shirt. I had topped this off with a red and white neckerchief, dark glasses, and rigidly gelled hair. I looked clean, moneyed, sure of myself and, I thought, terribly, terribly young. Outwardly I had an arrogant, set expression that covered a timid sexual insecurity visible only in my eyes, so neatly obscured by Ray Bans.

Tonight, beneath my painfully inscrutable expression, there was some kind of tidal force at work. It had been instigated by the removal of my father's pictures and was gradually building up inside me. It was a flow away from my mother, away from the house we shared, away from the cosy security of York, and into that dark, abstract world that had so completely obscured my father. It was a world that contained frightening choices, frightening perspectives. A world bounded by that jagged, enormous word: 'art'.

Art. It is something that gives me no clues, that suffocates me with conflicting viewpoints. It destroyed my father, but in its squalidness and baseness there is a grandeur that rises above all else. I would have given almost anything to have been a painter too, and resented the fact that I had no artistic talent. Martin, however, had talent enough for both of us and was following his creative vocation, studying on an art foundation course in Leeds.

On one hand I was absurdly jealous of him, and on the other I felt myself to be above the rather immature way that artists often behave. Whatever my feelings, Martin's creativity was the root of our friendship. Through him I could feel that I was associated with the art world – and consequently my father.

But artists are strange. They deal in the contradictory currency of feelings. On one hand they analyse and analyse, and on the other they are spontaneous and intuitive. Martin was no exception. I could see an emotional instability in him, and could feel one in myself. The difference between us was that I was trying to live without provoking my instability, whilst Martin was prodding his, poking it, exacerbating it in order to gain inspiration from it. Even now, without ever having seen a life devastated by the burning intensity of internalised emotion, I could sense the danger of it.

Martin was waiting in the hallway of his digs when I arrived. He was wearing a wing collared shirt, white bow

6

tie and tails.

'Do you like them?' he asked, flicking up his tailcoat. 'All I need now is a piano stool. Or a dance floor,' he added, giving an impromptu and almost convincing impression of a tap-dancer, clattering his shoes over the tiled floor of the hall. He stopped, smiled, then pushed me through the front door. Once on the street, he took my elbow.

'I found this lot in a second hand shop down behind the market today. Steph and I skipped life drawing. We had more important things to do.'

'Like what?'

'This and that. We went and had tea in a brilliant café near the station. I'll take you there when you're next in Leeds. We talked about all sorts of things, but mostly men. Actually, we spent a long time talking about you.'

'Me?'

'Only because we were bored.'

'What did you say about me?'

'Oh, the usual. That you're insanely attractive, blushingly innocent, still cooped up in your mother's house. I told Steph that you were ripe for a tragic love affair, a passionate romance with a decadent painter. She thought I was referring to her, but of course I wasn't. I was referring to myself.'

I laughed.

'Don't flatter yourself,' I told him. 'And don't forget Anna.'

'She doesn't count,' he said dismissively. 'She's still at school, and besides, you've hardly even kissed her yet.'

We walked through the sepulchral darkness, past the many churches on Bishopshill, and on up The Mount. There was something nostalgic about the breath that misted round my lips; something surreal about walking through night-time streets whilst wearing sunglasses. Martin was only being scathing about Anna because he was jealous that, after years of the opposite being true, I had a lover and he didn't. But tonight he was cheerful to the point of spontaneous laughter and I watched him as he walked quickly, blatantly, his dark eyes only just discernible in the deep shadow across his face, his dark, straight hair limned by passing headlights.

"Insanely attractive," I thought and tried to smile. But I was feeling suddenly dull, tarnished by the news of the forthcoming auction. I walked on, making an attempt to respond to Martin's high spirits.

'Okay,' Martin said, stopping beside a wildly overgrown privet hedge, 'what's the matter, Peter? Why the sudden gloom? You're not worried about tonight are you?'

'No, no,' I said, 'it's nothing like that.'

I brushed my hand along a trailing branch, causing a spray of cold drops to scatter across the pavement. I looked down at my hands which glistened, wet and streaked with grime from touching the ancient hedge.

'It's my father,' I said quietly.

I explained about the sale. I also tried to explain something of my feelings, but they were too complicated for me to understand, let alone to put into words for someone else. I felt a sense of loss, of betrayal, of tragedy and, more strangely, rejection. I jumbled together a vaguely coherent sentence or two, my confusion and misery quite obvious.

'This is ridiculous!' he exclaimed. 'Your mother must be mad. She can't sell all of them.'

'She can,' I assured him.

'But they must be worth a packet. She doesn't need to sell them all.'

I shrugged, feeling suddenly overwhelmed by a powerlessness that was dangerously close to lethargy.

'Sod it,' I said, kicking at the low wall in front of me, 'let's go to the party.'

Martin put his arm round my shoulder for a moment. I looked at him, his profile etched against the sky – full lips, thoughtful chin, rounded nose.

'I know,' he said. 'I know how much they mean to you.'

And I knew he knew. Of all the people I had ever shown my father's paintings, Martin was the only one who had felt their strength, their dark sensuality, their pull. Before our 'A' levels, he had brought round some incense and we had sat in front of the three paintings in my bedroom, Martin meditating about art and me worrying about my exams. It had been like that always, Martin seeing a deeper sense in things, trying to capture different feelings, different atmospheres. Now, as we stopped to buy some wine, I realised how completely I had taken him for granted through all those years at school.

'Come on,' I said, feeling suddenly tired of brooding, 'let's go and have some fun.'

'Good,' Martin replied, nodding. 'That's better.'

I could feel a reckless cheerfulness welling up in me that bordered on hysteria, and we walked up the last rise singing together as a ragged moon, smokey yellow and low on the horizon, pulled itself free from the rooftops. We stopped at a detached Victorian villa overshadowed by beech and holly, its sandstone porch streaked with green, its short drive soft with leaf mould; an entrance to some gothic dream. It was an image not lost on Martin, who paused to absorb the moment before entering the building.

'Alan only owns a part of this,' he said as he rang one of the five bells. 'It's a shame. This place must have been magnificent before it was turned into flats.'

'It still is,' I said, impressed by the stained glass surrounding the front door. I caught Martin's smile then, as he looked at the approaching figure through the door.

'Yes,' he whispered, taking me by the elbow.

TWO

The door opened to reveal a tall blonde woman of about twenty-five.

'Hello Steph,' said Martin, stepping through the door and kissing her. 'I didn't think you were coming.'

'I'm staying the night here,' she said, 'so I don't have to worry about getting back to Leeds.'

She stepped aside to let us past, turning her head to look out of the door before closing it. She had shoulder length hair, tousled and ravaged by overbleaching. But she was attractive, with long arching eyebrows, a wide mouth, cool eyes.

'Hello,' she said, 'you must be Peter.'

'Yes,' I said.

She held out her hand with sudden formality, and I shook it, feeling without any particular reason that this moment was more important than I could ever know. Then she dropped my hand, leaned forward and kissed me on the cheek.

'There,' she said, smiling a wide smile, 'it's always so much easier to be on kissing terms.'

She reached out almost shyly and eased my sunglasses off, folding them and putting them in my shirt pocket.

'That's better,' she said. 'A person thinks through their eyes, and it's so mysterious if you can't see them. You have such beautiful eyes too.'

'Of course he has,' laughed Martin. 'But don't embarrass him.'

'I'm not embarrassed,' I said.

Steph took our bottles of wine, then led us across the clinically clean hallway and into the nearest flat. It was disappointingly characterless, having been restructured, replastered, redecorated. It could have been any expensive flat anywhere, except for the magnificent bay window in

10

the lounge which reared up to the ceiling like an exhibit in a museum, so old and characterful, and so out of place in that immaculate room. It had no curtains, only shutters which had yet to be closed. On the newly upholstered window seat sat a girl, all brightly dressed in dazzling bits and pieces. She was wearing a scarf, a shawl, a skirt with a drape over it. Bright strands of material were twisted through her long, ringletted hair, tied round her wrists and ankles, pinned to her clothes.

'Who's that?' I whispered, struck by her peculiarly timeless appearance.

'Coll,' Steph whispered back, 'she's eighteen. She's on the foundation course with me and Martin. She's one of Alan's little finds.'

Martin said something that I didn't catch, then a drink was thrust into my hand and Martin dragged me off for a round of introductions. He knew about half the people there, almost all of them from the art world. But the introductions were useless to me because they came too fast and I ended up remembering no one. I drank two large glasses of wine very quickly, but they didn't help me to relax.

Alan, the host, turned out to be a formless man, physically average in every way. He was of medium height and medium build, with light brown hair and tired, hazel eyes set in a gently ageing face. He was the sort of man you would have trouble describing later, because everything about him was deferential, receding, diminishing. Yet he commanded the biggest arts budget in Yorkshire, and maybe the North of England.

'Is he gay?' I whispered to Martin, after looking round the room for clues and finding none.

'Yes,' Martin nodded, 'and absolutely rampant I'm told, though he hasn't tried anything on with me. Yet.'

I smiled and looked at this benign middle aged man. I couldn't imagine him being rampant about anything.

'So, what's his story?' I asked.

'No good,' Martin said. 'He's not inspiring enough. Pick someone else.'

It was a game of ours to try and guess the private lives of other people, a habit we had developed over years of travelling to and from school by bus.

'That girl over there?' I suggested.

'Coll? Okay. You first.'

'Fine,' I said, thinking hard as I looked her up and down. 'Of course, she's the result of an immaculate conception, found starving but quite composed beneath a rock in one of the remotest corners of the Amazon rainforest. Her discoverers were an Austrian princess and an Eastern cloth manufacturer, though quite why they were in a remote corner of the Amazon rainforest remains one of the great unsolved mysteries of the Twentieth Century. She was taken back to Europe, but could not conveniently be passed off as their child because they weren't married – Austrian princesses still being frowned on for begetting bastards.

'She went to school in England, chosen because it provided an excuse for the two to meet clandestinely outside their own countries. Coll's adoptive mother would send her parcels of exotic food, and her father bales of the most beautiful cloth – bright silks and satins that she cut up and made into dresses and ballgowns. As time passed, her father fell on hard times and the supply of beautiful new cloth dried up. Now she is down to her last few scraps, which she wears to the greatest possible effect, by attaching them here and there to the rest of her clothes. She's reasonably happy, waiting for her mother to whisk her back to her castle outside Vienna, where she can live a virginal life, and clothe herself in the style to which she used to be accustomed.'

'Very good,' said Martin, 'but quite wrong. She's not nearly so virginal as you seem to think. She's a heartbreaker. See the way she's listening to that man, her mouth slightly open as though in innocent wonder. Well, it's all a front. She's out for a challenge. She lost her virginity aged fourteen to a senior at her school. She accepted his money, presents, and adoration, then discarded him for someone else. That's what she's like –

will always be like... '

The man who had been talking to Coll moved off to speak to someone else, and she crossed the room to where we were standing.

'Come on,' she said, 'I know I'm fascinating, but I'm not that fascinating. Why are you two so interested?'

'We were wondering about your inner secrets,' Martin told her.

'I don't believe you Martin,' she said, then turned to look directly at me.

'Who are you?'

'My name's Peter,' I told her. 'I work in a museum.'

'Mmm,' she said, then turned to Martin.

'Right,' she smiled. 'I want to talk to you about Alan. Come on, over here. We'll sit in the window.'

Martin gave the slightest of shrugs as he looked at me, then he followed her. They sat together in that great window as though posed for a classical portrait, Martin fastidiously neat in tie and tails, and Coll such a surfeit of colour as to be almost overwhelming. Her fragile face was pale to the point of being geisha, and her eyes, darkly edged, trailed their way round the room as Martin spoke. She glanced at me, paused, asked Martin a question, then laughed. He laughed too, and turned to smile at me.

I wondered what they were saying, feeling madly curious and infuriatingly excluded. I wanted to be sitting with them, to be included in their laughter. It made me feel unsure of myself and aware that, apart from Martin, I knew no one here. I drained my glass, feeling uncertain about what to do next. The obvious thing was to go and introduce myself to someone, but I was too shy – couldn't think of anything to say. I closed my eyes and started to count to ten.

When I open my eyes, I thought, I'll do something.

On seven I felt a hand touching my arm. It was Steph.

'Are you alright?' she asked.

'Yes, fine,' I told her.

'You just looked a little strange, standing there with an empty glass in your hand and your eyes closed.'

'I was plucking up courage to go and talk to someone,' I said.

'Problem solved,' she smiled. 'Come and talk to me. What are you drinking?

'White wine,' I told her and she took my glass, steering me past several groups of people to an array of bottles jostling on a small table.

'Can I ask you a question?' she asked as she filled my glass.

'Of course.'

'Are you gay?'

I smiled a kind of off-beat smile.

'Why do you ask?'

'Because you're a friend of Martin's. I thought that might be how you met him.'

'No, we were at school together,' I said. 'I've known him for years.'

'I see,' she said, with a gaze of intimate knowledge. 'You're not like Martin,' she said mysteriously, without further explanation.

We talked about York and my work at the museum, but I wasn't interested in talking about myself and soon turned the conversation. I now knew from Martin that she was twenty six, and that seemed old to me. I couldn't imagine ever being twenty six. I was like a junior who had just arrived at school trying to imagine being a prefect. It seemed a lifetime away.

'Why did you decide to go to art school?' I asked her. 'After all, you must have done other things first.'

'I'm a dancer,' she said, then winced slightly as if at a gaffe. 'That is to say I was a dancer. I should have had a good few years in me yet if I hadn't been injured. It's my knee, you see. I've always had a weak cruciate ligament at the back, and it finally gave up last spring right in the middle of a performance. It was a spectacular exit, but painful. I was in plaster for a month, which left me jobless and careerless. Still, it could have been worse – I might have been a talented dancer.'

She laughed an ironic laugh.

14

'The injury doesn't affect my walking, but it's stopped me from ever dancing again.'

'Isn't there some sort of cure?'

'There are two treatments, one which works and one which is more dubious for someone who is going to work their knee as much as a dancer does. The first isn't available in this country, and the second is. I can't afford to go to the States for a private operation. So here I am, at art school.'

'I'm sorry,' I told her, wondering what it must feel like to have a career slip from one's grasp, and thinking of the empty spaces on the walls at home.

'I don't regret it,' said Steph. 'I was always torn between dancing and painting. Now I'll have had a chance to do both. Not many people can say that about their lives.'

'You seem to have taken it all very well.'

She dipped her head in assent, an assertive light in her eyes, an almost aggressive happiness visible in her manner.

'I didn't see it like that at first,' she said. 'I even thought of killing myself at the time. But I respect myself too much to ever do something like that. I've known dancers who have just given up when they can't dance any more; people who rush into marriage or tedious jobs, then waste away in their own self-pity. I've always rather despised people like that, so it was only pride that made me drag myself back up. Now that I have, I don't care what the reason was. I feel stronger than ever.'

She touched my arm again, lightly, affectionately, then kissed me on the cheek.

'I don't usually tell people this,' she said, 'but you've got a non-judgemental face that makes me want to confess things to you.'

This seemed terribly funny and I found myself laughing at her.

'Don't laugh,' she said. 'I mean it. I know these things because I'm the same. There are some people that other people open up to.

'And it's not easy being a born listener,' she went on. 'Not in the long run. At first you get very close to people very quickly, and that's a good thing. But then people start making demands on you, calling round late at night, or phoning you for hours on end. And of course, the biggest problem for people like us is that we can never bring ourselves to tell other people to go away and leave us alone.'

Perhaps she was right. I wanted to believe that she was right simply in order to believe something about myself. And talking about "people like us" in that way made us fellow conspirators. I seemed to already have a certain intimacy with her, an instinctive connection with her. Of course I was unused to being kissed in the way that she had kissed me a minute or two before. It hadn't been a formal kiss, nor a sexual kiss. It had been a simple expression of tenderness, of warmth, and I responded by feeling an absolute trust in her, perhaps even the first glimmerings of an infatuation with her.

I now realised something about my relationship with Anna. This evening – this conversation with Steph – would have been impossible in her presence. She inhabited a separate part of my life, compartmentalised into an exquisite box that I could remove and open at will, but which I hid from those around me. It was as if I still feared to be laughed at for going through the kind of adolescently incompatible fling that others had grown out of years before.

We talked some more about other things that I can no longer remember. Afterwards I was left with a vivid recollection of Steph's face – open, interested, intelligent – and a memory of Coll sitting talking to Martin and glancing at me from time to time. But what stays with me most is the haunting impression of having been opened, of having some previously closed space inside me prised apart, fractionally, painfully; not enough for revelation, but enough to give me an inkling that there was a space. I felt as though I had become active, like an unexploded bomb. Steph had somehow reached into me and lighted a fuse. I could feel it sparkling away inside me, feel instinctively that there must inevitably be an explosion, but I was unsure as to what it would be, when it would happen, and why.

THREE

I walked to work the next day feeling hungover and lingeringly randy. I had masturbated on waking – a desultory pleasure fogged by sleep and the pulse of a headache – but it hadn't relieved my lust, which still lay inside me like an unscratched itch. It clouded my brief walk with Emily, made me feel a whole world apart from my mother.

Three mugs of tea and half a litre of orange juice at breakfast helped to clear my head, but I didn't have time to masturbate a second time, and so left for work with an erection. I wasn't usually as keyed up as this, and put it down to my meeting with Steph the previous evening. She had certainly captivated me with her talk, her easy intimacy, and her relaxed confidence. It had surprised and flattered me when she had said that I was cool, handsome; someone to confide in. I was not good at taking compliments and blushed now at the thought of her sincerity.

I took the back entrance to the museum, remembering the thrill I'd felt only three months before when I'd started working there. Then, it had made me feel that I'd crossed the invisible dividing line between adolescence and adulthood, and the symbol of this transition was the simple notice on the back door which said: PRIVATE. STAFF ONLY.

Through that door lay the esoteric world of adulthood, in all its formality, bureaucracy, responsibility and triviality. In becoming familiar with it I realised that nothing had changed from my school days; that people were exactly the same. They had a new set of codes by which they expressed themselves. This closed grown-up world had impressed me when younger, but I now realised that these codes were invented to give the appearance of friendly cooperation, whilst preserving a complete estrangement. In the three months I'd been there I hadn't got to know anyone. Careful observation had revealed that ambition, rivalry and petty jealousies still existed, but were masked in a politeness that smacked, to me, of hypocrisy.

There were eight people in the Social History Project, as my department was called, and I was the youngest by seven years. They treated me as a child, and I didn't know how to make them change their attitude towards me.

The work itself was interesting enough – trying to work out what people's lives were like at various times in the past, so that accurate reconstructions could be made. There was drudgery; working through index files, catalogues and so on, but there were times when something fascinating would crop up, or when I had to deal with objects and original manuscripts. There were also trips to other museums, visits to archives, and field work, so I felt satisfied that I was embarking on the right career, and had even surprised myself once or twice by feeling a hint of vocation.

The first thing I did on arrival that day was go to the toilet and masturbate as briefly and as functionally as possible. It was satisfying in a certain sense, but even this kind of satiety didn't completely dull my physical ache for some kind of meaningful sexual contact. When I came, I found myself besieged by a feeling of depression and wasted opportunity, of life passing me by. I wanted more than this. I wanted more than my one-evening-a-week relationship with Anna. I wanted more than the quiet understatement of our lovemaking – the childish play-acting that we had fallen into.

As I sat at my desk, I wondered what my colleagues would think if they knew that only moments before I had wiped a nacreous strand of semen from the highly polished wood of the toilet floor. Perhaps I was not the only one that used the toilet for this purpose, but I didn't think of my colleagues as capable of that kind of thing. They were all too old, too unattractive, or too boring for me to be able to imagine them as having any kind of sexual

19

feelings at all.

My sexual feelings were so expansive and uninformed as to be more confusing than anything else. They encompassed an image of myself as a small boy waiting to be seduced, but also of a grown man ready to do the seducing. I tried not to become obsessed by thoughts of sex and ended up sublimating them into yearnings for a new relationship, though I didn't have a clear idea what kind of relationship I might be looking for.

Shrugging at these thoughts, I turned to my work: a register of employment at Nelson's brickworks from 1855 to 1865. Not the most gripping of documents, but it would give another angle on the local population. I looked round the room to see if there were any possible distractions before I settled down to work. But there were only three people in the office this morning. Maggie, my boss, who looked fiercely intent on searching for information on the departmental computer; Judy, who was working on producing an authentic wardrobe of clothes for a Victorian gentlewoman – to be used in future social history projects – and myself. The others were either out, or in the basement store rooms.

Today, before finally starting, I managed to find a distraction. On the desk next to mine there was a small pile of black-bordered envelopes. They were held together by an elastic band and accompanied by a note addressed to me. I picked them up and read the message:

> Peter,
> Thanks for letting me see these. They are certainly strange, but otherwise of no great value to us. I've taken photocopies of them just in case, and trust you don't mind.
> Mark B (Archives)

I now removed the elastic band and spread the letters out on the surface in front of me. There were ten in all, each addressed to Mr and Mrs R B Shanklin, Marston Farm, Nr Upper Poppleton, York. The stamps were pale orange or light green, and bore the heads of either Queen Victoria or King Edward VII. They were dated from 1897 to 1905.

Each envelope contained a letter of sympathy. I took one out:

Hammerton House
August 7th 1902

My Dear Robert and Mary,
Arthur and I were so sorry to hear of your terrible loss. Margaret will always be remembered as a gentle child, a kind member of the community, and a dear friend to our son James. Please accept our deepest sympathy, and do not hesitate to call on us if there is anything we can do.
Yours Sincerely
Miriam Eardly.

The letters were all like this – bland sympathy notes concerning different people who had died – but they brought back a trail of memories. I could clearly recall finding them with Martin when we were perhaps ten or eleven. We had gone for a seven mile walk from Martin's house and had set off cross-country. After a couple of miles or so, we had found a derelict farmhouse. The front two rooms were being used for storing sacks of fertilizer and were locked, but the back room and the kitchen were open.

It was a bizarre moment of time dislocation to walk through that back door into the kitchen. Thick dust lay over everything. There was a sturdy kitchen table in the centre of the room, a cracked pudding bowl, an ancient bottle of iodine, an almost disintegrated tube of Vim and, rather alien amongst these domestic objects, a gas mask with a rotten leather strap. A pile of old syringes – the large sort used for vaccinating cows – lay beside the rusted sink. Martin picked up several and stuffed them in his pocket (to be used as water pistols later). Then we turned to look at the gas mask. Neither of us were shy about trespassing, but that mask seemed to be sitting there watching us with its great round eyes and pig-snout mouthpiece. My memory of that kitchen is like that of a faded photograph, or a film in slow motion. It was like one fantastically long held breath, walking round the place, frightened to touch anything because our fingerprints would be so visible in the dust.

There was a simple door on the other side of the fireplace, which we opened. Inside was a pantry with empty shelves and a red-tiled floor almost completely obscured by letters. All of them were black-edged and ancient, greying in the dry air. Martin and I stood and stared at them for a long time before I slowly bent down to pick some up. The letters themselves were uninteresting, written on smart stationery. What was extraordinary was the quantity – there must have been hundreds – and the fact that they were here in this old farmhouse.

We took ten letters each, and referred to them ever afterwards as the Death Letters. We bragged about them at school and, a year or so later, went back to get some more. But by then the farmhouse had been gutted by builders and was being renovated. The incident made a strong impression on me, despite the trivial way we glamorised it to our peers. I kept my letters virtually untouched, whilst Martin cut out the stamps for his collection and threw the envelopes and their contents away.

I kept one letter on my mantelpiece and made up stories about the man – Reginald Shanklin – who had died. I imagined that he had been killed in the Boer war. That he was drowned in the Ouse whilst out boating. That he'd committed suicide as the result of a love affair. I built up a strong visual image of Reginald and, as time passed, he became more and more like my father, whose face I had only seen infrequently in magazines. (My mother didn't keep photos of him in the house.) I took comfort from this other man, because I could invest him with the personality that I would have liked my father to have had, but which I couldn't project onto him for fear of turning him from an image of perfection into a human being.

Reginald had had a whole life, completed by the facts of

his birth and his death. I was determined to make my life whole too, in a way that my father's life had never been. Of course he had died, but his life had been so unfairly truncated that death wasn't the final settling of a full life, as I then thought it should be. Death for him had been a harbinger of unfinished business. Business which included his painting, but which also included me. Reginald, I decided, had been a father – a good father – and he'd had a son just like me.

After work I went to see Anna with Martin's words still echoing in my ears – "She doesn't count."

'Hi,' she said when I arrived, 'mum and dad are going on from Asda to play bridge tonight, so they won't be back before nine-thirty at the earliest.'

She had cooked a mushroom quiche which we ate whilst watching Neighbours on tv. Afterwards we made love upstairs like the shy adolescents that we were, trapped within our own indecipherable sexual language and bound by the confines of ill-conceived endearment. And for the first time I felt that it was all empty. It wasn't what Martin had said about Anna that plagued me – it was the absolute certainty with which he'd said it. And in the light of his certainty, I became certain too. Something about our relationship was a sham. We both wanted to play at being in love, and we had fallen into the trap of never asking each other what we felt or what we wanted. Our lines of communication had never been established and I was making love to a stranger.

It brought a sad smile to my lips when we went downstairs again and Anna produced a cake. It had two candles on it.

'Two months,' she said. 'One candle for each month. One for you and one for me.'

She blew out the first candle and held the cake out to me. A single flame wavered before my eyes, the very essence of vulnerability and, as I blew, it seemed that life's precariousness was perfectly illustrated in that moment of extinction.

'There,' I said and smiled again at Anna's complete seriousness.

It struck me that there was something obscene about Anna's childish vision of what love was and what love should be. As she cut the cake, her long mid-brown hair falling forwards, I realised that for her the cake represented her love for me. She placed her love in material things because material things couldn't tell her what she didn't want to know – that she was being childishly idealistic by falling in love with an image that I conveniently fitted, so long as there was no close emotional inspection.

Perhaps I was being cynical. But I knew that love could never be like this. I knew that people like Anna would always look for fairytale princes instead of human beings, and find them in the most impossible places. I could look at her pale complexion and her dark eyes and know that she didn't see me. She saw her vision of someone else that she had superimposed on me. She saw in me her hope that I might be perfect.

There was something unbruised and patiently virginal about the way she smiled, and it made me feel sad and guilty to know I would be the first of many that would hurt her. It made me angry too, because I knew I could never be perfect, that because of her peculiar emotional blindness, no matter how hard I tried, I would inevitably hurt her.

But I needed her to prove to myself that I was sexually responsible; that I was not insecure. I proved nothing, of course, except that orgasms are not the final or utmost pinnacle of life's achievements.

I left her house at twenty past nine so as to avoid her parents, who didn't like her seeing me during the week, not with 'A' levels coming up. But instead of going home to those lonely bare walls, I called round at Martin's digs.

'Come on in,' he said when he opened the door. 'I'm just having a beer with Geoff and Lynn.'

He steered me into the little front sitting room. Geoff and Lynn were Martin's landlords. They lived in a small terraced house just within the city walls. They were

24

intelligent, congenial, and happy to have Martin as a lodger, accepting his homosexuality in a way that surprised me and, strangely, slightly shocked me. I liked them, but found them too serious at times.

Their sitting room was decorated with African carvings and wall hangings, and looked alternative in a pre-packaged sort of way. Geoff and Lynn were sitting together on the sofa. A middle aged man was sitting beside them on an upholstered bamboo seat. Geoff jumped up as I came into the room.

'Hello there,' he said, smiling broadly. 'How about a beer?'

'Thanks.'

'This is Sam Meakin by the way. He's an antique dealer.'

'He was very interested to hear about your father's paintings going up for sale,' Martin told me.

'Oh,' I said, 'I'm not sure anything should have been said about that yet.'

'Don't worry,' Sam told me with flagrant insincerity, 'I won't tell anyone.'

Geoff handed me a glass of beer and held my eye for a second longer than he needed to. He had an unfashionable Eighties' haircut, untidy on top and short at the back. He had a thin nose and pursed lips so that he seemed to be passing incisive judgement on everything. I often caught him giving me sideways glances when I went round, and wondered briefly whether he fancied me. But I'm no good at working out that sort of thing, so didn't pursue the idea.

'So,' Sam asked, 'what's your mother going to do with all the money she's going to get when she sells the paintings?'

'I don't think she's thought of it. I don't think she's got any real idea how much they're worth. And neither have I for that matter,' I added, sadly aware that this man was thinking of the paintings merely as saleable products.

'Paul Ellis is doing rather well in London at the moment,' said Sam. 'Not that there's much of his work about. I only really know something of him because I sold one of his pictures once.'

'Oh?' Martin asked, interested. 'For how much?'

'It was about five or six years ago – I picked up one of his early landscapes for a couple of hundred at a house clearance near Durham. There was quite a lot of artwork there, some of it way beyond my pocket, but I'd heard of Paul Ellis and so I took a gamble. We sold it by auction in Manchester a month later for fifteen hundred. I would have kept it for myself if I'd known how it was going to appreciate over the next few years. The only way I'd be able to acquire a Paul Ellis now would be if your mother was giving them away.'

'She hasn't even offered me one,' I said. 'She wants to get rid of the whole lot.'

Sam shrugged.

'I'll be interested to see how it goes,' he said, 'but not as a dealer. Paul Ellis is out of my league now.'

'Tell me,' I asked him, 'do you know if my father had any reputation for sculpture?'

'I'm no expert,' said Sam, 'so I couldn't say. Why?'

'It's just that my mother has a little marble sculpture that he did at one time. It's about seven inches high, with an abstract design on it. I've always liked it and I'm wondering if it's worth much. Maybe I could buy it back at the auction.'

We talked some more about my father's work, discussed the merits of antique dealing, and then Martin and I left to go upstairs.

His was a pale room, full of drawings, watercolours, prints and paintings that he'd done – pale, subtly worked as though he had been afraid to touch the surface. It was through them that I could see his gentle side.

'Look at it all,' Martin said, referring to the piles of paper, pencils, brushes, odds and ends, trinkets... 'I'm going to have to move out of here sooner or later. There isn't enough room. Besides, it's such a hassle getting from here into Leeds every day, and it's expensive too.'

He sat on his bed whilst I reclined on the floor, resting my head against the end of his mattress. He lit a stick of rose scented incense and we watched as the threads of

26

fragrant smoke twisted between us. I felt as though something inside me was being violated. Sam's talk of having made money out of one of my father's paintings left me cold. He had never once mentioned the content, the quality or truth of the picture. He had seen it in terms of return on an investment. It made my skin crawl.

Martin turned over and lay behind me on the bed so that his face was next to mine. He took my head in his hands and kissed me at the base of my skull.

'Don't worry,' he said, 'this world's full of people like Sam. It doesn't stop there being people like us. It doesn't make your father's paintings any less, just because Sam doesn't appreciate them – can't appreciate them.'

'God,' I sighed, 'if only I could be clear exactly what I feel about all this.'

Martin sighed with me, and it seemed as if nothing was ever going to be clear again.

'I'm in a bit of trouble too,' Martin told me.

In losing myself in my own worries I had become too self-orientated. I turned to Martin and found that there was a touch of misery in his expression.

'Come on, you can tell me,' I said.

'It's Geoff,' said Martin. 'I think I'm falling in love with him.'

'Oh, surely not,' I said with a quiet laugh, thinking how only half an hour before I had decided that he wasn't attractive. But then I remembered the way he had caught and held my gaze.

Martin turned over again and lay on his back, his head lolling down over the end of the bed so that he was looking out at the silhouette of the church across the road.

'It's true,' he said. 'I wish it wasn't, but it is. And the worst thing is that I think he fancies me too.'

'But he's married,' I pointed out. 'And he's old.'

'Thirty-one,' said Martin. 'That's not old, and being married never stopped anyone. I had sex with a married man when I was fourteen.'

'You never told me.'

'No.'

27

I looked into Martin's upside-down eyes as he stared into the darkness outside. Was there the first glimmerings of a tear in the corner of his eye? His long lashes made it difficult to tell.

'Move out,' I told him. 'It's the best thing to do in the end.'

'I know,' he said. 'I know that's what I should do. But I can't bring myself to do it.'

I leant over and carefully kissed his cheek.

'Be careful,' I told him, 'that's all.'

A real tear welled up this time and he sat up abruptly to hide it.

'That's the first time you've ever done that,' he said.

'Done what?'

'Kissed me.'

'Surely not.'

'It is,' Martin assured me. 'I should know.'

'Okay,' I shrugged. 'So what?'

FOUR

Saturday was a cold dry day after a week of rain. The River Ouse rolled turbulently through the city, mud brown and restless as it sucked vigorously at the arches of Lendal Bridge. I was feeling vulnerable again. Bratt's, the auctioneers, had fixed a date later in the month for taking my father's paintings away, and I was sick of feeling bad about it. My mother's pleasure at the prospect of their removal had erected a barrier between us that was fast becoming insurmountable. I was finding it difficult to bring myself to speak to her, let alone act as if nothing had changed.

I was passing the grocery on Blake Street when I saw Coll coming out of the Stonegate Arcade. I recognised her immediately, though she was dressed more subduedly in jeans and a thick, dark coat. I speeded up and caught her as she walked into St Helen's Square.

'Hello!' I said brightly.

She stopped, turned round, then smiled.

'Oh, hello Peter. What are you doing in town?'

'I had to get a new set of headphones for my Walkman,' I said. 'And you?'

'Nothing much. Have you had lunch?'

'Not yet.'

'Have you got any money?'

'Some.'

'Do you want to take me to lunch at the Gillygate Bakery?'

'I'd be delighted,' I told her, impressed that she had the nerve to invite herself to lunch with a virtual stranger.

Coll was exactly what I needed right now – an intelligent, lively person who could draw me out of myself. I already felt I knew her, though when I thought back to the party I realised that the only words I had said to her

29

were, "my name's Peter, I work in a museum." It did her credit that she remembered my name.

When we got there we had to wait a few minutes for a table, and stood around talking. I noticed she was carrying a copy of Lady Chatterley's Lover.

'Haven't you read it?' she asked.

'No.'

'You should. It's part of our history now, our heritage.'

'I thought it was just a dirty book.'

'Don't joke about it,' she told me. 'It's a great novel. Besides, sex isn't dirty. It's ignorant to say it is.'

I nodded in meek agreement and sat down opposite her at a small table in the window. We ate lentil and celery soup with crusty wholemeal rolls, a single carnation in a jar between us.

We talked about my father, whose troubled shadow was casting itself through all my conversations these days.

'It's fate,' Coll breathed. 'I knew there was some connection between us. And how wonderful to have a painter for a father.'

'He died when I was only a year old,' I pointed out.

'All the better,' she said. 'I wish my father had died when I was that age.'

She smiled a hard, mischievous smile.

'It's awful to say that,' she said. 'But I hate my father and I don't see why I should pretend about it. Take it from me, you're lucky you haven't got one.'

'I've got a mother though, and living with her is bad enough. Especially at the moment.'

'Leave home then.'

'I can't afford to. I'm not earning enough to buy a place of my own.'

'You don't have to buy a place. Rent a room somewhere where you can be yourself. That's what I'm doing. I've got a bedsit near the station in Leeds.'

'Moving out sounds very easy when you put it like that.'

'It is easy.'

I remembered telling Martin to move out of his digs only a few days before, and realised how simple it is to seem objective about these things when you're on the outside. Martin had said he was having problems, so I'd said "move out". As easy as that. Now I had to admit that I was in the same position – but living at home was too convenient. And then there was Emily. How many people would share a house with me if I brought a dog along?

'Come on,' said Coll, 'come back to my parent's place. It's not far from here. I'm staying the weekend, but they're away until this evening.'

'Okay.'

It seemed a good idea. I didn't fancy going home at the moment, and Martin was spending the afternoon with his parents, so there was no one else for me to visit. I followed Coll under the portcullis of Bootham Bar, down High and Low Petergate. The Minster reared up beside us, crisply silhouetted against a bright expanse of sky. Pavement artists were out in force, kneeling on the cold flagstones and drawing old masters, landscapes, the faces of pop stars, or modern designs, in chalk. I looked at their pinched faces and raw hands, and thrust my own hands deeper into my coat pockets. Coll was withdrawn, and I was happy to walk in silence, happy to let the afternoon drift past.

Coll's house was newly built, samey, semi-detached, in a close of other identical houses in the shadow of the city wall. Planners, I suspected, would one day regret that such a bland cul-de-sac had ever been built in the centre of such an extraordinarily beautiful city. Coll let me into the house and waved me on up the stairs.

'First door on the left,' she told me, then disappeared into the kitchen.

I went into her room. It was dim already, with a small north facing window, walls covered in sashes, headscarves, drapes. It looked like an eastern boudoir which had been crammed into a box ten foot square. There was a deep, ingrained scent of incense to the room which made me think of Martin, though where his room had been pale, Coll's was seductively dark, richly fragrant, overwhelmingly feminine. I found it hard to believe that such an assertive person could have a room like this.

31

Coll came up a couple of minutes later, carrying two mugs of coffee. She put them on her black bedside table, then turned her convection heater full on, though the air was already warm.

'Do you like it?' she asked.

I looked round the room.

'Very much,' I told her truthfully.

'It took me ages to give it some sort of personality. But I like it now. Of course, I've taken a lot of my stuff to Leeds. I'm hoping to find a good house-share, and then I'll take the rest too.'

We were both still standing just inside the door, which Coll now closed.

'Wait there,' she said whilst she kneeled to pick a packet of incense from the floor.

'Martin burns incense too,' I told her as she lit some. She looked disappointed at this, as though her use of it should have been fascinatingly unique. She put the incense in a holder and placed it on the floor in front of the heater, then stood for a moment to watch the smoke drift upwards, catching in the warm updraught. She crossed over to her dressing table, took two short, squat candles out of the drawer and lit them, placing them on her bedside table.

She came over to me then, calmly.

'Kiss me,' she said.

I felt somehow suspended in the second before she had spoken. In some strange way it was as if she hadn't spoken.

'Kiss me,' she said again, and I couldn't suppress a smile at the suddenness of her request. As with Steph, I found myself unable to do anything but respond, without thought or judgement. Coll was five or six inches shorter than me and so I had to stoop to reach her lips. I didn't have time to worry about what I was going to do. I just kissed her.

Sex with Coll was different from sex with Anna. Coll had a control that impressed me. What she wanted, happened in a seemingly effortless way. And she liked nudity. She wanted to look at me, to watch me, and to be watched. She was unshy in the way she touched my penis; the way she dug her fingers into my thighs as though trying to squeeze something out. I was impressed and slightly shocked by her physical aggression and the way, at times, we almost seemed to be wrestling. But there was still a fundamental lack of communication. There was something unnegotiated. I was just being seduced, and though that was a thrill in itself, part of me recoiled at the thought that I was ultimately helpless.

I was disappointed at the brevity of our sexual assignation. Orgasm had arrived for me long before any real feeling of release. But Coll seemed to have derived some secret fascination from our encounter. She leaned back against her bed, sipped her lukewarm coffee and smiled at me.

'That was your first time, wasn't it?' she said.

'No,' I replied, surprised that she should make that assumption.

'Martin told me that you were a virgin.'

'Well that's typical of Martin I'm afraid.'

It annoyed me to hear this. I wondered why Martin had been so devious and I felt a flush of embarrassment creep through me.

'Don't worry,' she said.

She handed me my coffee and I took a gulp.

'As a matter of fact,' I told her, 'I have a girlfriend at the moment. Anna.'

This amused her.

'Does that matter?' she asked.

'I don't know,' I replied.

'I see,' said Coll and her eyes glinted wryly. She rolled over onto her stomach, reached for another stick of incense; lit it in the candle flame.

'When I saw you at the party,' she said, 'I knew I was going to seduce you. I decided then and there that I was going to meet you, take you home, and make love to you.'

She held the incense in front of her as she spoke, watching the glowing tip.

'As simple as that?' I said with a smile. 'But what if I

33

hadn't bumped into you?'

'Then I would have phoned you up or something. I hadn't really thought about that side of it, I knew it was going to happen. That it was our destiny.'

'Our destiny?'

'Yes. I knew it was our destiny to love each other.'

I walked home that evening with a feeling of having started something I might not be able to stop – some blind emotional momentum that had a stark inevitability about it. Anna was coming round to the house in Bernard Terrace the next day and I didn't know what I was going to tell her.

But detached from my immediate worries, there was a part of me that ignored these superficial ideas, that couldn't have cared less what happened tomorrow. It boggled about what I had just done, crowed excitedly that I was unusual, enticing, that I had obviously captivated Coll with my looks. I hadn't talked to her at the party, so there was nothing else that it could have been.

'Insanely attractive,' I said aloud as I walked, and laughed to find that there was a plausibility to that statement now, where before it had been an empty compliment.

I walked home via Martin's house and was pleased to find him in.

'Mum and dad are here. They came round to have a word with Geoff and Lynn, but they're out somewhere.'

We went through.

'Peter!' Mrs Armstrong exclaimed, jumping up and giving me a warm hug. 'How are you? How's your job at the museum going? We haven't seen you since you started.'

'I must have seen you, surely.'

'No,' Mr Armstrong told me. 'You went camping with Martin at the end of September, then stayed the weekend when you got back. That was a week before you started your job.'

It was amazing that I could have gone four months without staying at Martin's house. It was a second home to me, and I had always regarded Mr and Mrs Armstrong as surrogate parents. They were what I regarded as normal people; normal in a way that my mother wasn't and had never been. They did normal things like have dinner parties, friendly conversations, arguments about who was going to do the washing up. They enjoyed watching good films, reading good books, getting happily drunk. And there was Martin's younger sister, Caz, and her friends, so there was always plenty of activity. In many ways it was the complete antithesis of the house that I lived in, which had always been unnaturally quiet, with a kind of death-like stillness to it that managed to wheedle its way into one's soul.

'The job's fine,' I told Mrs Armstrong, and left it at that. I wasn't in the mood to talk about my work, having come here to talk to Martin about Coll. I sat and waited for them to leave, without annoyance because they were congenial enough. They both had that sleek look of understated affluence. It showed in the cut of their clothes and in their immaculate grooming. I wondered, as I talked to them, how often I would see them now that Martin had left home. Not often, I supposed, and felt suddenly sad how life can change in ways we wouldn't choose.

Mr and Mrs Armstrong stayed for another half hour or so.

'Tell Lynn we called round,' Mrs Armstrong said as she left, kissing us both, and squeezing my hand affectionately. At the last moment, when Mr Armstrong was out of sight, she stepped back into the hallway and pressed two twenty pound notes into Martin's hand. It was something that my own mother would never have done.

'Come on upstairs,' Martin told me as soon as the door was closed, looking curious and amused. I followed him into his room and sat on the bed.

'Alright, what's happened to you then?' he asked. 'You look like you've been in a car accident.'

'It's nothing like that,' I said. 'It's just that I bumped into Coll in town today. We had lunch at the Gillygate bakery.'

'Ah,' he said slowly. 'I see.'

35

'Yes, I spent the afternoon round at her place.'

'So,' he said, looking round the room, 'that's that, then.'

He pulled at the shoulder of his sweater for a moment.

'Of course,' he said, 'I knew she was after you. She told me as much at the party.'

I didn't know what to say. I'd come round here to tell Martin what had happened, but now I was here, I couldn't.

'Did you enjoy it?' he asked after a moment.

'Yes,' I said. 'Yes I did.'

'And you're keen to repeat the experience with her?'

'Actually, I don't know what's going to happen now. That's the thing. I've lost part of myself – the part that I was sure of.'

I looked over at him.

'Why did you lie, and tell Coll that I was a virgin?'

'It was hardly a lie, Peter. Just an exaggeration.'

I felt at a loss for words.

'I really came here to ask you what I should do now,' I said after a pause.

He shrugged at that as though he had an ache across his shoulders. He looked suddenly young – childishly vulnerable – and I felt bashful asking him for advice. It occurred to me, then, that despite our desperate attempts to prove otherwise, we were still trapped in our adolescence; Anna was a schoolgirl and Coll barely six months older. It seemed presumptuous to ask Martin for advice, presumptuous because I knew so little of his sex life.

Martin had always been discreet about his relationships and I had only once met a lover of his, a shy librarian of indeterminate age who had loved Martin in an overprotective way when he was seventeen. That meeting, and the subsequent oblique references that cropped up now and again in conversation, led me to believe that he had a kind of sexual wisdom that would be made available to me on request. But Martin seemed unwilling to give advice. He sat there, staring blankly at his shoes, silently preoccupied with his own thoughts.

'Well?' I asked him. 'What do you think?'

'I don't think anything, actually,' he said, dragging his feet across the carpet. 'I'm sorry, but I don't.'

'I don't know what's going to happen now,' I said. 'Anna's coming round to the house tomorrow afternoon.'

'That's what's going to happen, then.'

'I don't mean that. I mean, how do I deal with situations like these?'

'Okay,' Martin said with a sigh. 'The question to ask is: do you want to see Coll again? Now that you've been to bed with her, is there still any curiosity?'

'Yes, of course there is.'

'Then you've answered your own question,' Martin told me. 'The next thing for you to do is get to know her better.'

That sounded simple enough, and good advice as far as it went, but I was cruelly unsure as to what to do about Anna.

Anna's visit was an anticlimax. She was quiet, lost in her own idea about the two of us. In the end, to get some reaction, I took her to the stack of my father's paintings and asked her for an opinion – something she'd never offered of her own accord.

She didn't like them. I had known she wouldn't. She could respect the obvious feeling in them, the sureness of their style, the technical brilliance of their simplicity. But she still didn't like them.

'They're too dark and sinister,' she said as she looked at the array of canvasses that I had propped up around the room.

'But they're full of life,' I told her. 'Look at the tension in the figures. Look at the sweep of the lines, the taught expressions.'

But she couldn't see it.

'You said they were figurative, but they're more abstract than anything else.'

I realised I was being unfair, so didn't say anything as I felt anger welling up in me. She hadn't had the years of familiarity with them that I had. Looking back to my childhood, I remembered that they'd frightened me then, with their black backgrounds, with their weirdly twisted human forms. It was only after years of intimacy that I had begun to see their inner life – the humorous way they laid bare our twistedness. It was a black humour, an esoteric humour, and it was wrong of me to judge Anna because she couldn't see it.

'Come on,' I said, 'let's go upstairs.'

My mother was in the bowels of the house, pottering in her usual disinterested way. She had come out briefly when Anna had arrived to see who it was, and had then left us alone. She'd said hello, picked up two empty coffee mugs and left.

'I keep forgetting,' Anna whispered as we started on the second flight of stairs, 'what a huge house you have.'

'It's pointless,' I said.

My mother had the large bedroom suite on the first floor, and I had the front room on the second. There were a further four bedrooms, including two in the attic, which had become dusty, shabby spaces in our lives. Martin had seen all sorts of possibilities for converting the attic into a studio, but it was only a dream. He would never have wanted to live in the same house as my mother, and she would never have let him.

'I hate the waste of space,' I told her. 'All these empty rooms.'

For as long as my father's paintings had been on the walls, there had been at least some point in having the extra rooms, even if the only time they were ever used was when I went in to dust them. Now there was something obscene about all this unused space, something selfishly impersonal.

Despite the convenience of having as much room as I needed, I began to realise that this place was no longer a home for me. I was going to have to move sooner or later so that I could keep my head above the mordant atmosphere that was beginning to contaminate the house. The whole building felt like a desecrated mausoleum, and Anna's presence brought into sharp focus the fact that I shouldn't be there.

38

We walked into my room and Anna looked up at the cornices, the tarnished brass light fittings, the open fireplace. Then she turned to me with a trusting expectancy that bruised me somewhere inside.

We kissed in our usual hesitant way, Anna wriggling out of her clothes like an animal shedding its skin. She didn't look at herself; her small breasts, her skin slightly mottled in the cool air, the tumescent ridge of her hips. I saw all these things, but they were secrets. Secrets, I realised, that Coll would have wanted me to share. But this was Anna, and Anna curled away from me, yielding with a kind of pathetic inevitability. Parting her legs to receive my erection, she gave no outward indication that she felt anything at all. She simply lay there, in taut concentration as though holding her breath under water.

After we'd made love she leaned over and whispered 'I love you' gently in my ear. It was the first time she had said it and I was surprised to hear the words directed at me with such conviction. I swallowed hard because I almost said it back.

The one and only serious promise that I'd ever made to myself was that I would never say "I love you" to anyone until I truly meant it. It would have been so easy to say it now – so convenient, and ultimately so damaging.

And yet it was cowardly to lie there and not say anything, not to reply in any way to her statement. I cradled her head against my elbow, stroking her hair. She had a trust that frightened me. It made me curl up inside to realise that I couldn't feel the same in return. There was something hard in me. Something solitary that wanted to shut people out, just as another part of me was yearning to let them in.

Two months was far too short a time to be clear about anything. But can people ever be objective about their lovers? One thing I realised, even then, was that I should be experiencing these things and not thinking about experiencing them. The fact was enough. I would have plenty of time for post-mortems later, once I'd decided what to do.

'You seem quiet,' Anna whispered to me as we lay in our protective silences. 'What are you thinking about?'

'Nothing really,' I said.

'I'm thinking about how nice it is to be here. About how your bed is too small – except I like that, because it means we have to squeeze together. I was thinking that you're the most beautiful person I've met. No really,' she went on, pinching me as I smiled in disbelief, 'I mean it. You're going to have to learn to take compliments, Peter.'

She lay back and looked up at the dusty cornice.

'I think you have low self-esteem or something,' she said.

I laughed at this for a moment.

'I'm just going through a vulnerable phase,' I replied.

FIVE

On Monday Coll came to the museum as I was about to take my lunch break. She was shown in by Ian, the cataloguer, and she looked out of place. Then she saw me and smiled.

'I didn't go into college this morning,' she said. 'I came over to see when your lunch was.'

'I'm just finishing,' I told her. 'Sit down here, I won't be long.'

I was filling in a list of occupations of the residents of Robertson Road from the 1871 census. I had nearly finished the column I was working on. Coll sat upright in her seat whilst I worked. She was wearing a bright blue and green skiing anorak over jeans and looked ready for anything, eyes bright from the cold breeze outside.

'This is brilliant,' she said as I put my pen down. 'All this history!'

I looked around at the shabby bookshelves bulging with papers. There was an open trunk in the middle of the floor full of Victorian bric-a-brac. Glove stretchers, boots, a chatelaine, various books, items of clothing... It had all become a part of my job to me. I had lost the initial thrill of handling objects that for most people are shut away behind glass. My pleasure was more specific now, more to do with information that could be gleaned from objects than with the objects themselves.

'Come on,' I said, getting up. 'Where shall we go?'

'Out,' she said, opening her shoulder bag for me to see inside. 'I've brought sandwiches and coffee. We'll eat them by the river.'

'Okay.'

She put her arm through mine with a kind of mock girlishness and smiled at Ian and Maggie, whose eyes followed us with curiosity. As soon as we were outside, she pulled at my elbow and kissed my cheek.

'You didn't introduce me.'

'No. I don't know any of them well enough. It would have been silly to introduce you. They never introduce their friends to me.'

We walked out into the early February sunshine. The river was looking more sluggish today, more peaceful. It was pleasant to be out in the fresh air, walking beneath the bare branches of chestnut trees. We passed the long warehouses that had been converted into hi-tech apartments – buildings that spoiled this part of the river. There was something unpleasantly overt about them, something blatantly, disrespectfully wealthy. But we were soon past them and out into the fields.

'We can't go too far,' said Coll. 'I've got to take the two o'clock train to Leeds.'

There was a willow, long since fallen, yet still struggling to survive. We sat on the trunk and watched as a motor launch came purring along the river, its wake whispering along the bank as it washed against the grasses there.

'Here,' she said, reaching into her bag, 'I've got something for you.'

She took out a cellophane covered tube of incense. I took it from her and looked at the label: INDIAN BOUQUET.

'You do like incense?' she asked.

'I've never used it.'

'Well, now's the time to start.'

'Don't worry,' I said, handing it back to her. 'Keep this for yourself. I'll buy my own.'

'No, you keep it. I bought it for you. Anyway, it hardly cost anything.'

'Okay.'

I began to eat my sandwich.

'This is one of those places,' she said. 'You could come here to die. Or get stoned. Or curse the fact that you've got such fucking awful parents.'

'Or walk. Or think,' I said.

'Walk, yes,' she said. 'You could do that too. Long walks designed to make you a little more tolerant of your

42

surroundings. A little saner. Maybe even a little nicer.'

'Clarity,' I told her. 'That's what I come here for. Life is always so murky. I bring Emily here every weekend. We go for a long walk out to Bishopthorpe, and sometimes down to Acaster.'

'I'll come with you next time.'

'Okay,' I agreed, privately disappointed at the idea of someone else sharing my solitude. I didn't even let Anna come with me. The walks were the only time that I really managed to unwind. They were times that I looked forward to throughout the week, and which I relished all the more as my homelife became more and more constricting. The only person who had ever come with me was Martin, and even then not very often.

By the time we had to leave it felt as if I'd spent years of my life with Coll, rather than just one afternoon. But she invited this feeling by treating me as an established partner, by speaking her mind, by kissing me, by holding me with a kind of sureness that suggested a depth of time.

We wandered back towards the museum, talking about Emily, my home, college. On reaching the back door of the museum, I was about to say goodbye to Coll when I noticed Anna leaning against a nearby railing. She was finishing a sandwich and looking bored.

Coll noticed my sigh and caught my glance.

'That's Anna is it?' she asked.

'Yes,' I said, 'she sometimes comes over to see if I'm around.'

Anna, seeing us, stood and walked our way, with a look of annoyance and curiosity. But before she got to us, there came a shout. I ignored it, assuming it wasn't directed at me, but it came again. I turned and saw three youths of my own age approaching from the riverside car park. My heart sank. One of them was Dave Boothe, a brash, aggressive troublemaker that I had been at school with. He was tall, with cropped hair and a broad grin that might have looked friendly on someone else, but which on him looked lethal. He had left school after 'O' levels and I'd seen him around every now and then ever since. He despised me about as much as I despised him. Whenever I saw him, there was always some kind of unpleasant scene.

With him was Paul, his nonentity side-kick of several years standing, and another boy whom I didn't recognise. Coll and I remained motionless, unsure what to do.

'Well,' Dave sneered, 'if it isn't Peter arsehole Ellis. Peter I'm-better-than-you Ellis.'

'Hello Dave,' I said, bracing myself for a quick dash into the building.

'So this is where you work, eh? Nice cushy number?'

I didn't reply. I knew from experience that if I didn't say anything, he'd call me a few more names then go away. If I was rude back, it might lead to violence. Anna came up to us at this point and took my arm, but she didn't say anything.

'So you're doing pretty well for yourself are you?' Dave asked. 'Still living in bliss with mummy?'

He glanced at Anna, a dismissive look that obviously angered her.

'I was only looking,' he said with a sneer. 'Anyone can look.'

Anna shrugged, feigning indifference and looked away.

'Don't expect me to be interested,' she said.

'The feeling's mutual,' he laughed. 'Don't worry. I'm only interested in darling Peter here.'

'Why?' she asked. 'What could someone like you want with someone like Peter?'

'A talk maybe.'

Anna laughed.

'It would be a waste of time waiting round to listen to your conversation,' she said.

'Oh, I see you've got a friend with an arsehole for a mouth,' he said to me. 'Is this your girlfriend? You've decided to try fucking girls now, then? It makes a change from boys, doesn't it?'

He turned to Coll.

'What's a nice looking girl like you doing hanging around with the likes of him?' he asked her.

'It's none of your sodding business,' she said.

'Oooh,' he sighed, 'all these aggressive women!'

He looked back at Anna.

'Take it from me, darling. Don't waste your time. He's trash, that's what he is. He's a fucking disease!'

'I only take advice from people I respect, and that doesn't include you,' she said slowly.

'Ha ha,' he laughed without humour.

He took a step closer and thrust his face towards Anna.

'Why don't you fuck off back to cookery classes.'

He turned to me, and as he did so, Ian came round the corner with Mark from archives. Dave hesitated.

Mark saw my expression and nudged Ian.

'Having trouble?' he asked as he came up to us.

'This person here,' said Coll, 'is being abusive.'

Dave looked at Ian, then at Mark who stood well over six feet tall and looked as though he'd have no trouble if it came to a physical confrontation. Dave smiled, shrugged, then splayed his hands in a conciliatory gesture.

'No offence,' he said. 'We were just larking.'

'Well go and lark elsewhere,' Mark told him.

Dave and his two companions walked off, talking quietly together. Dave said something and the other two laughed derisively.

'Are you okay?' Mark asked.

'Yes,' I said. 'Don't worry. I'll be in in a minute. Thanks.'

They left us on the doorstep. As Dave got to the other side of the car park he turned and cupped his hands.

'Fucking pervert!' he shouted. 'Fucking Aids carrier!'

'What does he mean?' Anna asked. 'Why did he say that?'

'Oh, it's ancient history,' I said. 'A misunderstanding. I'll tell you later.'

But Anna was suspicious, and not only about Dave. I could see her looking sidelong at Coll with an expression that I didn't want to interpret. She was about to say something, but decided against it. She looked at Coll instead.

'Hello,' said Coll. 'I'm a friend of Martin's. I was in York for the weekend, so I thought I'd pop in and see Peter before I went back to Leeds.'

'I'm sorry,' I said. 'I didn't realise you'd be coming over today.'

Anna shrugged.

'Tell me about it later,' she said quietly. 'I've got to go. Where shall we meet?'

'Let's meet in town. How about The Bishop, eight-thirty?'

'Make it nine, then I'll have finished my homework.'

'Fine.'

She kissed me goodbye, touched by a troubled expression. I watched her go, and it struck me again what absolute strangers we were. Coll readjusted the strap of her bag and looked at me.

'I'd better go too,' she said, kissing my cheek. 'Don't let boys like that get you down. He's an ignorant prick.'

She turned to walk away, then paused.

'Life's never easy,' she said. 'I know that's a cliché, but actually it's true.'

SIX

The next afternoon I had another visit at the museum. I was unprepared to see Martin and Steph when they turned up at five o'clock. Steph kissed me warmly, soliciting curious glances from Maggie and Ian.

'We've come over to have a look round the museum,' Martin said. 'Any chance of a guided tour?'

'I can't,' I told them. 'Besides the museum closes in half an hour.'

'Never mind. Actually, we really came to see if you wanted to go out for tea somewhere.'

'I don't usually finish before five thirty,' I said, looking up at Maggie, who could clearly hear our conversation.

'If you want to knock off a few minutes early today, Peter,' she said, 'go ahead. I don't mind. But please,' she added, looking at Martin and Steph, 'this is a private department. It isn't open to the public.'

'Oops,' said Martin. 'Sorry.'

He looked at me with a smile in his eyes.

'I hope we're not getting you into trouble,' he whispered.

We went downstairs at Betty's in St Helen's Square and sat in the warm expensive atmosphere, subdued conversation buzzing round us.

'Look at this,' said Martin.

He took a copy of Square Peg magazine from his holdall.

'It's a back number,' he said. 'I got it from Steph's flatmate.'

He briefly searched for an article, then passed it to me. On the pages he handed over were two paintings, illustrated in black and white, of garishly haunted faces. The first picture was of one face on its own. The second, of two together. There was something deathlike about them, something horrible about their gaping, dark eyes, their

47

empty expressions, their utter hopelessness. They were painted by a man called David Ruffell; a man, the article said, who had Aids. The caption on one of the pictures read: BY HIS DEAD SMILE I KNEW WE STOOD IN HELL. It sent shivers down my spine.

'Why have you shown me these?' I asked, realising that I would remember the images for a long time.

'They remind me of your father's work,' Martin said.

'Surely not.'

'Yes. Look at the way the faces are simplified, brought down to basics.'

'But,' I said, 'these are full of unhappiness.'

'So are your father's, in a way. At least that's what has always struck me about his work – the fact that it's bubbling somewhere deep down with sadness and resentment. Like David Ruffell's work, only taken to an extreme.'

I looked carefully at the pictures in front of me and nodded. There was some truth in what Martin said. Something in these pictures touched a nerve; a subtle sub-text that was shared with my father's work – a sub-text that I was incapable of reading.

'I can see where this man's fear comes from if he's got Aids,' I said, 'but where did my father's fear and anger come from?'

I saw by the way that Martin and Steph exchanged glances that they had asked themselves the same question.

'I don't know,' said Martin with a hooded smile. 'Curious, though, isn't it?'

I handed Martin the magazine.

'I don't suppose there's any way I could get hold of a copy of this?' I asked.

'Yes, there's a back issue catalogue. I could order one for you.'

'Please.'

I thought of the article, and felt shocked that my life was so muffled, so submerged in trivia. My own feelings were an emotional anaesthetic in comparison to the screaming rawness of the pictures I had just seen.

'Which brings me,' said Martin, 'to the other reason why Steph and I came over this afternoon.'

'You have another reason?'

'We were wondering when the auctioneers are coming to take your father's work away.'

'The end of this week,' I told him. 'Why?'

'Can we come round and see them? I'd like one last chance to look at them before they're dispersed.'

'And I've never seen them before,' Steph said.

'Of course,' I told them, pleased. 'I'd love to show them to you.'

'Great,' Steph smiled. 'I've heard so much about them from Martin.'

This was the first really positive feeling I'd had about my father's work for a long time. Until now I had been going through a subtle bereavement about it, a bereavement that I felt I shouldn't be feeling – because after all, they were only paintings.

Now I would have a chance to look at them with Martin, who was a great believer in my father's talent; and Steph, who was at least another artist and not a salesman. I only now realised how disappointed I had been that Anna disliked the paintings. By being so unresponsive, she had somehow denied my grief.

As soon as we arrived home, I went through to the kitchen, leaving Martin and Steph in the hallway to try and cope with Emily, who was jumping around excitedly and barking. My mother was sitting at the long oak breakfast table reading a magazine. She looked up as I came in.

'I won't be eating here tonight,' I told her. 'Martin's come round and we'll be going out.'

'Good,' said my mother absently. 'I'll have a microwave dinner by myself then.'

She smiled a distant smile before going back to her magazine. I left feeling completely disconnected from her.

'Come on in,' I said, coming back into the hall and leading the way into the front room. There lay the stack of thirty-four canvasses, leaning slightly against each other like a row of dominoes. They took up the whole of one

49

wall, and I lifted them one by one and propped them up on the sofa, chairs, against the walls, mantelpiece, window ledge...

We stood and looked in silence at the twenty that I had displayed, and as I looked, the image of wasted faces came vividly to mind. "By his dead smile I knew we stood in hell," I thought, and saw for the first time the private intensity of anguish that lay in the spreading darkness on the canvasses. How strange that I had never seen it before.

'I had always seen a kind of humour in these before you showed me David Ruffell's work,' I told Martin. 'Now all I can see is pain.'

'There is humour here,' he said. 'But it's a dark gallows humour.'

'Like Francis Bacon,' said Steph, 'only more simply graphic.'

'Do you like them, though?' I asked her.

'Like them? How can anyone like pictures like these?'

She walked over to a canvas that was larger than most and looked carefully at the sure lines, the subtle colouring, the dark, dark background.

'I'm moved by them, challenged by them. But do I like them? I don't know.'

'If I were to say you could have one,' I said, 'would you accept it?'

'Oh, well,' she said, shrugging, 'of course I would. You didn't ask me if they were good. You didn't ask me if there was a weight to them, an emotional truth to them. You asked me if I liked them. Well, that's something different. I've only seen them for a few minutes, but I can already tell you that they verge on the brilliant. Of course I would take one. I'd put it on my wall to challenge others – and myself.'

I was pleased with Steph's reaction. To have said 'do you like them?' had been simplistic. They were pictures that were meant to make you feel uncomfortable.

'Martin says you know hardly anything about your father?' she said to me as I put the paintings back and set out the others.

'Almost nothing,' I said. 'My mother never talks about

50

him. I haven't mentioned him for years. It's not worth it. It only makes life miserable between us.'

'But surely there are other ways of getting information about him.'

'Yes,' I said. 'I've read a number of articles in arts magazines like The Artist and Studio International, and I've seen his work listed at art sales in London. But that's about all. All these things just talk about his work. I've read very little about him as a person, except for hints that he was unhappy.'

'You'd have to be blind not to see that,' said Steph, glancing round the canvasses.

'Quite. And maybe that's why my mother is so reticent to talk about him.'

'How old was he when he died?'

'Twenty-nine,' I told her.

'Twenty-nine! So young... '

She looked at the pictures again.

'Only three years older than I am now, and he'd done all this.'

'He started out younger than you, don't forget,' Martin pointed out.

'But even so, it's still incredible. Just think what he might have come up with by now if he was still alive.'

'Exactly,' I said.

'Except there's something about this work that makes you wonder how much longer he could have gone on,' Martin said quietly.

Steph looked intensely across at Martin for a moment.

'He didn't commit suicide did he?' she asked suddenly.

'No,' I said.

'How did he die?' she wanted to know.

'Actually, he died of alcoholic poisoning on the night of his first major exhibition. I know it sounds improbable, but he drank a whole bottle of whisky for a bet.'

'And it killed him,' said Martin. 'I think people usually die of respiratory trouble when they've drunk too much.'

'Mmm,' I said. 'Sounds awful.'

'What a waste,' Steph murmured.

51

I nodded.

"By his dead smile I knew we stood in hell," I thought and felt a tickle of fear like a haunting.

Why had he done it? What happened on that last night to make him so reckless?

'I can't believe you've never bothered to try and find out more,' Steph said.

'I just drew blanks from my mother and the articles I've read, so I didn't see any point in looking further.'

'You should be more methodical about it,' she said. 'You should get in touch with the people who wrote these articles and ask for more information.'

'Maybe,' I said, knowing that I wouldn't look further, knowing that the image I had of my father would collapse as soon as I had any detail to flesh it out.

Later, we bought a hamburger in town and dawdled by the river as we ate, ending up in The Bishop just after eight. The burger I had eaten lay queasily on my stomach and I now felt nervous about seeing Anna again, because of the inferences she had so obviously taken from my meeting with Dave Boothe earlier in the day.

Martin was still preoccupied with the paintings.

'Perhaps some of them will go to art galleries rather than private collections,' he said hopefully. 'Then we'd get to see them again.'

Steph was more realistic.

'Unlikely,' she said. 'Public money these days is so middle class, so safe, so uninspired. I'd be surprised if more than a couple end up in public places.'

'Maybe,' Martin conceded. 'Victorian values seem to be the order of the day, I guess. They'll be taking the non-classical nudes down from our galleries soon if public opinion gets any more prudish. Maybe a painter like Paul Ellis no longer has a place in a country as culturally barren as England.'

'And they'll end up abroad,' Steph suggested. 'That's where a lot of interest in genuine art is. It's also where the money is.'

'But this is all conjecture,' I said. 'We'll find out for sure the month after next.'

'When exactly?' Martin wanted to know.

'Either May 17th or 24th. It's still to be confirmed.'

'Do you think we might be able to get in and see the auction?' Martin asked. 'Is it a public thing, or is it by invitation? Either way, your mother ought to be able to get us in if we ask her.'

'What, and see them go under the hammer?' I asked, horrified. 'I couldn't bear to see them go. It would be like... like... oh, it would be awful.'

'It was just a thought,' said Martin.

He sipped his pint.

'So what's happened about that little marble sculpture?' he asked me. 'You were talking about it the other night, but it wasn't out with the paintings.'

'No,' I told him. 'It's been sent down to Sheffield for valuation. Apparently there's a man there who's an expert on that sort of thing, and he's familiar with my father's work. He's taking a look at it for Bratt's.'

'Then he's your man,' said Steph. 'If he knows something about your father's work, he might know something about the rest of your father's life. Why don't you go and talk to him? A talk would be much more informative than a magazine article.'

'I don't know,' I said doubtfully. 'Sheffield's quite a long way.'

'Of course it isn't,' Steph said. 'But it's up to you.'

'It's a brilliant idea,' said Martin. 'You should do it.'

I didn't say anything, but felt a momentum building, formed of my curiosity, but also of Martin's and Steph's. I felt that they were pushing me into trying to talk to the man in Sheffield. The man who might tell me all.

'But he might not know anything about my father's private life,' I said aloud.

'So?' said Steph. 'You still won't have lost anything by asking.'

'I know,' said Martin. 'I know how difficult this must be for you, Peter. It's like trying to open a door that you

53

always thought was locked. It's not easy.'

'I'm really hoping,' I said, sidetracking, 'that I can buy the sculpture. I know I can't afford one of the paintings, but maybe I could afford that. I've got some savings... '

'Surely your mother would give it to you if you asked.'

'No way,' I said. 'She's signed the whole lot away. She told me so herself so that I wouldn't bother asking for anything.'

'It's like the final stage of exorcism,' said Steph. 'Getting the last of your father out of her life. I wonder why.'

'Because she's insensitive to his work,' I said. 'And she's insensitive to me too. She promised me that sculpture, and she deliberately signed it away.'

I felt a sudden and almost overwhelming bitterness towards her. I had a choking feeling of hating her and not being able to do anything about it. It made me feel powerless and humiliated, and very, very angry.

I was about to say something uncharitable, when Anna came in. She saw us immediately and looked disappointed that I wasn't alone. I got up quickly.

'Anna,' I said. 'You know Martin. And this is Steph.'

'Hello,' she said.

'Right. Good. What do you want to drink?'

'A half of Guinness please.'

I went to get her drink as she sat down. She didn't say anything and I saw, as I ordered the drink, that an uneasy silence had descended at the table. I turned back to the bar and waited, realising with increasing nervousness that this was going to be awkward.

'Here we are,' I said brightly a couple of minutes later, proffering her drink. But my words fell absolutely flat. There was a sudden dull atmosphere, as though an echoless mist had fallen around us. Anna had brought a pall with her, an aura of impatient disquiet. I sat down beside her and lapsed into silence myself. Martin looked wary and uncomfortable.

'Look, I'm sorry to barge in like this,' she said. 'I've obviously ruined your conversation. But I've got to ask Peter about this afternoon. About what that boy said about him.'

She turned to me.

'You said you were going to explain.'

'Yes, I know,' I said.

But I didn't know where to start.

'What was this?' Martin asked.

'Some guy this afternoon,' said Anna. 'He was saying that Peter was an Aids carrier.'

'It was Dave Boothe,' I said quickly.

Martin made a soundless 'ahh'.

'It was just something stupid that happened at school,' I said.

'Yes?' asked Anna. 'And?'

'Martin was involved in it too,' I went on. 'It wasn't very pleasant... '

'What happened was this,' said Martin. 'In the build up to taking my 'O' levels it became generally known at school that I was gay. I didn't mind particularly, except that it led to a lot of aggravation. Most of it was verbal, but unpleasant enough. And some of it was physical. The most aggressive of the people who used to victimise me was Dave Boothe. One day he and someone else from my year, Paul Short, set on me. They got me down on the ground and started kicking me.'

'Which is when I turned up,' I said. 'I reckoned I could have a pretty good go at them, so I jumped on Dave from behind, and then it got pretty nasty for a while. I got a bloody nose, but in the end it turned into a shouting match more than anything else. It happened just outside the school grounds, so we got quite an audience. Dave started shouting abuse at Martin. You know, along the lines of what he was saying today. And then I just shouted back to him that I was gay too.'

'Mmm,' said Martin. 'I never did figure out why you did that.'

'Because it was an us and them situation. I didn't want you to be on your own.'

'You said you were gay, although you're not gay?' Anna asked, disbelievingly.

'That's right. Martin's my best friend. If people were against him, then they were against me. That's how I saw it. I wanted to be on his side. I wanted to be seen as separate from people like Dave Boothe.'

'Is this true?' Anna asked Martin.

'That's what happened, yes.'

'So nothing happened between you?'

'Our friendship happened between us,' he said.

'You know what I mean,' Anna snapped.

'No, not really. What do you mean?'

I could see an open hostility appearing between them. Martin's eyes had narrowed, whilst Anna sat as tall as she could.

'I mean,' said Anna, 'is Peter gay?'

'You should know better than me,' he said.

'Did you sleep with him?' she asked quietly through almost gritted teeth.

Martin paused for a long time before saying: 'No, I didn't.'

Anna looked Martin in the eyes, then stood up and walked out of the pub. I glanced at him in annoyance and hurried after Anna.

She was walking quickly up the street and ignored me as I called her name.

'Anna, wait!' I shouted, running up to her and grabbing her elbow to make her stop. 'What is all this? Why are you so angry?'

'You make me sick,' she said turning to me. 'As soon as I walked into the pub I could see what there was between you. It's in the way Martin looks at you all the time. It's disgusting.'

'What do you mean? There's nothing between me and Martin.'

'How can I believe that? I saw.'

'What do you mean, you "saw". You saw what?'

'I saw him looking at you as if you were lovers.'

'You saw Martin looking at me, that's all,' I said, angry in my turn. 'You put an interpretation on it that I think was wrong, but even if it's not wrong, it doesn't make any

56

difference. I don't feel that way about Martin, whatever he feels about me.'

'Then why did you look back at him like that?'

'Like what?'

'Like you were lovers.'

'I happen to like Martin. That's what you saw. You saw a look of friendship. You're just feeling insecure after what Dave Boothe said this afternoon.'

There was a certain logic here, and Anna paused, looked less certain.

'I mean it,' I said. 'I don't want Martin as anything other than a friend.'

'But that boy Dave. He seemed so sure of himself when he was shouting those things at you.'

'If you're going to believe people like that,' I said, irritated, 'then we might as well give up on trust altogether. He's a liar and a troublemaker. And besides, we explained how he came to think I was gay.'

We stood there on the pavement in the cold, clear evening, our breath fogging, our eyes tentatively searching for trust – and failing to find it.

'And then there's that girl that you were with today. What about that?'

'What about it? She's just a friend of Martin's.'

'God, Peter, you're such a bad liar. Wake up and listen to yourself, just listen to yourself! You stand there saying these things and you expect me to believe them. But I can see in your eyes that what you say and what you feel are two different things.

'Look,' she went on, 'I don't care whether you've been to bed with Martin, or with that girl today. That doesn't matter. The fact is that you feel more for them than you feel for me. That much is obvious at least.'

What could I say? I couldn't deny it.

'Okay,' I said slowly. 'So where does that leave us?'

'It leaves me with plenty of time to revise for my exams.'

As she walked off, I felt a depression-edged feeling of relief. I felt stupid, tired and empty. That's all.

SEVEN

The following week, at the museum, I was helping Maggie sort out a box of Victorian clothes when there came a loud crash from downstairs. Ian, who was working by the window, looked out, then turned to me.

'It's those delinquent aquaintances of yours,' he said, hurrying to the door.

I followed him downstairs, Maggie behind me. When we came to the back exit, the porter was standing, a brick in his hand, looking at a splintered panel in the door. We all stood for a moment, speechless, standing absurdly motionless. Maggie was looking at the damage, as if trying to think of something sensible to say. Ian looked shocked by the gratuitous stupidity of what had happened. But, for me, it wasn't the physical damage to the door that was shocking. It was the large silver words that had been written over the dark wood in aerosol spray-paint; in rounded, childish joined-up letters. Bold, imperative and vicious, they smacked of ignorant vindictiveness and petty prejudice. They said: PETER ELLIS HAS AIDS.

It would have been laughable if it hadn't been sprayed in such a public place. In fact, despite everyone else's horrified expressions, I couldn't help smiling at how utterly, pathetically juvenile this vandalism was, and how devoid of personal threat. Of course, it was a complete untruth, so I could safely ignore it. I didn't have Aids, and that was that. There were other statements that Dave might have sprayed which would have been more embarrassing, and more difficult to shrug off.

I stared at the words and my feeling of safety faded as I began to question the implications of Dave Boothe's behaviour. Perhaps this incident meant that Dave was after me in some nasty way. Perhaps this was a precursor to violence. Or maybe it was nothing more than a silly prank

58

that wouldn't be repeated. I looked questioningly at Maggie.

'Presumably,' she said, 'you know the people who did this?'

'Yes,' I nodded.

'Right, George,' she said to the porter, 'you'd better call the police.'

Talking to the police was hardly inspiring. They were too preoccupied to take me seriously. Maggie made more of an impression, I think, but even so, grafitti on a door is hardly a major crime. They left after a short time, having taken statements from Maggie and myself. But during the afternoon, I knew that things had changed. News travels fast at work, and the museum was no exception. When Judy came in after lunch she looked at me as though she'd discovered that I had a criminal record. Even Maggie seemed to be treating me with some suspicion, as though I must have had a shady past to have provoked Dave's petty attack. The others, who all put in an appearance at some point in the afternoon, gave me hooded glances, but no one mentioned anything.

Maggie sent me home at four thirty, complaining that I was too preoccupied to be of any use, and I walked back feeling pensive. It was incredible how volatile people's personal loyalties were. I suddenly realised with absolute certainty that if the police were to come in to work tomorrow to arrest me for murder, people at the museum would put their heads together and say: 'Yes, I'm not surprised, I knew there was something odd about him.' I knew this, as I knew that if I was accused of murder and then proved innocent, they would say: 'We knew all along that he didn't do it.'

I hated that impersonality. Beyond a certain superficial friendliness (Mark helping me out when threatened by Dave Boothe for example) there was nothing. And yet, we all colluded – myself as much as anybody – to hide our real personalities from each other, to remain impersonal at all times. No one had asked me why Dave Boothe disliked me so much, and I didn't feel inclined to tell them.

As I walked under Micklegate Bar, I saw Mat Gow walking towards me. I hadn't seen him since school. It was only seven months since we'd left, but already he had changed. He was taller, more purposeful, yet somehow fragile with it. He looked directly at me without surprise, then held out his hand.

'Hello Peter,' he said. 'I was wondering when I would bump into you.'

It was absurd of me to be surprised, but I was and felt obscurely uncomfortable. Mat and I had never been particularly close at school. The strongest link between us had been our friendship with Martin.

'Hi,' I said, taking his hand, 'how's things?'

He shrugged. 'Okay.'

We stood about a yard apart, not speaking. I wanted to say something, but there was a seven month silence between us that was insurmountable. He was wearing smart but casual clothes, and looked self-conscious in them; slightly shorter than me, with a long face, a wafer of a nose, large pale eyes and sticking-out ears. The sum of his eccentric features were strangely attractive in an off-beat kind of way. He smiled in embarrassment at our silence.

'Where are you going?' he asked.

'Home,' I said. 'To walk the dog.'

'Can I come along?' he asked. 'I'm at a bit of a loose end right now.'

'Of course,' I told him. 'Come on.'

We walked back together, in silence again. I was still too full of thoughts about Dave Boothe and Anna to be able to launch into a conversation without warning, so it took me time to think of something to talk about.

'So what are you doing now?' I asked as we reached the turning into Bernard Terrace.

'I'm working down in the dole office,' he said. 'It's tedious, but I didn't have any choice. I was signing on, so I couldn't pretend I wasn't available for work when they offered me the job.'

'Still living at home?'

'No. I left there as soon as I got my job. I've moved into a bedsit round the corner from you, actually, by Scarcroft Hill.'

I couldn't imagine Mat living in a bedsit. I think he sensed this, because he suddenly looked shy again.

'It's a bit dingy where I live,' he admitted, 'but it's very cheap. I'll start looking for somewhere else as soon as I've paid off the debts I got into whilst signing on.'

'You should have given me a ring,' I said, 'if you were hanging around at home with nothing to do.'

'I didn't know whether I should,' he said. 'I mean, I didn't know whether I'd be welcome.'

'What do you mean?' I asked with a laugh. 'Of course you'd have been welcome.'

Mat gave another slight shrug. He seemed unwilling to talk about the past.

'Have you seen anything of Martin?' I asked.

'No,' he said. 'I've lost touch with everyone from school.'

'But you two were so close.'

'Maybe not so much towards the end. And anyway, there's something a bit incestuous about hanging round with old school friends.'

'It depends why you're doing it,' I said, unable to resist adding: 'Besides, I'm an old school friend.'

'There are always exceptions to every rule,' he replied.

I took my keys out and unlocked the front door. As soon as it was open, Emily raced out excitedly, leaping up and pawing Mat.

'Hello there Emily,' he smiled, bending over and stroking her ears. 'I haven't seen you for ages.'

'Come in,' I said, switching the hall light on.

Emily followed us and barked as she ran between our legs.

'Do you want to stay for something to eat?' I asked.

Mat looked uncertain at this.

'Won't your mother mind?' he wanted to know.

'She's in London,' I said. 'That's why Emily's so excited.'

61

She's been on her own in the house all day.'

'Okay then,' said Mat.

'I'll be with you in a moment. I've got to make a quick phone call. Go in and sit down.'

I phoned Anna. To apologise? To ask to see her again? I wasn't sure. Perhaps it was just so that I could feel I'd made an effort. Mrs Lowe answered and told me bluntly, but with sympathy, that Anna wouldn't talk to me and didn't want to see me again.

Well... I'd at least hoped to speak to her. Now I stood, uncertain, with the expectation of conflict still racing my pulse.

On impulse, I phoned Bratt's to ask about the marble statue.

They suggested I go and bid for it myself if I wanted it, but when I told them that I was the artist's son, they eventually agreed to see me on Saturday with a view to buying it privately.

It appealed to me that I should buy the sculpture, because through my financial sacrifice I would exorcise the involvement of my mother in the artwork of my father; I would feel at least some connection with my father's work, and I would somehow get Anna's indifference out of my system. I had no idea how much Bratt's were going to ask for the statue. They had been cagey when I phoned them, saying they hadn't yet had the valuer's report. As a wild guess I estimated its value at a thousand pounds, then steeled myself to pay double. It was a sum I could just about afford, because of an inheritance from my aunt Joyce that I had expected to spend either on a car or a deposit on some property.

'So where have all your father's paintings gone?' Mat asked when I came back.

'Gone to London with my mother,' I said, and started to explain about the auction. Mat followed me through to the kitchen and I thought to myself, it must be like this when someone dies. You think you've told everyone the bad news, then someone else crops up who doesn't know.

I picked up Emily's lead and we went straight out. As

we walked down to the park, Emily panting and straining, I was thinking how relieved I was that the paintings had finally gone. They were no longer stacked up in the living room to remind me of their imminent sale, and at last I could start getting used to their absence.

When I unhitched Emily, she raced off and we stood and watched her go.

'So you're working down at the museum,' Mat said, as I idly swung the lead round my wrist. He glanced at me with a slight smile and looked, I thought, thinner than when I had last seen him. He'd always been thin, but now he looked as though he might snap in the middle with the slightest pressure.

'Yes I am working there,' I said. 'How did you know?'

'Mum found out from your mother. They bumped into each other at Christmas.'

'Oh.'

I was beginning to wonder why I had invited Mat to stay for a meal. Neither of us seemed able to relax.

'Are you still in touch with Martin?' he asked as we began to stroll across the grass. It was dark, the park furtively lit by pools of orange light.

'Yes,' I said. 'He's the only one I keep in touch with from school. I'm meeting him for a drink later. Do you want to come?'

Even as I said it I realised I'd have been better off keeping quiet. But there was something so lost about Mat that I couldn't help feeling protective towards him, and even, absurdly, responsible for him. He was surprised at my offer, shocked almost, and thought about it for some time before saying, 'thanks, I'd love to.'

We ate microwaved baked potatoes and a salad in the kitchen, and talked about school, my job, Mat's job. I don't think either of us felt comfortable and the conversation was hesitant. The thing I was most conscious of was not the embarrassment of long silences, but the sheer weight of Mat's loneliness. He had always been a loner, and now, living in a bedsit, I could imagine life being unbearable for him. It made me feel that he was clinging to me, even as I felt a strong sympathy for him. But I had a capacity for loneliness myself, and I could imagine that, in his situation, I would be desperate for company too.

When the time came for us to leave Mat wanted to walk into town via his bedsit.

'I'm going to have to change,' he said. 'I much prefer jeans.'

It was only a two minute walk to his place, and he was right about it being awful. There was a one-ringed cooker in the corner smelling of rancid grease, a scuffed wardrobe of some dark veneer that was peeling at the edges, filthy curtains, a dark green carpet worn thin at the door. There were two sagging easy chairs, a bookcase, a small, cracked porcelain sink, and a bed with a bright, clean bedspread on it. The room was a reasonable size, but that's about all it had going for it. The window looked out over some shabby allotments, and the plaster of the ceiling had some disquieting cracks in it.

'It won't be so bad when I get it properly cleaned up,' Mat said. 'A couple of rugs, a coat of paint and some new curtains will help.'

I sat in one of the easy chairs and browsed through the bookcase whilst Mat changed. He had a heavily illustrated book about the artist Henri Gaudier-Brzeska, which I took out and flicked through. It was illustrated with simple line drawings, carvings, plaster reliefs. I knew Martin very much admired Gaudier-Brzeska and had made a point of seeing his work when he'd visited Paris. Now, I was suddenly vividly reminded of my father's work; and especially of his little sculpture.

Along with this recollection came a further, deeper recollection – an incident from my childhood that I hadn't remembered for years, that popped into my mind with such a visual sense of clarity that I was totally caught up in it.

I remembered cradling the statue in my arms and telling it how much I loved it. It was the only objective connection I had with my father – that I could pick up and hold. My mother came in when I was doing this and, smacking me, dragged me straight to bed. Her fury had mystified me then, which was presumably why I had forgotten the incident. But now, looking at these Gaudier-Brzeska drawings, the memory of my mother's annoyance came strangely complete.

It was shortly after this incident, I realised, that my mother had relegated the sculpture to the bottom of the bathroom ottoman – a place where it had remained until Bratt's took it away.

'Okay,' said Mat. 'Ready?'

'Yes,' I said, putting down the book, feeling that I had inexplicably found a jigsaw piece of my father's life from the depths of my memory. A new fraction of information amongst other fractions. I felt a raw emptiness inside me again, and tried to shut it out.

'I didn't realise you were interested in Gaudier-Brzeska,' I said as I stood up.

'It was Martin who was really interested in him. I think some of his enthusiasm rubbed off on me.'

He had put on a pair of jeans, a designer sweatshirt and a peaked cap, and looked suddenly like the Mat I had known at school. This, more than anything else, made me finally begin to relax with him. I had never been to the pub with him before and decided that it might be interesting to try and get to know him better. I could never get used to the distances that school life placed between people, nor how different people are at school from the way they are away from it. Perhaps school had got between us, that was all. As we were leaving the door, I smiled at him.

'You know,' I said, 'it's good to see you again.'

We left the house and walked down The Mount back to Micklegate Bar.

'What are you doing with your life now?' Mat asked. 'I mean, when you're not at the museum.'

'Well, I see quite a lot of Martin still. And I'm seeing a girl called Coll... '

'Is she going to be at the pub tonight?'

'No. She's in Leeds tonight, but she's coming over tomorrow. My mother doesn't come back from London

65

until late Sunday.'

Mat nodded and we walked on for a while.

'I've also had a bit of trouble with Dave Boothe,' I told him.

'Oh? What sort of trouble?'

I explained about the brick incident, but didn't tell him what the grafitti had said. It wasn't the sort of thing I wanted to talk about right now.

'Do you remember that terrible fight at school,' said Mat, 'between you and Martin, and Dave?'

'Yes,' I said. 'Absolutely.'

'I wish I'd had the nerve to join in,' said Mat. 'I think I probably would if it happened now.'

When we got to the pub, Martin was already there with Steph. Mat stood in the doorway, hollow eyed and haunted, and I could see the thin line of a pulse in his neck. His agitation seemed ridiculous and I ignored it, walking over with a smile.

'You two,' I said, 'you're always together.'

'She's my side-kick,' Martin said.

'He's my side-kick,' Steph said.

Mat stood behind me, and I took him by the elbow, propelling him forwards slightly.

'Mat,' I said, 'this is Steph. Steph this is Mat. Now what do you all want to drink?'

At the bar, I looked back to see Mat sitting down, self-consciously I thought, on a stool beside Steph. The pub was already pretty crowded and there was a smoke-haze between us that made the three of them, Martin, Mat and Steph, seem somehow unreal – as though I was watching them on tv. Steph was laughing at something, but Martin looked as though he was switched off; closed down and turned inwards. His usually expressive face was blank. He'd put up this same barrier when Anna had turned up at The Bishop. His look of reservation and disguised animosity was directed, presumably, at Mat. I was intrigued.

When I came back with the drinks, Mat looked as though he was on the verge of either tears, or a spontaneous scream. But when he spoke, he sounded completely calm.

'You never phoned,' he said to Martin, who shrugged.

'Yes, well,' Martin said as though that was all the explanation he was going to give.

'You never wrote.'

'I'm bad at letters.'

'You never came to see me.'

'No.'

Mat picked up the beer I'd placed in front of him and took a long gulp.

'Look, Mat,' said Martin quietly, leaning towards him slightly, 'that's all so ridiculously in the past. Let's forget it, okay?'

Mat dipped his head in assent, but his expression carried the unspoken scar of pain. I felt suddenly stupid, realizing how blind I was never to have seen this between them.

Martin looked at me quizzically, with a hint of suspicion, as though I might have deliberately brought Mat as a kind of unpleasant prank. Of course, now they were together I could see that they had been lovers – or at least had had a sex thing going. Looking back, the signs were all there. The way Mat had hung around Martin that last term at school. The way he'd suddenly developed an interest in art (buying that book about Gaudier-Brzeska for example). All the signs had been there but I had never read them because I hadn't been looking for them.

'Perhaps I'd better go,' said Mat. 'I wanted to find out how I stood. It's alright Martin, it's not your fault. I'm sorry to have butted in on your evening.'

He stood up, but Steph reached out and took his elbow.

'Stay,' she said. 'Come on, sit down and finish your drink at least.'

He sat down again with a mixture of relief and anxiety. I felt responsible again, and tried to smooth the situation with a flow of conversation. But I've never been good at superficial banter and everyone knew I was being false.

'Come on, Peter,' said Steph eventually, 'we don't have to be bright young things all the time. Why all this

67

insincere good humour? Let's be honest about that at least.'

I was still young enough to be idealistic about love. To see such estrangement resulting from a physical relationship was something that I found profoundly disturbing. It was an awful thought that Anna and I would become like Mat and Martin – a negative quantity.

'Seen Anna recently?' Steph asked.

'That's all over,' I said.

'Good,' said Martin.

'Martin!' Steph exclaimed.

'It pisses me off that people can think that being gay is such a big deal,' he said. 'I'm disgusted by the fact that Anna was disgusted by it.'

'That's not fair,' I said. 'I don't think Anna gives a toss whether you're gay or not.'

'Oh yes? You could have fooled me. She looked at me as if she thought I was shit.'

'It's one thing to wonder whether someone else is gay,' said Steph, 'but it's quite another to wonder if your boyfriend is gay.'

'Peter's her boyfriend, not me,' said Martin, 'so why should I be dragged into it?'

'It doesn't matter now,' I said.

Martin shook his head in a dismissive way.

'Yes it does. It's obviously why she's left you.'

'Don't be simplistic,' I told him. 'You're just annoyed that she didn't like you.'

'But why didn't she like me, Peter? She was okay when we first met. But when she realised that I'm your best friend, I suddenly became a threat.'

'Oh, come on,' I said dismissively.

Martin glanced at Steph, a look rich with bitter misgiving.

'Now it's you who's being simplistic,' he told me.

'Okay,' I said. 'We're not going to get anywhere talking about this. Let's talk about something else.'

Martin smiled inwardly and glanced at Steph once more. A look that I chose to ignore.

'How's your work going at college?' I asked him.

'What do you think?' he asked Steph.

'I think work's going well,' she said. 'Martin has loads of talent, of course, and if he gets some scale to his work he'll walk onto any Fine Art course in the country.'

'My problem is that I tend to do quiet sorts of things,' said Martin, 'like pale life-drawings, and watery watercolours.'

'Like the stuff you've got at your digs,' I said.

'But I need to get more feeling into my work. It's not the technique or the style that I've got to change. It's the content.'

'When I said that Martin needed more scale,' said Steph enthusiastically, 'I meant emotional scale.'

'Sounds like you've come a long way since school,' said Mat.

'God, the work I was doing at school is like kiddy scribbling compared with what I'm doing now,' Martin said. 'I've thrown out everything I did then. It was too embarrassing.'

'I thought it was good.'

Martin shrugged.

'I'd very much like to see what you're doing now.'

'Come round sometime,' said Martin.

'Okay,' Mat nodded.

We lapsed into silence for a while – a silence far more comfortable than my earlier attempts at cheerfulness. We drank; listened to the juke box. Mat looked happier. Martin looked pensive. Steph looked as though she was carrying on a conversation in her head.

'And how about you?' I asked her. 'How's your work going?'

'Me?' she glanced at Martin. 'What do you think?'

'Steph has loads of talent, of course,' he said. 'But this foundation course is too limited for her. It's performance art and set design that she's going to be brilliant at, and she needs more space for that.'

EIGHT

I drove to Sheffield in a nervous trance. The brightness of the day made me feel lightheaded and I sped along in my hired Ford Fiesta as though to some charged reunion or bright, long awaited destiny. Bratt's had been almost dismissive when I'd called in to see them earlier, saying they hadn't got the sculpture at the moment, that they hadn't even had a valuation on it yet. But they'd agreed to put a call through to Mr Munro, the valuer, to get me a preliminary estimate. After a brief discussion in which both the auction had been mentioned, and the fact that I was Paul Ellis' son, Mr Anderson had changed his approach completely.

'Okay,' he'd said when he put the phone down, 'I think perhaps we can do you a deal after all. Mr Munro feels that we should try to sell the statuette separately if possible. Given that there are thirty-four paintings on offer, to put the statuette alongside might make it seem an oddity – especially as your father has no reputation for sculpture. The catalogue is going to the printers on Monday, and it might be as well not to include the piece that you are interested in... Actually we've been at a loss about handling it, and how best to present it at auction. I'll be glad to get it off my hands.'

So I was now the proud owner of an original Paul Ellis and on my way to collect it from Mr Munro. This was exhilarating, but there was a nervousness too. At the back of my mind was the knowledge that Mr Munro knew more about my father than I did. Martin and Steph stood somewhere in my consciousness demanding that I pump him for all the information he could give me. It was a great opportunity to find out more. But it was scary too.

As I drove, I inwardly gasped at the price I'd paid. £2,500. All that money for something that could be held comfortably in the palm of my hand – that had probably taken my father only a few days to make. But Mr Anderson had assured me it was a bargain, that if I had the money I should make the most of the offer.

And in spite the price, I hadn't hesitated. I would have paid double if necessary and gone to the bank on Monday to beg for a loan. I had to possess a piece of my father's work, and the sculpture was my only chance. There was no point even thinking about buying one of his paintings. Apparently, Mr Anderson told me, one of his early abstract landscapes had been sold for £17,500 before Christmas.

It was strange to know that my father was now edging his way into the history books; that he was one of those artists who achieve posthumous recognition. Perhaps in the future he would be studied on courses like Martin's; be talked about in the context of his time – recognised as an important, though not great, painter of the mid-Twentieth Century. Maybe postcards of his work would be on sale in the galleries in which his paintings hung... maybe. He deserved it. He had deserved it when he was alive, and it oppressed me to know, with absolute conviction, that there was no such thing as life after death, that my father wasn't somewhere "up there" relishing his spreading fame.

I reached Dore, a village on the outskirts of Sheffield, just before two. Mr Munro lived in a post-war house in a tree-lined cul-de-sac, in a slightly shabby looking pebble-dashed detached building. It was not what I'd expected. I had imagined something eccentrically arty, or at least not quite so middle class and suburban. There was a short concrete slip that sloped steeply down towards the house. I parked here and went to the door, annoyed at myself for having had any expectations. After all, this man was not my father. He had probably never known my father personally, was probably indifferent to his life and personality – only interested in him from a technical point of view as an art valuer and historian.

The man who came to the door was of medium height and indeterminate age. He might have been around forty and had short, greying hair, a trim moustache and dark,

dark eyes. He had a straight, slightly small nose and the taut skin of the extremely fit. He had an intensity about him that made it clear that he was an intelligent man.

'Mr Munro?' I asked hesitantly.

Mr Munro beamed the disarming smile of the genuinely happy.

'That's right. You must be Peter Ellis. Come in.'

I stepped into the hall and stood for a breathless moment looking around. The floor was bare polished wood. The walls were covered with paintings. I could see into the sitting room to an array of wallcoverings, ornamental plates, ceramics, paintings, drawings, etchings, screen prints, unframed sketches pinned up here and there... it was overwhelming, and so different from what the outside of the house had implied.

'You like it?' he asked, noticing my expression.

'It's incredible,' I said, looking briefly round the walls.

'Come through.'

We stood for a short time in the doorway of the dining room. Here the paintings were sparser – all landscapes in muted colours.

'This room is my room of unity,' he said, a mild, educated Scottish accent discernible as he spoke. 'Eating and inspiration have a certain unity, and there is too much clutter in the rest of the house. Here I've got a theme. Landscape.'

He turned with a smile and gestured for me to follow him as he entered the sitting room.

'I'll show you round the rest of the house later, if you're interested,' he said. 'But first, tea.'

I sat on the edge of a heavily embroidered chaise-longue and looked around in amazement. It was at the same time like an art gallery, and not like one. There was something about the informal way the art was jumbled onto the walls that was absolutely unlike a gallery. There was a surfeit of colours, styles, subjects, impressions. Across the longest wall, amongst other smaller works, were three paintings by my father. They were a connected sequence of landscapes in vibrant blues and subtle greys, framed in simple black

72

wood. I had never seen them before, but had seen pictures of other work from this period of his life. In the flesh they held such a glowing power that I was transfixed, rooted to my seat in admiration. It was some time before I slowly, reverently crossed the room for a closer look.

'I thought you'd like those,' said Mr Munro coming in with the tea. 'I tried putting them in the dining room, but they overwhelmed the other landscapes in there.'

'They're so much brighter than any of the ones we had at home,' I said.

'Yes,' he nodded. 'The darkness came later.'

He put the tray down on an intricately carved and inlaid Indian table and picked up the marble abstraction which stood almost indiscernible amongst a group of other small sculptures. He sat down on a chair opposite me and gestured towards the statuette.

'So, you're particularly interested in this?' he asked.

'I'm particularly interested in all my father's work,' I replied. 'It's just that this is the only work of his that I can afford.'

Mr Munro nodded.

'I remember when he did this. It was in 1971. He'd been to the gallery at Kettle's Yard in Cambridge and came back raving about the artist Henri Gaudier-Brzeska... '

'I know his work!' I exclaimed, surprised. 'A friend of mine thinks he's brilliant.'

'Your friend isn't the only one,' Mr Munro assured me. 'Paul, your father, was far too caught up in it all for his own good. His pictures were all heavily influenced for a while, until he managed to get his own voice back. He destroyed a whole series of works at that time because he thought them too derivative. In fact, the only surviving piece from then, is this... ' He held out the statuette. 'It's a kind of in-joke, a puzzle. The seemingly abstract lines etched into the marble are actually a Gaudier-Brzeska drawing wrapped round and round the marble so that all the lines overlap. I can't remember which drawing it is. It might be fun to try and work it out sometime, although it might be too complicated.'

73

He looked at me and laughed.

'In fact, this is really a kind of lucky charm – a talisman. Your father was trying to exorcise the influence of Gaudier, whilst at the same time retaining his presence.'

There was something thrilling about this inside information, this human face to the statue. But the weird thing about it was that it didn't come as a surprise. It was as if I was already aware of what Mr Munro had said, even before he'd said it. There was something unnerving about it, something psychic or, stranger still, some kind of intrinsic knowledge direct from my father that made it somehow obvious. I swallowed back the intensity of my emotion, aware that this was something I couldn't talk about. Mr Munro was watching me carefully, but he didn't say anything, turning instead to pour the tea.

'So,' I asked carefully, 'you knew my father personally?'

'Yes. We were friends.' He gestured towards the three paintings on the wall beside him.

'I commissioned these,' he said. 'It was Paul's first professional commission. I specifically asked for three because I had a large wall in the flat I was renting and I wanted to cover it up. It was 1970 and everyone was into bright colours – but Paul had some kind of real depth with it, a kind of natural touch that I liked. I was only twenty-one at the time, and new in the art business. But I had a bit of money and it was great to think that I was actually becoming a patron of the arts.'

He smiled to himself at the memory.

'Of course,' he went on, 'in financial terms I would make a fabulous return on my investment if I ever wanted to sell them. But I shall never do that. I don't like to see the art in my possession as a product, but more as a slice of an artist's psyche – a slice of his inner life. I'm very choosy, incidentally, about what I'll put on my walls.'

He sat for a moment and drank some tea. I felt absurdly tongue tied in his presence and the silence seemed to buzz with unasked questions.

'I expect your mother's told you most of this anyway,' he said.

'Not at all,' I replied. 'My mother never talks about my father. I used to mention him when I was younger, ask questions and that sort of thing. But I soon learned not to. I soon learned not to ask why there were no photos of him around the house, why he was never talked about – why he was such a blank in my life.'

'It was a big blow to your mother when he died,' said Mr Munro. 'Especially on the night of his first big success. It wasn't easy being the wife of a struggling painter. Paul was suddenly on the verge of making a living – not a very good living, but a living nevertheless – and then he died. It was tragic. Tragic for your mother, but tragic in other ways as well.'

'Tragic for the art world,' I said.

'Of course,' Mr Munro agreed, 'that too.'

We continued to talk around the subject of my father, but I never asked any of the really burning questions. Mr Munro kept on looking at me as if to say "ask me, ask me", but I couldn't. The questions lingered somewhere, unspoken, in the air between us: What was he like? Where did he get his inspiration from? Was he really unhappy like the articles said, and if so why? There was other information that I wanted to know but which I couldn't pin down with specific questions. Part of me wanted to say, "tell me about him". But I didn't. I made an excuse to leave almost as soon as I'd finished my tea. Mr Munro was far too intimidating in his energetic openness to be really approachable, and I made some excuse about having to get back. In fact, I did have to get back to see Coll, who didn't know anything about this visit.

'Well,' said Mr Munro as I stood to leave. 'I expect I'll see you at the auction.'

'No,' I said. 'I can't bring myself to go. There's no point, seeing as I can't afford to buy any of the pictures. I don't think I could bear to see them being sold.'

'I can understand that,' Mr Munro said. 'You must do what you feel is right for you.'

As I left, I opened the window of the car to say goodbye and he shook my hand.

75

'Take care,' he said, handing me a book, 'and read this, there's a chapter on your father. Give it back sometime, it's the only copy I've got. Come again if you want to. I'm sure there's a lot more that you might be interested to know. Don't forget, if you've got any questions about your father, just ask.'

I agreed to do so and set off feeling disorientated and rather sad. The statuette was on the seat beside me and I patted it absently as I eased out into the fast lane of the motorway. What intrigued me was Mr Munro's offer to tell me more about my father if I should have any queries. He had so obviously seen my curiosity, and was making it easy for me to go back and ask the things I hadn't been ready to ask today.

But I couldn't understand my feeling of sadness. I had the sculpture after all – had discovered someone who knew my father personally. I had found three of his paintings that I'd never seen before. (I must ask to photograph them, I thought.) But somehow it all added up to an anti-climax. Because I hadn't asked the right questions? Because I hadn't really found out anything new? Because the sculpture had not changed, become more special, now that I had paid £2,500 for it?

I picked up the book that I'd placed above the glove compartment. It was titled, rather pompously I thought, Twentieth Century Scottish Painting: A Perspective.

NINE

I was already at home by the time Coll arrived at six. There was an aubergine casserole cooking slowly in the oven. I had followed an imprecise recipe and wasn't sure of the outcome. The first thing I did was take her through to the dining room to show her the sculpture which I'd set in the centre of the table. Fortunately I had expected her not to like it, though as an art student I'd hoped for better.

'The marble's nice,' she said picking it up and weighing it lightly in her hand, 'but the sculpture is a nothing. It doesn't even look like anything.'

'It's abstract,' I pointed out.

'That's not what I meant. It doesn't have any form – not even an abstract form.'

'It's not form that counts,' I told her, 'but feeling.'

'Maybe that's true, but there's no feeling in it either.'

'In your opinion,' I said.

'In my opinion,' she agreed.

Because I'd suspected that she would dislike it, I was somehow endeared by her honesty. I would have been much more upset if she'd said it was very nice and had left it at that.

'What do these letters on the base mean?' she asked, handing the sculpture to me. There was a series of letters and numbers: LUTT G. P.E. 70.

'As far as I know,' I said, 'the G stands for Gaudier, the P.E. for Paul Ellis and 70 is the date he carved it. I don't know what LUTT means. I should have asked Mr Munro.'

'It's curious,' she said. 'I'd like to know.'

'Maybe I'll phone, then,' I said.

We ate our aubergine casserole by candlelight in the dining room. I had hoped it would be romantic, but I'd oversalted the dinner and we sat and nibbled at it with pursed lips and our resultant thirst made us drink too much wine. I talked some more about Mr Munro, but Coll wasn't interested. What truly amazed her was the price I'd paid for the sculpture.

'Two and a half thousand pounds!' she said with incredulity, drawing out the words in a kind of elongated sneer. 'I can't believe you paid so much for this... '

She gestured towards the sculpture which stood on the table between us, looking touchingly precious, I thought, in the candlelight.

'You can't have the same feelings about it that I have,' I told her. 'I have all sorts of memories wound up with it.'

She shrugged.

'I think it's awful, actually. I'd be embarrassed to have it on my mantelpiece. It's useless. It's too narrow at the base too be a paperweight, too small to be a doorstop. Too ugly to be an ornament. I think you're crazy to have bought it. If I had £2,500 to spend like that, I'd have spent it all on having a decent photographic reproduction made of each of the thirty-four paintings that your mother's getting rid of. I know you're attached to them.'

'Let's talk about something else,' I said.

Instead, I went to get the dessert – fresh oranges in caramel, doused liberally with Grand Marnier. I had to leave the room to swallow my anger at Coll's antipathy. It was all very well for her not to like the statuette, but it was too much for her to ridicule it – ridicule me for buying it. But she had a point about photographing the paintings. Even if I couldn't afford expensive reproductions, I could at least have used my own camera and taken a snapshot of each one. It was so obvious, and so tragically too late to do anything about it.

When I came back, Coll's mood had changed. I was surprised and pleased to find her apologetic.

'Look,' she said. 'I'm sorry about what I said. It doesn't matter what I think. So long as you like the sculpture, then I'm happy. I was amazed by the price, that's all.'

I served her dessert and she took the collar of my shirt, pulling me down towards her. When we were only inches apart she said, 'I love you Peter,' and kissed me on the lips.

I was still too upset to respond, and felt suddenly pathetic and young and stupidly close to tears. Why hadn't I photographed the paintings? I was insane. I was an idiot, and Coll – seeing my expression – stood up, put her arms around me, and kissed me again.

'God, I'm sorry,' she said, 'I forgot how much this means to you.' 'Don't worry,' I said. 'I'm okay.'

There was something between us at that moment that must have been dangerously close to love. There was an intensity and a charge that seemed to spark between us, but I couldn't translate this feeling into coherence, so let it go unquestioned. We sat down again to eat. The oranges were light, delicious and quickly eaten. In the silence that remained when we'd finished, Coll looked at me and smiled.

'It's nice and warm in here. What's the rest of the house like?'

'Cold.'

'I thought so,' she said. 'In which case we could either go upstairs and shiver in your bed, or we could stay here.'

'Let's stay here.'

'Good.'

She got up and came over to me, sitting gently on my lap and undoing my shirt buttons. I responded by doing the same with her blouse.

'I've never done it on a dining room table before,' she whispered.

'I don't think it'll be very comfortable,' I whispered back.

'Who cares.'

I don't know why I was whispering – we were alone in the house. I carefully stacked the plates and put them on one of the chairs. Pushing the place mats to one side, Coll lay on the dark, polished mahogany and pulled off her tights. We lay on the cool wood and kissed.

Having sex in front of the statuette gave me a feeling of startling intensity. There was something brashly unconventional about it, something adolescent and rebellious. Coll broke off as we were finding our rhythm and pushed me back, sitting up and reaching for the two candles beside us. She knelt on the table and held them over me. Gently, with a secretive smile, she poured molten wax in two long trickles across my chest. It was searingly hot, and I could feel the wax prickle my skin as it hardened. I closed my eyes and let her pour more, drop by drop, as it melted. It was sensual, uncomfortable and very erotic. I lay and gave myself up to the experience. When she dropped some wax on the head of my penis, it was genuinely painful and I sat up suddenly with a cry. Coll laughed and pushed me back down, straddling me, and peeling the cooled wax from my skin piece by piece, leaving a lattice of red marks across my chest and stomach.

'Ready?' she whispered with a sigh, 'let's start again?'

Coll had a certain aggression that I had only occasionally noticed when we were together. It showed in her verbal assertiveness; and it showed now, as I lay on my back, cool wood against my spine. She grasped my shoulders, clutching me and squeezing as though some kind of transformation could result. She pummelled my chest, then massaged it so hard that my muscles tingled with relief when she stopped. She ran her fingers through my hair, twisting it round so fiercely that I cried out in pain. She seemed unaware of any discomfort that she was causing, and I was not inclined to ask her to stop, being so caught by the intensity of her attention.

I held her firmly round the waist, but she took my hands and placed them elsewhere. Against her rib-cage, cupping her breasts, cradling her throat. She wanted to be described in terms of the movement of my fingers, and I obliged, even down to her finger tips which I rolled in mine, placing them in my mouth and biting gently against the fleshy pads.

My orgasm, when it came, left me partly relieved and partly released. I felt relieved by Coll's continuing lust, by her undiminished interest in me; and released in some weird way from the absurd reverence I had felt for the house. It was entirely due to the respect I had for my father. But now the last traces of him were gone – and making love on the dining room table reduced the room,

80

and consequently the rest of the house, to being simply a place in which to get on with my own life. Fast on the heels of this realisation came the secondary knowledge that it was only my mother's absence that had made this evening possible.

Afterwards, I went through to the sitting room and turned on the gas fire, then went back to Coll.

'Let's wait for it to warm up a bit through there. Coffee first?'

'Mmm,' Coll murmured.

I started to put my shirt on, but Coll objected.

'No, don't,' she said. 'Let's stay like this for a while.'

'I've got to get at least partly dressed if I'm going through to the kitchen,' I told her.

'Don't be stupid,' she told me. 'Who's going to see you?'

'Okay, then.'

With my mother gone I felt free of having to conform to my image of what she wanted from me – namely for me to be discreet and quiet and to disturb her as little as possible. It seemed odd that I had accepted as normal the fact that we were two estranged people, that in spite of our estrangement we had made no effort to get away from each other. We had become settled into a stifled acceptance of each other, an inert nothingness between us.

Naked, I poured the coffee and, now that we'd finished eating, I let Emily come with me to the dining room. I could sense, for the first time, what a freedom it would be to live away from home. To have this feeling of personal space was a persuasive reason to move away.

Sitting in the candlelight, hair pulled back, wearing no make-up, hugging herself with arms crossed, Coll looked almost boyish as she smiled at me. She dropped her hands as I came in and her breasts dipped in a gentle movement, destroying the impression.

'Come on,' she said, 'let's go next door.'

'It won't have warmed up yet,' I said.

'Never mind.'

We went through and pulled the sofa up to the fireside. Emily immediately lay down as close to the fire as she could bear, and proceeded to ignore us as we sat in a loose embrace on the worn embroidery of the cushions and sipped our coffee.

'I'll have to go round to Martin's tomorrow,' I said, 'and show him the sculpture. He'll be so pleased that it's finally mine.'

Coll didn't say anything for a while. She looked at me with a touch of annoyance, and then put her mug on the floor.

'Don't go tomorrow,' she said. 'We're spending tomorrow together. I want to go for a long walk with you and Emily.'

'There'll be plenty of time to call in on him,' I said. 'Besides, I want to tell him about Mr Munro.'

'I don't want to go.'

'Okay,' I said. 'You can stay here. It won't take long.'

'No, Peter,' she said. 'I want to spend this time with you.'

'I'll go and see him on Monday, then,' I conceded. 'You can come along too, if you like.'

'No,' she said firmly.

'Why not?'

'What point would there be in me going round to see him. I see him at college anyway.'

'But he's my best friend,' I said. 'I spend a lot of time with him.'

Coll shrugged. I felt a peevish anger at her for being so negative. What was it with the women that I slept with? Why did they object to my friendship to Martin? It mystified me, annoyed me, and made me determined not to let it get in the way of my friendship.

'You liked Martin okay at Alan's party,' I said. 'So what's changed?'

'Nothing. I feel indifferent to Martin, that's all. I'm polite to him, but that doesn't mean I want to make friends with him.'

'I'm not going to stop spending time with him,' I told her.

'In that case you'll have to decide whether to spend time

82

with him, or time with me.'

'Come off it,' I said, 'you're being unreasonable.'

'No I'm not. Martin would say the same. I bet he doesn't want you to see me.'

I felt sad again, and suddenly naked. I looked down at my winter paleness, at the way our limbs touched so softly in the warmth, at the way the blond hairs on my legs caught the flickering glow from the fire.

Emily snuffled in her sleep and Coll dropped to her knees, moving away from me, and began to stroke the inert dog, tickling her ears and gently waking her. Emily leaned her head towards her in appreciation and they murmured to each other. I looked at Coll's back, so smooth and young.

It came as a shock to me then to realise that if it came to a confrontation and I was asked to choose between Coll as a lover and Martin as a friend – I would choose Martin. I knew this absolutely and it frightened me. Of course, I'd known Martin for years and years. We had a lifetime of friendship ahead of us. But Coll? How well did I know her? And how long did we have together before we would drift apart? We had already started imposing on each other the images that we wanted to see. But we were no more than chance acquaintances at a party. There was no reason why we should be destined to love each other, just because we were sex partners. Coll had already said I love you, but only in an internal kind of way, as though she was exercising her own ability to say it to another person.

'I'm going to leave home,' I said, the words slipping out before they had properly registered. Coll looked at me, nonplussed by the stark immediacy of my statement.

'What's made you suddenly decide that?' she asked.

I thought carefully before replying.

'Because I've realised that I can't do what I want to do in this house,' I said. 'It's only because my mother is away that we're sitting here like this at all. It's too much of a compromise. For as long as I was alone, it didn't seem to make much difference. Now you're around, it's time I made a move.'

Coll left Emily to sit beside me. She put her arms round

83

my neck and kissed me several times, very slowly.

'I'm glad,' she said between kisses.

Coll stayed the night as planned. My single bed was inadequate and we both had a disturbed sleep, but it was fun all the same to be together. I felt clandestine and it pleased me that I would keep this secret from my mother. She might be hovering round my father's paintings like some cruel bird of carrion, but I would ignore the setting up of the sale, just as I would ignore the auction itself in two months time. I was pleased to have done my own thing this weekend, and I looked forward to showing my mother the statuette on her return.

We took Emily for a walk the next morning. It was one of those blustery March mornings, a threat of showers never far off, with spring hanging in the brightness of the day. It was only half way to Bishopthorpe that I realised I had promised to take this walk with Martin. Last weekend I had arranged to phone him at ten thirty this Sunday. It was now midday.

Emily raced about as usual, dashing ahead only to stop and look back in exasperation at our slowness. Coll, warmly wrapped in her thick tweed coat, seemed touched by permanence. She might have always been here, silently absorbed by the grasses and the bare hawthorn, the silent river and the clogging mud of the path. It was as though she had been on every walk I had ever taken.

I felt a touch of guilt about Martin, but I couldn't pretend that I would have wanted this morning to have been otherwise, and I put thoughts of him to the back of my mind, mentally preparing an apology for later. All I wanted of today was an invigorating walk, a quiet lunch in town, a long, deep bath to fill the afternoon, and to make love again as the day faded.

TEN

'Woman trouble,' Martin told me. 'That's what it is. It's always hard when a woman gets between friends.'

I had told him that instead of walking the dog with him the day before, I had gone with Coll. The news depressed him.

'When I arranged to go with you, I didn't realise I was going to have her staying for the weekend.'

'You could have phoned me anyway, to say what was going on. I had an invitation to go to Leeds for the day, as a matter of fact, and I ended up sitting at home doing fuck all.'

'Sorry.'

Martin puffed his cheeks and gracelessly took a mouthful of lamb passanda.

'Forget it,' he said.

We were sitting in one of the better Indian restaurants in town. I was treating him to a celebration meal – a celebration of the purchase of my father's sculpture, which stood between us on the table.

'Look,' I said, 'can't you cheer up even slightly? This is supposed to be a happy occasion, for me at least. I am now the owner of an original Paul Ellis.'

'Which is great, I know,' said Martin. 'Look, I'll try to cheer up, but I'm in trouble at the moment and it's hard.'

'Trouble?' I echoed. It sounded ominous coming like that from Martin, especially when he looked so genuinely depressed.

'Yes, with Geoff.'

'Ahh,' I nodded. 'You've slept with him.'

'Yes,' he said, grinning slightly for the first time that evening. 'It's crazy. I don't know whether it was me that seduced him or him that seduced me. I don't suppose it matters.'

'But what about Lynn?'

'Quite,' he agreed. 'I don't suppose we can keep it a secret from her for long. Besides, I hate the momentum of this kind of secrecy. The whole thing started out as a slightly drunken grope, but I think he's falling for me, and that makes it dodgy.'

'I can see that,' I said.

'Can you?' he asked. 'Well, I suppose it's not so uncommon. What I hate is that Geoff can't be honest with himself about what's going on. He keeps on saying it doesn't mean anything, but he says it in that hysterical way that means exactly the opposite. The last thing I ever wanted was to get involved like this. I quite like him, and he's reasonably attractive, but I don't want to get into a relationship. Certainly not on these terms. And especially seeing as he's my landlord. No, now all I want is to get out.'

'That's no problem, surely,' I pointed out. 'You've always said you're going to have to go and live in Leeds. You've got a perfect excuse to go.'

'Mmm,' said Martin thoughtfully.

'There's no Mmm about it,' I told him. 'There's no reason for you to stay. It can't be that difficult to find digs, surely?'

'But I don't know if I want to.'

'What? You want to stay and have a messy affair with someone you're not even in love with?'

'Well...'

'And you can't keep that sort of thing quiet,' I said. 'People pick up on these things pretty quickly. You knew instantly when I first started going out with Coll. Have you thought about what's going to happen when Lynn finds out?'

'You're right,' he agreed. 'I should have thought about all this first. But the sex is so good, that's the thing, and Geoff seems so grateful for it.'

I shook my head.

'Get out,' I said.

Martin nodded, but still looked unhappy.

'I hate feeling down like this,' he said.

'Use your head for a while,' I said. 'Look at it from the outside. It's not that big a deal.'

'But love is never easy. Even when it isn't really love.'

He returned his attention to his food then added, as though continuing the same thought process, 'how is Coll by the way?'

'Okay,' I said, 'though I'm coming to the conclusion that she's a little strange.'

I hadn't told him about the candlewax.

'What do you expect, going out with an art student,' he said.

'I could say the same about married men.'

Martin laughed, at last, a brilliant flash of a smile and a genuine touch of humour in his eyes.

'God, why is everything so bloody complicated?' he groaned, and drank some lager.

'You'd be bored to death if it wasn't.'

'This,' said Martin, 'is true.'

I called for the waiter and ordered more drinks.

'Now tell me about Mr Munro,' Martin said. 'I think I'm just about ready to be enthusiastic.'

So I described my visit. It was like a bright moment in my past, weighted with significance, but when I tried to talk about it, there wasn't much to say. I'd arrived, picked up the statue, looked round an amazing house (you would have loved it, Martin), drank two cups of tea, and then left.

'He was a personal friend of your father's?'

'Yes, apparently.'

'And you didn't ask him all the questions we've been asking ourselves ever since we were so high.'

'I was too shy.'

'Too shy! Too shy to ask why your dad was unhappy? Too shy to ask if Mr Munro had any photos of him, to ask for details of their friendship, information about how your father worked – why he painted such extraordinarily weird pictures?'

'I didn't ask, okay,' I said, feeling pinched by Martin's incredulity. 'You weren't there, so you can't appreciate how intimidating it all was. At least he's said I can go back and

87

see him if I want.'

'Take me next time,' said Martin. 'I'll ask the questions. I'm an artist too, you know. I'm not just interested for your sake. I'm interested for me.'

We ended up in a pub by the Minster. It was a mixed pub with a number of people there who were obviously gay. A month ago I would have been intimidated by the place, but now I had the security of my relationship with Coll.

The first person we saw on our arrival was Alan, the man with the arts budget.

'Hey,' he called to where we stood in the doorway, 'come and join us.'

Martin raised his eyebrows at me in an ambiguous question. I shrugged back, equally ambiguously I hoped, and we wandered over with our drinks.

'Sit down, boys,' he said. 'Let me introduce you to my friend Jerome – another painter.'

Jerome shook our hands and smiled an openly friendly and perhaps slightly seductive smile. He was tall, with light brown hair, and a large, unruly moustache that focussed attention on his mouth and his extremely white teeth. I guessed him to be in his mid-thirties, which seemed ancient to me, though not as ancient as Alan. There was a lightly freckled paleness to his skin, a flawless smoothness between the wrinkles that made him look not quite real.

'Hi,' he said with a slight mid-Atlantic accent. 'If Alan says I'm another painter, can I take it that you're both painters too?'

'No,' I said, 'I'm not a painter. I work in a museum. Martin's the other painter.'

'Peter's father was a painter,' Martin added. 'Paul Ellis. We're having an intriguing time at the moment trying to find out more about him.'

'Paul Ellis?' Alan murmured, 'isn't there going to be a sale of his work in London soon?'

'Yes,' Martin said eagerly, 'do you know anything about him?'

'Not really. Only what I've heard from Bratt's. They

always send me advance notice of their sales, in case I want to organise a purchase.'

'So you're going to buy one?'

Alan shook his head.

'No, it's not really up to me. I'm far more involved in setting up exhibitions than in buying works of art. Once a gallery has its budget, I don't have any more to do with it.'

'So what do Bratt's say about my father?' I asked.

'I can't really remember. Not a lot. Some hype about investment potential and international interest. The usual. I think it says he died in the early seventies.'

'That's right,' I nodded. 'I was only one at the time. I know very little about him.'

'How mysterious,' said Jerome, smiling his broad toothy smile.

We sat and drank for a few moments before Jerome spoke again.

'So you're a painter?' he said to Martin.

'Yes, I'm an art student, actually. I'm doing a foundation course in Leeds.'

'I'm living in Leeds, too,' said Jerome. 'You must come round. I haven't been there long, so I don't know many people yet. I was in New York before that. I lived there fourteen years, up until Christmas.'

'What brought you here?' I asked. 'Surely New York has much more to offer than Leeds?'

'I hate that,' said Jerome. 'People can be happy anywhere, and people can be unhappy anywhere. I came to Leeds because it was somewhere to go. I had to give up my studio space in New York for several reasons – to do with emotional problems – so I was free to move on. As a matter of fact, I have relatives who live near here. They fixed me up with somewhere to live.'

'But it can't be a patch on New York,' Martin insisted.

'What about all those trees, and parks, and open spaces you've got here?' Jerome asked. 'Have you any idea how long it takes to get into the countryside – I mean real, wild countryside – if you live in New York? I sometimes stop beside a tree or a bush when I'm walking somewhere and bury my head in the leaves. Have you ever really looked at a tree or a bush? Have you ever spent half an hour losing yourself in the smell, the touch, the experience of a single plant? Everyone takes it all so much for granted. And it's not just nature, it's everything. I want to experience everything. I want to sit in the window for an hour in the morning and watch the sunrise. I want to walk through the evening and see the frost begin to settle on the pavement. I want to savour every moment of going into my local newsagent to buy the daily paper. I want to put all this down on canvas, all these riches that come to us by simply being alive.'

He leant over and placed his hand over Martin's.

'It doesn't matter where you live. You can live in New York, or Leeds, or anywhere. Life is still an amazing thing.'

Martin smiled at Jerome, embarrassed, impressed by the force with which he had spoken.

'You're right,' he said quietly.

'Of course I'm right,' he said. 'Isn't that so, Alan?'

'Quite,' Alan agreed. 'But most people don't feel anything as intensely as you.'

'How sad for them,' he said.

I could see that Martin had been impressed by Jerome. It was difficult not to be. The passion with which he spoke was infectious, and as the evening passed it seemed that everything touched him with its intensity. Mere experience gave him pleasure – the taste of his beer, the company of others, the simplest of discussions. It was humbling to meet someone who could derive an honest sense of fulfilment from life. I thought of my dissatisfactions and felt embarrassed by them.

Towards the end of the evening, with sudden inspiration, I took the statuette from my pocket. I hadn't thought to produce it before, because I had a peculiarly personal feeling towards it. I didn't mind Martin sharing it with me, because his respect for my father's work was beyond question. But there was no reason for me to be closed about it here.

'Look,' I said. 'Here's a small sculpture that my father

made in 1970. I bought it on Saturday.'

Jerome took it from me and proceeded to examine it closely, to run his fingers along the grooves in the marble, to feel the coolness of its touch.

'That's a first even for me,' said Alan. 'Someone pulling a valuable sculpture from their pocket in the middle of a crowded pub. Do you do this sort of thing often?'

'No.' I blushed. 'I only brought it into town to show Martin. I didn't expect to see anyone else.'

Alan took it from Jerome and looked at it carefully.

'I love marble,' he said. 'I know it's difficult to work with, but it's worth the effort.'

He stood the sculpture on a beer mat and we all stared at it as if it had some strange religious significance. It remained on the table for the last half hour that we were there, a centrepiece for our conversation. Even when we talked about other things, it was still present between us. I felt so proud knowing that it was mine.

I had a late coffee at Martin's place. I took the statue out again once we were in his room, and Martin lit some incense. I smiled to think that my whole life had been wrapped in fragrant smoke lately. Since I'd met Coll, there was something vaguely erotic about the scent of sandalwood or rose, something soporific too.

The statue looked at home here, surrounded by the paraphernalia of an artist's work. I sat on the floor and hugged my knees. Martin looked pensively out of the window.

'What did you think of Jerome?' he asked.

'Very American,' I said. 'Very vibrant.'

'I think,' said Martin slowly, 'that he's the most incredible person I've ever met.'

I looked at Martin's serious face and thought, this is probably what religious conversion looks like – or love at first sight?

'I think,' I said, 'that Jerome isn't actually human. I think he comes from another planet where everything is so deeply dull that all things human are a wonder by comparison. I think he transmits vibrant energy back home in instalments, to stop all his relatives from dying of terminal dullness.'

'Yes,' said Martin, 'he does seem to give off energy.'

'He'll end up as some great earthly religious figure with a fanatical congregation of acolytes. They'll all have to bury their faces in the leaves of trees for an hour every day as part of their devotions.'

Martin laughed. 'Don't be so cynical,' he said. 'I wish I could do that. I wish I could be so fired by everyday things.'

'So do I, really,' I admitted.

'I think I'll go round to see him,' Martin said. 'I want to see what kind of paintings he paints.'

We sat and watched the incense burning, listening to a clock ticking downstairs. Geoff and Lynn were in bed and the rest of the house – the rest of the street – was deadly quiet.

'So what are you going to do about Geoff?' I asked.

'I don't know. I'll have to try and cool off a little, but it's so difficult with us living in the same house.'

He breathed a long slow breath and then looked at me.

'I don't really want to talk about it,' he said.

He leant forwards and picked up the sculpture, looking at it fondly, then smiling.

'What did your mother say when you told her you'd bought it?'

'She was furious,' I said, 'though she tried not to show it. It's none of her business whether I bought it or not, and she knows it.'

I took the sculpture from him and felt the weight of my pleasure in owning it as I gently passed it from one hand to the other.

'I wonder how she'll feel getting all that money from her own son.'

'Love it, I should think,' said Martin.

ELEVEN

Even if I hadn't been thinking about Dave Boothe on a conscious level, it still wasn't a particular surprise to meet him during my lunch hour on Wednesday. Nor did it surprise me when, along with Paul, he jumped down from the dirt-streaked sandstone wall below Skeldergate Bridge and sauntered towards me. There was a rotting wooden structure just out from the near arch of the bridge – a kind of mooring perhaps, or an architectural prop for which there was no longer any use. As I glanced at it, three or four ducks shot out from underneath in a squall of noise, making me jump. Dave saw my discomfort and laughed at me as he approached.

He was idly carrying a short plank of wood, but I didn't feel physically threatened. Now that the police had intervened once, I assumed that he would be more careful in his dealings with me. He held the wood as though unaware that it was there, and he looked calm and disinterested.

'I just got a warning,' he said to me, pleased. 'I bet you thought I'd be arrested or something.'

I didn't say anything. As a matter of fact, I already knew this from Maggie.

'Where's your girlfriend today then?'

Again I didn't reply. Dave looked at me with subdued aggression. I got the impression that he wanted to hit me, but was scared to. I didn't know what the police had said to him, but they'd obviously told him to leave me alone. We stood looking at each other, Dave with a pitiful, impotent insolence, and me with growing confidence.

'Fuck,' Dave said quietly to himself, then turned to Paul.

'Let's go,' he said, looking sidelong at me with contempt.

'Queer,' he breathed as he brushed past.

'I hope you have a nice time paying your seventy-five pound fine,' I said.

This startled him, as I'd intended it to. He was surprised that I knew about his fine, and his forehead pinched in a frown as he glanced quickly at me. His reaction was immediate, almost reflex. He swung the piece of wood that he was carrying, neither viciously, nor particularly fast, but with a calm, unconcealed violence which seemed to say that under other circumstances he would be ready to go a lot further.

I raised my arm to protect myself and the rusty, but still sharp nail at the tip caught the fleshy edge of my palm and bit a gash there almost two inches long. I winced and doubled up, clutching my palm with my uninjured hand, jamming it between my knees.

Dave laughed, not realising he had cut me. There seemed to be an unnatural silence for those few seconds as I gasped with pain. Even the ubiquitous rumble of traffic ceased to register. I stood slowly, gingerly releasing my good hand. A small reservoir of blood that was caught in the palm of my hand fell with a barely audible spatter as it caught my trousers and shoes on its way to the flagstone quay.

'Shit,' said Paul quietly. Dave looked at the plank, only then noticing the nail. I began to breathe in the shallow way that accompanies shock.

'Come on,' Dave said quietly to Paul, turning to go. It was impossible to say from his expression whether he was worried or not, but as he began to walk away, he threw the plank into the river with a startled movement, as though it had burned him.

I stood, unable to move because my mind had gone completely blank. The cut hurt, of course, but the blood scared me far more than the pain. It was falling as a steady drip-drip-drip from my little finger. When I began to think coherently, I felt the embarrassment that people feel with injuries of this kind. Part of me wanted to rush to the casualty department at York District Hospital and get immediate treatment; another part was convinced that they

94

would laugh at me for being ridiculous; would tell me not to be such a baby and to go home and put a plaster on it.

I couldn't tell how deep it was – how serious – and I quickly decided that the best course was to return to the museum and try to clean myself up. If the bleeding didn't slow down soon, then I'd consider going to the hospital.

It was only a couple of hundred yards to the museum, but I left a neat trail of blood all the way, the drops spaced about eighteen inches apart. As soon as I got into the building I bumped into Maggie.

'God,' she said, 'what's happened?'

'I cut myself,' I said, rather obviously.

She took my hand for a moment, glancing at the cut.

'Right,' she said. 'I'm taking you to the hospital.'

She took a small, perfectly white handkerchief from her bag.

'Here,' she told me, 'press that against the cut and hold your arm above your head.'

I felt stupidly self-conscious following Maggie across the car park wearing bloodstained trousers and holding my arm in the air.

'How did you do it?' Maggie asked as she pulled out of her parking space.

'It was Dave Boothe,' I said.

Maggie sighed, and we drove on in silence.

Of course, at casualty they didn't tell me to go away. They took a good look at the cut, cleaned it out, put five or six of those sticky surfacial stitches on it, and then gave me a tetanus injection. I was there for about an hour.

Now I'd told Maggie that it was Dave who'd been responsible, it was inevitable that the police would be involved again. She was adamant that I should press a charge of assault. I was less sure, knowing that Dave had been unaware of the nail. But Maggie pointed out that he shouldn't have been hitting me with a plank, whether it had a nail in it or not.

'Stand up for yourself,' she told me as I sat waiting for my injection.

The police were more interested this time, and I gave a full statement of what had happened. Maggie was pleased, and told me so. I secretly dreaded what was going to happen to Dave, not wanting to be responsible for getting him a criminal record – if he didn't already have one. Would he get another warning? A fine? Or would he end up in prison, or remand care, or whatever it was that they did to people like him... But, as Maggie said, he should have thought about that before.

Maggie was sensitive and kind to me that day. I could see that she was curious to find out why Dave should dislike me so much. But I was unable to open up enough to tell her of the episode when I had told Dave that I was gay. I didn't want to put that possibility into other people's minds – didn't want them to see something in me that I couldn't.

I was split in my feelings about Dave. I knew, of course, that he was now in real trouble, but I didn't feel good about it. One part of me felt bad about having gone to the police in the first place, and the other part felt bad because I wanted Dave to be punished for what he'd done to me – not just at Skeldergate Bridge, but over the years since the brawl at school. This part of me genuinely wished him ill, and it upset me that I could feel so negatively about another person. If I was strong, I decided, I should be able to shrug it all off.

That evening was the first time I met Coll's parents. I went round for a meal, and felt trapped.

'You've got to help me out,' she had explained. 'I hate going round to see them, but they won't pay me my allowance if I don't. You can give me emotional support.'

First of all, Mrs Palmer made an absurd fuss about my hand. I lied and said I'd done it whilst trying to get a Victorian piece of machinery to work. She kept on asking me how I was, whether the cut hurt, how long before the stitches would be removed. It wasn't as if it looked impressive – covered by a padded pink plaster. Coll was short tempered, and told her mother to be quiet.

'Don't talk to your mother like that,' said her father – the first thing he'd said since I arrived, bar a surly mumble of greeting.

Coll was seething. I could see that, though I couldn't understand why. Her parents were dull people, that's all. Polite, kind, thoughtful – but dull. But then perhaps that was the problem. Maybe dullness was the worst thing in the world for Coll.

We sat in the sitting room, the medieval city walls visible through the window, glowing a warm, deep orange in the last light of the sun. Coll kept looking at me as if to say, yes I know this is hell, but we're going to have to get through these introductions sooner or later.

When we sat down to eat, at least the food was good – a seafood lasagne with salad. Mr and Mrs Palmer occasionally spoke to each other in short, unconnected sentences. I remained silent. Coll gave a brief account of her work at college. The meal was mercifully short and afterwards, when we went upstairs with our coffee, Mr Palmer gave me a deeply distrustful look as if to say: don't have sex with my daughter whilst I'm in the house.

As soon as we got into the bedroom, Coll closed the door and kissed me. I kissed her back carefully, nearly spilling my coffee.

'Sorry about that,' she said. 'You've just experienced a typical meal at home. Boring, huh?'

'Yes,' I nodded.

We sat down on the bed.

'So how did you cut your hand?' she asked. 'And don't tell me it was on a piece of machinery, because I know it wasn't. You're such a bad liar, Peter.'

So I told her about Dave and the police. Strangely, she was thrilled.

'Good,' she said. 'I'm glad he's in trouble. I hope he goes to prison.'

In Coll's room it turned out to be pretty well an extension of the evening downstairs – dull and soporific. We had little to say to each other, so we talked about my hand and the likely demise of Dave Boothe. I know that this desultory mood was at least partly because Coll was at home, but I felt that somehow, after only a short time of knowing each other, we had run out of conversation. The only thing we had left was to sit and be bored together. If I had been with Martin there would have been no problem about silence, because somehow my silences with him were full silences, whereas with Coll they were empty and uncomfortable. Of course, Coll was suffering from her antipathy towards her parents and couldn't really relax. It was as though she was in a kind of limbo, waiting for them to go to bed or something. I felt I hadn't achieved anything constructive that evening with my time.

Perhaps, I thought, all relationships are like this. Once you've got used to each other, you drift on together, without much excitement, without much of anything except the comforting presence of a partner. It was an unpleasant thought, because through all my stifling life at home I had imagined a vibrancy out there that I would one day find the courage to go and intercept. The thought that life might actually be a rather dull affair in the end was deeply depressing.

Coll surprised me when we made love. She was trembling, as though nervous or desperate. She relinquished herself to me completely that evening, and this sudden change of behaviour made me nervous too. She was vocal, which was surprising with her parents downstairs, and when she came, she cried out. It was peculiar and embarrassing knowing that I'd have to face them later in the knowledge that they had heard us.

After sex we sat around whilst Coll put on some music. Then she became listless and agitated.

'Shit,' she said at half past nine. 'Let's go.'

'I thought you were going to stay the night.'

'I can't face it. I'll take the train back to Leeds.'

We went downstairs. Mr and Mrs Palmer were in the front room.

'Look, I've got to get back,' said Coll, standing in the doorway. 'I'll take the nine fifty train.'

'Why don't you stay here?' her mother asked. 'You can

98

have breakfast with us and take the train in the morning.'

'No, it's okay mum, I've got a day return.'

'See,' said her father, 'she had no intention of staying. She says, yes, yes, I'll stay and then she never does. She drags these young men in here like some local tart and then buggers off back to Leeds.'

'He's right, you know,' her mother said.

'I know you don't like the way I live,' said Coll.

'No, we don't,' her father replied simply.

'It's not that we want you to live your life in any particular way,' Mrs Palmer said, 'it's that we wish you'd do that sort of thing elsewhere. When you come and see us next, why don't you come on your own?'

'Because I'm bored shitless,' she told them. 'I can't stand to be here on my own because it's like some kind of death. I feel like I'm suffocating in boredom by walking into this house.'

Her parents seemed less shocked by this than I would have imagined – than I was. Perhaps they'd heard it all before.

'Next time you come,' said her mother quietly, 'I hope you have the grace to apologise for what you've just said.'

'Fuck off,' said Coll, and shut the door.

I walked in silence with her to the front door.

'Ha,' she said to me as we left, 'that's that.'

'And are you going to apologise?' I asked her.

'Of course.'

We parted by Skeldergate Bridge and Coll went off to the station. My walk home took me past the house where Mat had his bedsit. I was anxious to redeem something from this bland, bizarre evening, so I rang his bell.

As it happened, he was there.

'Hi,' I said. 'Are you busy? I was just passing.'

'No,' he said, 'I'm not busy. Come in.'

He led me through to the bedsit, which already looked better. He'd hung new curtains, and had painted the room white.

'Sorry about the smell of paint,' he said. 'I did most of the brush-work at the week-end, but I've been finishing the last bits off this evening.'

There were some brushes in the sink, and the old jeans and sweater that he was wearing were spattered with white flecks.

'Do you fancy going out for a drink?' he asked.

'I was going to suggest that,' I said.

'I'll change.'

I sat again in the easy chair and picked up the book on Gaudier-Brzeska, idly wondering whether any of the pictures might be the one that my father had used when making his sculpture. None of those illustrated suggested themselves as likely candidates and I soon lost interest.

'How's work?' I asked.

'Boring,' Mat replied.

He dressed more smartly this evening, perhaps in response to the rather formal clothes that I was wearing. He put on a pair of well pressed dark trousers and an earthy green sweater. The dark colours accentuated the paleness of his face, which in turn accentuated the lucent blue of his eyes. I couldn't decide whether he was attractive or not. Last time I'd seen him, I'd decided that he was. This time he seemed a little too strange and too frail to fit my usual idea of good looks.

We went to the pub by the Minster again, and again there were a lot of gay people there – which is presumably why Mat had suggested it. On Monday, when I'd come here with Martin, I had felt inviolable in my heterosexuality, Coll somehow a solid symbol that I was straight. After the dinner round at her house, and the subsequent rather tawdry non-communication between us, I felt more vulnerable to my old doubts – doubts that had previously been obliterated by the sexual connection I had with Coll, and Anna before her.

I am living in a world where I am a stranger to myself, I thought. I felt as though there was a long, loud scream waiting somewhere inside, gently working to the surface like a small bubble in thick liquid. I wanted so much more from life than a job in a museum and a relationship with Coll, but I didn't know what it was that I wanted, and

100

worse, I didn't know how to go about finding it. I felt stuck in the rut of my own existence, in the inertia of my own limitations.

Mat was seemingly unaware of my preoccupation and conversed with me about current affairs, and the books he'd been reading. I started off feeling bored, but after a very swift pint of beer I gradually cheered up, warmed by his good humour. We laughed about the Prime Minister for a while, and I managed to ignore the emptiness that I was beginning to feel.

We walked back together, the air damp and surprisingly warm for the beginning of March. I accepted an offer of coffee as I wasn't even close to being tired. I was in one of those moods where sleep would be impossible before two or three o'clock. I was buzzing somewhere inside with dissatisfactions – the nourishing food of insomnia – and didn't want to be alone.

When we came into the bedsitting room, I was taken by surprise when he kissed me. It was a curiously sexless kiss, on the edge of my mouth, and it left a moist coolness that I instantly wanted to brush away. But I didn't. I stood and looked at him as calmly as I could, trying not to show that I had begun to tremble.

'Why did you do that?' I asked quietly.

'Because I thought you wanted me to.'

'No,' I said, 'I didn't want you to. I'm sorry.'

'Oh,' Mat turned from me in sudden embarrassment. He crouched down, opened the small cupboard beside the cooker and took out two mugs. I stood, unmoving, in the doorway, uncertain of what to do next. Should I act as if nothing had happened? Should I talk about it? Should I tell him the truth and say that, at that moment, I felt no desire for him – that I wanted, suddenly, to be in the reassuring arms of Coll?

The kettle began to rumble as it warmed and Mat, his back still turned, was opening a fresh jar of coffee. We had been in the room for some time now and it was becoming absurd that I hadn't moved. I took my jacket off as casually as I could and hung it from the back of the door, then went to sit in the easy chair.

When he'd made the coffee, he brought it over.

'Powdered milk,' he said. 'There's no point me keeping fresh here, because I don't have a fridge.'

'Thanks,' I said, taking the mug from him and blowing gently over the coffee's lustreless surface.

'Listen,' said Mat quite suddenly. 'Will you please forget what happened? It was stupid of me. I'm sorry.'

'That's okay,' I said. 'I don't mind. But it's not the sort of thing I want, that's all.'

Mat nodded. He looked as if he was trying to think of something to say to change the subject, but he involuntarily shuddered instead.

'No,' he said, 'this is no good. I'm not going to quietly shut up and say, I'm sorry, I'm sorry to you like that. I can't. It's too demeaning. I can't bear the idea that you'll go away and say, poor Mat, he tried it on with me this evening... '

He stopped and looked at me almost with hatred.

'You're a bit of shit, really,' he said. 'You seem so calm and reasonable on the surface, but underneath you're just a sexual thief.'

I looked blank at this, feeling uncomfortable.

'I don't understand,' I said. 'What have I done? And what do you mean by a sexual thief?'

'I mean that you give everyone the come on. You act so intimate and available, but it's only a front for your ego. You want people to fall for you, so that you can prop up your narcissism with the admiration of others. You steal something from us, and give nothing in return.'

'Look,' I said, 'this is ridiculous. I'm not like that at all. I've never been in this situation before.'

'No?' Mat challenged. 'What about Martin? What about the last year at school. You led him on, and then turned your back on him.'

'He's my best friend,' I said. 'I've never turned my back on him.'

'That's not the way he saw it. I know, because I got him on the rebound. He didn't want me at all, he wanted you.

You'll probably never know how humiliating that is – to fall in love with someone, only to find that they're in love with someone else.'

I opened my mouth to say something, but nothing came, so I closed it again.

'I thought you might have changed when I saw you again,' he said. 'But of course you haven't. You seemed so much more open and aware, but underneath you're as selfish as ever. I feel sorry for your girlfriend. You hurt people, Peter. You hurt Martin, you'll almost certainly hurt Coll, and despite the fact that I was half expecting it, you've hurt me.'

'I don't believe all this,' I said. 'I don't believe that I've hurt Martin.'

'Ask him,' he said. 'Go on. Ask him, and see what he says.'

I shook my head.

'I don't get it,' I told him. 'I've never given you the come on. This is all your own imagination.'

'No it's not,' he told me. 'Look into yourself, Peter, and think about it. It's not what you say to people, it's your manner. It's in the way you look at people. And looks are much more honest than words. You looked at me as though you wanted us to make love together. I don't expect you to admit it to me now, but if you really think about it, you'll know I'm right. I'm amazed that Martin still takes the trouble to see you.'

He looked at me now with sympathy rather than anger. I tried to ignore what he'd said, but found myself vividly remembering the night when Anna had run from the pub. What had she said – something about the way I was looking at Martin as though we were lovers?

'I'm right,' said Mat, 'and you know it.'

103

TWELVE

The episode with Mat left me more shaken than I would ever admit. Of course, I didn't believe him in a literal sense about Martin's feelings for me – he must have been exaggerating because he was angry, and it was only an opinion anyway. And yet, I couldn't bring myself to talk to Martin about it, which was perhaps the most telling thing of all. I feared what he might have to say. Instead, I asked Steph.

I met her for lunch in Leeds on Saturday. We were both going to go over and see Martin for the afternoon in his new digs. I was still amazed at how quickly this had all happened. Martin had met Jerome on Monday, gone to visit him on Tuesday, and had moved in on Thursday.

I met Steph in a small green and white failed imitation of a French café. She looked well and happy.

'Awful decor,' she said after ordering salad and a fruit juice, 'but good cheap food.'

'So,' I said, 'have you seen Martin's digs?'

'Yes. I helped him move in.'

'And?'

'Wonderful. Bright, spacious and rent free.'

'Rent free!'

'Yes. Jerome won't charge him.'

'That's brilliant.'

'Yes,' she agreed, 'though I don't know how long they're going to be able to stay there. The landlord's trying to evict Jerome at the moment.'

'At least it's a start. And it gets Martin away from Geoff.'

'Oh, he told you about that did he? Yes, it's a good idea for Martin to move.'

'Listen,' I said, 'I want to ask you something about Martin.'

I briefly explained what had happened between myself and Mat, and told her what he'd said about Martin. When I finished, Steph remained quiet for some time.

'This isn't really for me to talk about,' she said. 'Why don't you ask Martin?'

'I can't,' I said. 'I don't want him to suspect my motives.'

'What are your motives?'

'I want to know, that's all.'

'Do you remember the party when we met?' Steph said. 'I asked you if you were gay.'

'Yes.'

'You didn't directly answer me.'

'Didn't I?'

'No, you said you had a girlfriend.'

'Isn't that about as direct as you can get?' I asked.

'Not really,' she sighed. 'If only you knew... '

I ate my baked potato whilst she watched me.

'I want to remind you of that,' she added.

'Why?'

'Because it's important.'

'Anyway,' I said, 'I know Martin too well to want to risk our friendship over a failed sexual relationship. I don't even know if he'd want one.'

'He loves you,' Steph said. 'I can't believe you're not aware of that. I shouldn't have to tell you, but perhaps you would never have worked it out for yourself. What you do about it is up to you.'

She paused to crunch some lettuce.

'I love Martin,' I said. 'But not sexually.'

Steph shrugged.

'I'd never be nineteen again,' she told me. 'Thank God I've got through all my struggles over sexual identity. You'll get through it too, but you've got to work at it.'

'You make me sound like an immature child,' I said. 'You also sound as if you're telling me I'm gay.'

'No I'm not,' she said seriously, placing her knife and fork beside her plate so that she could stare at me with her abundant sincerity. 'All I'm saying is that you're confused about yourself. Anyone can see that. You're confused about

105

what you want. You'll sort it out one way or another, but only if you're properly honest with yourself.'

Steph always made me feel that she was looking right into me. It made me wonder where she'd got all her wisdom.

'Okay,' I said. 'I'll think about it.'

I resumed eating.

'What about you?' I added. 'Are you in love?'

'No,' she said with a slight edge of emotion that might have been pleasure, or regret. 'I'm deliberately going through a period on my own. I went out with someone for four years. I'm not ready to start another journey of discovery yet. I need time to myself for a while.'

'What was he like?'

'She,' she said. 'She was beautiful, demanding, dishonest, loving, vibrant, unconventional, consistently surprising, great fun to be with and, ultimately, self-destructive.'

'Ah.'

'It takes a long time to recover from being whisked into a life of such endless participation. I hardly had time to sit down and think about what I was doing. I was too busy doing it.'

'Do you miss her?'

'Sometimes. But no, not really. I only miss the good bits.'

When we walked to Martin's I kept thinking: she's a lesbian. I kept wondering why I was surprised, and why it made a difference.

Martin was in and ready for us. He had a cafetiere of coffee ready and some croissants in the oven.

'I thought I'd greet you with a French breakfast,' he said. 'Caf* au lait coming up. Jerome has these brilliant French coffee

bowls... '

The flat was in the roof of a great old crumbling Victorian house. The rooms all had sloping ceilings and looked out over parkland. The sitting room had stained walls from where the roof was leaking, and the whole place had an air of studied poverty. There were shabby art

106

books everywhere, an easel in the sitting room, novels, magazines and so on strewn haphazardly across the floor. Everything looked as though it had been picked up from second hand stalls and jumble sales. There was a pervasive reek of undried oil paint.

'These are the only occupied rooms in the building,' Martin told me. 'The owner wants to sell it for development into luxury flats, but Jerome is refusing to leave. They're taking him to court sometime soon to get an eviction order.'

'And what then?' I asked.

Martin shrugged.

'I'll find something else. I'm not going to think about it until it happens. I'm going to live in the moment, like Jerome.'

'It certainly seems to have done you some good,' I told him, 'moving here.'

'It has. It's so inspiring here. So... '

He looked around the room with great affection, then left to get the croissants.

'I've never seen Martin at a loss for words,' said Steph. 'It must be good.'

There came the sound of the front door being unlocked and Jerome came in a few moments later, followed by Martin carrying a tray of croissants.

'Just in time,' he told Jerome.

'Hello,' said Jerome. 'What a beautiful day to be visited by friends.'

He sat down, cross legged, beside the window and smiled at us whilst Martin served the food and coffee. When he'd done so, he lit some incense and then sat beside Jerome. I started on my croissant, still full from the baked potato I'd just eaten, but unable to resist the apricot conserve.

'I've started a new painting,' Martin told me. 'The light in my bedroom is absolutely right. It's as good as a studio.'

'Good,' I said, my mouth full.

'I want to try a figure painting,' he went on, 'and I wondered if you'd like to model for me?'

107

'And me,' Jerome added. 'You could sit for us both at the same time.'

'Okay,' I said, pleased.

Martin turned from me and, leaning over, kissed Jerome. Watching him do so sent a shiver down my spine. I was suddenly aware of two distinct feelings – first that I was envious of Jerome being so close to Martin, and second, that I wondered what it would feel like to kiss someone with a moustache. Steph glanced at me and smiled secretively when I looked back blankly.

In front of me was the copy of Square Peg that Martin had shown me in Betty's tea shop. I opened it at the article on David Ruffell and read once more the caption that had so haunted me: BY HIS DEAD SMILE I KNEW WE STOOD IN HELL. I looked at it for a few moments, then closed the magazine and put it back on the floor.

'David Ruffell?' Martin asked.

'Yes.'

So, Martin was having an affair with a man from New York that he'd met only a few days before. It seemed strange and insanely sudden. I wondered about Aids and other dangers – emotional dangers – and felt a thrill of fear, envy and rejection all rolled into one.

Later, after Steph had left and Jerome had gone to do some work, I mentioned Aids to Martin. He laughed.

'Don't worry,' he said, 'Jerome insists on safe sex with me, so there's nothing to worry about there.'

'Oh,' I said and shrugged, wondering why I didn't feel relieved.

'So when can you come and sit for me?' Martin wanted to know.

'When do you want me to?'

'Tomorrow?'

'Okay. I can come over after I've walked Emily.'

'Great.'

I sat, feeling that I ought to go but unable to do so. I could see that Martin was waiting for me to leave so that he could go and talk to Jerome. I felt excluded from him, for the first time ever, and was surprised to find how much it hurt.

'Okay,' I said, standing up, 'I'd better get off... '

Martin stood up, a little too eagerly I thought. He followed me into the hall and opened the door.

'See you tomorrow, then.'

'Yes,' I said. 'About two?'

'Good.'

When I got back to Bernard Terrace I realised with absolute certainty, as I walked into the hallway, that this was no longer my home. Even Emily's enthusiasm didn't make me feel any more comfortable. I'd have to find somewhere to live where I could take Emily with me – somewhere close enough to the museum so that I could get out at lunch times to give her a walk.

After so long of trying to convince myself that I should leave home, it came as something of a shock to find that just looking at these bare walls made me smart inside, as though scalded by my own feelings of captivity. I had to get out. As soon as possible.

The only consistent thing in my life was Emily. She was boisterous and energetic, as usual, and I ran with her down to the park. I felt silted up with croissants, and other things, and chased Emily in an attempt to invigorate myself. She responded by becoming over-excited, barking and jumping at me to affectionately paw at my thighs. It infected me with something of her energy, and over the next quarter of an hour, I managed to slough off at least some of my listlessness.

As I came back into Bernard Terrace, I saw a couple of youths hanging around outside the house. As Emily ran along the pavement, the youths turned away with a distinctive swagger and I realised with annoyance that they were Dave Boothe and Paul. Seeing them again deflated any positive feelings I had generated, and set me wondering how long it was going to take for me to find somewhere else to live.

My mother was cheerfully cooking the dinner when I came into the kitchen to make myself a mug of tea. This happy mood of hers oppressed me even more. It was so unusual for a start. It had settled on her since she'd come back from London, and hadn't left. Perhaps it was the knowledge that she was about to become a wealthy woman (at least by my standards), or that she had at last got rid of my father's work. I'd seen a set of carpet and wallpaper samples in the dining room and I cringed to think what the house would look like if it was redecorated to her taste – all swirls and floral patterns.

I was dunking my tea bag when a thought occurred to me.

'Oh, by the way,' I said. 'I've been meaning to ask you. Who is Mr Munro?'

'Mr who?'

'Mr Munro. Alasdair Munro. Apparently he knew my father.'

'How did you come to meet him?'

'He's the valuer in Sheffield that Bratt's asked to look at the marble statuette.'

'He's a troublemaker,' my mother said shortly. 'Keep away from him.'

'Why?'

'Because he's a liar.'

'I thought he was nice.'

'I know him better than you, and all I can say is stay clear of him.'

'He told me that if ever I wanted to know more about my father, then I should go and speak to him.'

'Oh no you won't,' my mother warned, angrily.

'I just wanted to ask a few questions, that's all.'

'And you want to hear lies?'

I couldn't bear the sanctimonious tone that my mother took when she was telling me what to do. I found myself almost shouting.

'Who else can I ask?'

'I'm not prepared to discuss this if you're going to raise your voice,' she told me. 'I've told you not to see him, and that's that.' I shook my head and left the room. Didn't my mother realise that I was too old to be commanded in this

110

way? Didn't she realise that, by telling me not to talk to Mr Munro, she had guaranteed that I would? The only thing she had achieved was to reaffirm my steely conviction that I must move out. I even considered taking a room in a guest house for a while, but decided I was being over-dramatic.

I went to bed early that night and read a book. I felt sleepless and frustrated and found I was reading page after page without taking anything in. I kept on thinking about registering with all the local accommodation agencies on Monday – putting ads in the paper to find a house-share. Maybe I could sleep on Coll's bedsit floor for a few nights...

It suddenly occurred to me that this was the first time I'd thought about Coll in connection with moving out. What would this mean for our relationship? Did we have a relationship? I hadn't seen or heard from her for days.

At around twelve-thirty Emily started barking. There was a public walkway on the far side of our garden fence and she often barked at people who walked there late at night. This time it sounded more insistent than usual and I considered getting up to see what it was. But she quietened down and I listened for a few moments before beginning to drift off to sleep. A couple of minutes later, I heard a stealthy noise from downstairs. I knew it couldn't be my mother because I'd heard her go to bed some time before. I lay in bed in that breathless elongation of time, waiting for the next sound. When it came it was so quiet and so inhuman as to make my hair prickle. It was something between a low moan and a whimper. I got out of bed, put my dressing gown on, and armed with the marble statuette, I crept down the stairs. When I switched the hall light on, there came a startled scuffling of feet and the scurry of a quick exit – then silence. I waited for at least two minutes before descending further.

The door into the garden was open, but nothing in the kitchen seemed to have been disturbed. Perhaps the intruders hadn't got as far as the sitting room, where the most valuable and easily portable antiques were. I went to close the door and noticed two things. First, the credit card

111

lying by the step, used – as I had done myself in the past when locked out – to push back the tongue of the yale lock; and second, the pale shadow of Emily lying on the path.

I stood looking at her, knowing instantly that she was dead, afraid to approach her for that confirmation. I stooped to pick up the credit card and glanced down at it. Scuffed from where it had been inserted in the crack of the door, it bore the name A G Clarke, and was almost certainly stolen.

Now, after staring for a moment at this unfamiliar name, I went to kneel beside Emily – placing my hand on her surprisingly warm rib-cage. She looked asleep out there in the almost complete darkness, with legs outstretched, but there was something absolutely inanimate about her that made me shiver once more. I remembered the whimper I'd heard from upstairs and, although I was emotionally blank, I felt the sting of involuntary tears.

I hadn't expected her to be so heavy as I picked her up to carry her back into the house, and I held her to me with something between a hug and an embrace. Once in the light I saw the nail, long and vicious, neatly hammered into her skull.

THIRTEEN

Any attempt to follow a particular trend or logic in Twentieth Century art is futile and hypothetical. There are so many cross-references, not to mention both conscious and subconscious influences, that no major artist or artistic movement can truly claim to have nothing to do with any other. In as far as any originality does exist in this melting pot of ideas, then one striking example must be the painter Paul Ellis.

I was lying in bed reading Twentieth Century Scottish Painting: A Perspective. Each chapter was by a different critic or historian. The chapter on my father was by Mr Munro. It was now nearly three in the morning and I was wide awake. Emily was in the kitchen, wrapped in a blanket, and I couldn't decide what to do with her.

It is interesting to note that on leaving Scotland, his native country, there followed a remarkable change of style. The figurative in his work came to the fore and he abandoned his earlier work in schematic landscape and geometric abstraction. "For me the abstract is just an intellectual exercise," he wrote to a friend. "It serves to please the eye, but does nothing to ease the soul. There should be a measure of the artist in every picture he paints. Not just the artist's ideas, but every part of him should be represented. His mind, body, spirit, emotions, prejudices and fears should all have a place... "
   In this short statement we obtain a succinct insight into Ellis' work. The simple compositions of his later paintings have a lively freedom of background, and along with the distortion of the human figure, go a long way to creating the strange atmosphere for which his paintings have become noted.

113

"The colour black has always intrigued me," wrote Ellis, "although it has connotations of fear and what the religious might term 'evil'. But I see many more symbols in the colour than these. For a start, black isn't really a colour at all – although to the painter this is an almost absurd notion. It dominates a palette and, consequently, a picture that contains it. It doesn't surprise me that the Pre-Raphaelite painters dropped it altogether from their palettes, preferring shades of brown to the extreme of black. It is a mysterious tone and one that can be used to suggest things that aren't there – concealment in shadow is one of the great artistic conventions. I like to use black to isolate my figures. To make them the only object in the picture. They have no space, or infinite space, whichever way you choose to look at it. This means that the viewer has no distractions from the subject. Unlike white, a black background makes a statement. A white background is often simply the surface on which the subject is represented. Black on the other hand shows some sort of intention on the part of the artist... "

Of course, it was Dave Boothe who had killed Emily. There was no doubt about that. In knowing this, I found I had a wealth of anger that came in waves and felt as intoxicatingly excessive as any emotion I have ever felt. I was transfixed with grief and anger, and only slowly able to think about either Dave Boothe or Emily without a protective numbness descending.

The question was – what should I do? Go to the police again? It was only because I'd made sure I got him into trouble that he'd gone out of his way to pay me back. If I hadn't gone to the police as Maggie had advised me, Emily would still be alive. I felt responsible for her death, and a desperate need to have as little to do with Dave Boothe as possible. Perhaps it was enough that he'd done this terrible thing, and now I should let it go.

But no, it was impossible! I couldn't walk away from this and let Dave get away with murder. Emily was far too important to be shrugged off. I had to go to the police. It was my duty to Emily – to myself. I felt tears again as I thought of her; the only close company I'd ever had at home, the only receptacle for my love through my early adolescence. I remembered her as a puppy arriving on my twelfth birthday, unsteady and immensely lovable. Instantly infatuated, I doted on her for months, never becoming indifferent to her as many of my friends had become with their pets. She had always rewarded my attention with loyalty and affection. And now she was dead.

Poor Emily. She hadn't bled at all when I'd carefully removed the nail. Maybe she hadn't suffered. All there'd been was that quiet moaning whimper, so subtle and so unforgettable.

There was a mark above her right ear where she had presumably been struck, by a stone perhaps, to initially immobilise her. Then she had been murdered. Dave hadn't come to steal things from the house – he'd had plenty of time for that before I'd turned up. No, he'd come to kill Emily. It was deliberate revenge. He'd decided how he could hurt me without laying a finger on me. And he'd succeeded.

I picked up my book again, to try and break the endless cycle of jarring recollection of exactly how Emily had looked out there on the path...

Perhaps one of the greatest tragedies for Twentieth Century Scottish art was the untimely death of Paul Ellis in 1973 at the early age of 29. There were several notable changes of style throughout his short career, the last being the most mature and deeply considered. The frustrations that dogged his personal life, however, prevented him from ever developing a style that properly fitted his nature and intentions, and it would have been interesting to see how his paintings might have progressed over the years had he lived. Perhaps he would have earned a place at the forefront of British painting, rather than remaining, undeservedly, in the background.

115

Whatever might have happened, one thing is certain – the loss is ours.

My father seemed to be staring at me through the blankness of time, through the fresh vision of death that shadowed my wakefulness. His sadness was suddenly palpable, and I could almost feel his disembodied emotion.

Tomorrow I would be gone. I couldn't bear the idea of another night in this house of murder and death. I would take Emily and bury her somewhere suitable and then leave forever.

I felt an anger against my mother, as though Emily's death was her fault; as though by having given birth to me she had set this inevitability in motion. I knew I was being irrational, but I wanted to be irrational. A part of me kept saying: She's gone, she's gone; whilst another, more shocking part, murmured, Why get so upset? She was only a dog. It was almost a refrain – only a dog. Why was I so upset – she was only a dog, not a human being.

But she represented so much more than flesh and blood and bone. She had understood my moods, had received and returned my love. She had been a valued companion...

I fell asleep feeling wretched and betrayed.

I did go to the police – at eight o'clock the following morning. By chance, I spoke to the officer I'd seen the last time I'd complained about Dave's behaviour. He believed me immediately when I told him that it had been Dave, but he pointed out that I hadn't actually seen him. Nevertheless, he told me, they'd look into it. The whole business took only a few minutes, and I was home by nine-fifteen, feeling disorientated and disappointed that the policeman had been so offhand about my distress. (I'd kept on expecting him to say something crass like: 'Why are you so upset? It was only a dog... ')

Martin and Steph were brilliant. Steph drove straight over when I phoned her and we took Emily out to bury her along the banks of the Ouse, out towards Bishopsthorpe where she had loved to explore. I felt sad, but released. It was as though Emily had been my last link with home, and the savageness with which that link had been severed was in keeping with my feelings about the place. But I found myself choking with anger every time I thought of Dave Boothe, and fought to put him from my mind.

We dug a shallow grave in the water meadow on the long curve of the river by Fulford. Although I'd brought a spade, it was far more difficult than I'd expected to dig a hole big enough for her. We all took turns for nearly an hour before we could bury her. Martin lit some incense and pressed the sticks into the rich, crumbling earth. It seemed peculiarly fitting, and I smiled, a sad brief smile, at the feeling of gentleness and love that the three of us managed to generate. Emily, reduced to this blank space of earth, would remain a fresh source of painful memory for a long time.

When we turned away, Martin put his arm round my shoulder.

'Come and stay with us,' he said. 'There's a spare room. It's not very large, but it'll do for a while.'

I nodded and we walked back to the car like that.

I packed as many of my things as were easily portable and we filled Steph's car with clothes, books, my music system, pictures, papers and, of course, the marble statuette. I felt clandestine, leaving like this without my mother's knowledge. She was away, as every Sunday, having an early luncheon with friends. She had been bemused and, I think, somewhat distressed when she'd found me making phone calls to Martin and Steph. I hadn't told her how Emily had died, though she'd asked. Nor did I tell her where I was going. It hadn't seemed important.

In the end I left a note:

Dear Mother,
I've found some digs in Leeds with Martin and have decided to move in. Sorry this has been so sudden, but I didn't find out about them until this morning. I'll come back for the rest of my stuff in a few days.
Peter.

117

I added the address, but not the telephone number, and we left. It had been as simple as that. I'd decided to leave, and now I was going. I was light-headed with grief and adventure and, for the first time, felt absolutely and utterly alive.

The drive back to Leeds was quiet and I spent most of the time looking out of the window at the flat landscape and the passing buildings. I felt introspective and, when I got to Martin's flat, ready for the light lunch that Jerome had prepared. We sat, the four of us, on cushions in the sitting room and ate bread and salad.

After lunch I was happy to sit for Martin and Jerome. It seemed like the start of a new life. They had playfully asked how many of my clothes I was prepared to remove, and I ended up lounging in a comfortable armchair in Martin's bedroom wearing only a pair of jeans. I felt absurdly daring, though my bare feet became cold in the draft from the door, and we had to keep Martin's two bar heater on full. It was strange to have to remain immobile for several hours, and more difficult than I'd imagined – despite being comfortable to start off with. Martin and Jerome concentrated hard, Jerome on a pencil drawing and Martin painting straight onto canvas with oils. But every time I began to drift off into a pleasant dream, the image of Emily, dead in my arms, came back to me with fresh clarity and made me start.

We had about three hours before the light began to fade and I was no longer needed, though both of them were set to work for a while longer. I decided to end my afternoon with an impromptu visit to Coll, who lived three or four streets in towards the city centre.

I walked to her bedsit feeling dislocated and homeless. Jerome's flat would never seem like home to me. It was too well stamped with his personality for me to ever feel like anything other than a guest.

I knocked on Coll's door and laughed at her surprise when she answered.

'How did you know where I live?' she asked, ushering me in.

'Martin told me,' I said.

There was a young man sitting on Coll's unmade bed, looking unshaved and dishevelled. He looked away in disinterest when I came into the room and leant over to pick up a pair of dark, much patched jeans.

'Peter, this is Eddy,' she said. 'Coffee?'

'Please.'

I sat down on a kitchen chair beside the small table that served as desk and dining table. The room was small and dim, but clean and comfortable, if messy. There was a tiny kitchenette and I could see Coll's back as she put the kettle on.

'We're neighbours now,' I told her. 'I've moved in with Martin.'

Eddy stood up and put on his jeans. He coughed a rasping, dragging cough that made his wiry, dark hair fall across his forehead in springy straggles. He looked sidelong at me, and I expected aggression. Instead he looked tired and vulnerable, and unhappy.

'Have I come at a bad time?' I asked.

'No,' he said, before turning to Coll's back. 'Look, Coll, I've got to go. See you later.'

'At the Union?'

'Yeah.'

He let himself out, giving me a curt but friendly wave. It made me feel adrift, unsure.

'Sorry about that,' Coll said, coming in and handing me a mug of coffee. 'Eddy's alright. He just needs some attention every now and then.'

'Are you lovers?' I asked.

'Why, are you jealous?'

'No,' I replied, surprised that this was true.

'Oh.' She sounded disappointed.

'What makes a man a lover anyway?' she murmured. 'Are you a lover? Is Eddy a lover? I don't know.'

'I've left home,' I told her. 'I'm sharing a place with Jerome and Martin.'

'See,' she said. 'It was easy enough once you'd decided to leave.' 'Yes.'

119

She sat on the bed.

'Oh, Peter,' she said, quietly, worn out. 'What a bloody mess I'm in.'

I'd thought of Coll as being energetically self-reliant. I had never tried to imagine what her life was like when she was away from me. She had existed in a bubble, had only been real when we were together. But she had other friends and other lovers. How many? I didn't know. I didn't know what she felt about me, what she wanted from me – what I wanted from her. It seemed as though this moment was either a beginning or an end. Our previous meetings had been some kind of extended greeting, and now we had to decide whether we wanted to get to know each other. Anna had been so sure that she wanted a straightforward text-book love affair with me – well-groomed boy and well-groomed girl blissfully in love. But I couldn't tell what Coll wanted, except that she wouldn't want that, and I didn't want her to want it. I yearned for something unconventional to happen to me. Something that would make me separate and different from people like Anna and my mother. That was why I had been so electrified when Coll had poured molten wax over me. Because it was different; because it made me feel individual. Better. Because it made me feel that I had secrets.

'Look, Peter,' she said eventually. 'I think you'd better go. I didn't get to bed until after six this morning, and I'm still feeling rough.'

'Okay.'

I stood up.

'I'll come round to Martin's and see you,' she said.

'When?'

'Tonight. After I've talked to Eddy.'

'Are you sure?'

'Yeah.'

'So you knew about this Eddy, then?' I asked Martin later. I was annoyed that he didn't seem surprised when I mentioned him.

'Everyone knows Eddy,' he replied. 'He's the sad guy on our course. He's the one with bags of talent who'll probably commit suicide before he really gets to grips with his own ability.'

'I don't know what to think about him,' I said. 'Coll and I never really talked about what we were doing, but I sort of assumed that we were going out together – whatever that means.'

'Quite,' said Martin. 'Whatever that means. And anyway, I don't think anyone ever goes out with Coll. As far as I can tell, the main reason why she sleeps with people is to get at her parents. She's very odd Peter. Don't take her too seriously.'

But I couldn't fail to take her seriously. I had slept with her. We had had sex together. That was a big thing for me – a vast and intractable connection, somehow, that made me incapable of being casual about her.

If our relationship ended now, then I could accept that, but unless or until that happened, I felt an attachment to her. It seemed that relationships are like being hit on unprotected flesh. A bruise is inescapable; the inevitable consequence. Once I had slept with Coll, I was involved to the extent that my emotions had to develop like a blank piece of exposed photographic paper. An image was set to appear. What it would be I didn't know, but it heralded the next stage of our sexual relationship – even if that stage was its ending.

She arrived at eleven o'clock, cheerful and controlled, with none of the vulnerability that had been so apparent earlier.

'Hi,' she said to Martin when he let her in, 'how's things?'

'Okay,' he told her, ushering her into the sitting room and leaving us alone. Jerome was working – he always seemed to be working – and Martin went off to talk to him.

'Sorry about Eddy and all that,' she said. 'I've sorted it out.'

'In what way?'

'Oh, you know.'

She sat down beside me and obviously had no intention of discussing what her arrangements with Eddy were. It

121

didn't really bother me. Whatever she'd said, I suppose I would have assumed that she was having an affair with him, or someone else. I had heard too much about Coll now to expect otherwise.

She came with me to my tiny bedroom. There was a single mattress on the floor, a battered chest of drawers and a single wardrobe. That was all. It felt like a momentary haven to me, somewhere from which I would move before too long. Coll smiled when she saw it.

'A bit of a come down from your palatial bedroom in York,' she said.

'But a vast improvement,' I assured her.

'You look a bit miserable,' she said. 'Are you okay?'

'Actually, no, not really,' I said. 'My dog was murdered last night.'

I felt tears, but I knew they wouldn't spill. I was in control to that degree at least. Coll saw that I was upset, but seemed incapable of saying anything to comfort me. She was so wound up in herself that she didn't have room to expend energy on me.

We didn't talk much. Coll had a scarf which she tied in a blindfold over my eyes. I wasn't sure about this, but I didn't seem to have the strength to resist her will. She tied it tight and made me lie still on my mattress.

It was astonishing how much my sense of touch was heightened by not being able to see. It was also amazing how vulnerable I felt in the knowledge that Coll could see perfectly well. When she ran her fingers over my skin, it made me thrill in a way I hadn't experienced before. In submitting to her so completely, I knew that I was giving up responsibility for what was happening – and how seductive that was! To be taken charge of, to be unsure of what was going to happen next.

When I was about to come, Coll, sensing this, bit into the fleshy part of my shoulder, so hard that I cried out in genuine pain. She laughed when I pulled the blindfold off to look angrily at her, my erection drooping, my shock at this abuse of her power over me showing clearly in my face.

122

'Poor Peter,' she whispered, taking my penis in her hand and squeezing gently. She licked away the blood that was welling on my shoulder, tracing her tongue down and round until she settled for a moment at my nipple. I was still in pain, but began to regain my erection as she attended to me. She knelt over me and, eyes closed to try and simulate the blindfold, I came quickly.

Afterwards Coll smeared blood from my shoulder onto the sheet.

'There,' she told me, 'a memento of tonight.'

She stood up and started to dress.

'Aren't you going to stay?' I asked her.

'No, I don't think so,' she said, but didn't say why. I left it at that, realising that Coll was one of those will-o-the-wisp people who come and go without allowing rules to bind them. What fear of commitment must she have? What strange ideas about love and happiness. I watched her go and wondered when, and if, I would see this strange young woman again.

FOURTEEN

I took the train to York in the morning, along with a dreary trainload of commuters. I wondered if this was going to be my future – living in Leeds and working in York. In one sense it seemed like the fulfilment of my worst nightmare. To become a man who worked nine to five and commuted to work was an image that I had never had of myself. On the other hand, the freedom that I now felt was exhilarating. I could be myself at last; and outside work I could do what I wanted, with whom I wanted, when I wanted.

I walked to the museum along the river. As I approached Micklegate Bridge, a woman walked past me with a Dalmatian on a lead. I felt the tears well up suddenly and blur my vision as I watched the dog stride along beside its owner. I felt fresh pain at the way things had been torn from me and realised that, like a victim of poorly performed surgery, I would take time to heal, would remain perhaps forever scarred. Emily was gone, the last traces of my father were gone, my mother might just as well be gone. I felt like an orphan – something I had always wanted to be as a child. But now, this feeling gave me no pleasure; just a dull ache which lasted until I got to work. Then it was dissipated. The museum was so absolutely as it had always been that I couldn't help feeling grounded again. My choppy waters were spending themselves on the silt of work's routine.

My mother phoned me at ten to ask when I was going to collect the rest of my belongings. She sounded calm, disinterested. She had had the weekend to get over any emotion that she might have felt about my going, and had obviously decided to treat me in the same dead-pan way that I had treated her.

So, I thought, it has come to this. I phoned a van rental

124

firm and booked a van for five thirty that evening, wondering as I did so if I would ever see my mother again after I'd picked up my stuff.

She said almost nothing when I went round to pack. She must have known that I had to go. She must have known that I couldn't bury myself in that stifling house any longer. Perhaps I stifled her too. Perhaps she was as glad to see me go as I was to leave. I had never got to know her well enough to answer these questions.

There was a small pile of drawings that Martin had given me – which I now decided I was going to have framed – some books in the sitting room, a yucca, a disobedient cheeseplant and an unruly tradescantia. There was my bedding, a threadbare persian rug that I didn't like but which had been given to me by my aunt Joyce. Mat had admired it in the past and I took it now to give to him. It would look good in his bedsit.

When I'd packed up the small van, it was only half full and it made me feel sad to think how little I possessed. I had the trimmings of life. None of the essentials – the carpets, curtains, chairs, tables, fridge, cutlery and crockery. All these things would be provided in rented accommodation, but they would never be mine, just as the things in my mother's house were not mine...

She came out to say goodbye, asked if I had enough money, then waved me off without asking when we would next meet. It was as if, having seen that I had decided to go, she had sheered my moorings herself, pushing me away from her without ceremony and without remorse.

I drove round to Mat's only to discover that he wasn't in. I was disappointed because the rug would have made a good peace offering, and if I took it to Leeds it would be a bind to have to bring it back. I wrote a brief note to leave on the rug and rang the other ground floor doorbell. I waited for a while before it was opened by a suspicious middle-aged woman.

'Yes?' she asked.

'Hello,' I told her, 'I'm a friend of Mat's. I've got something for him. Can I come in and leave it by his door?'

125

'Mat's not here,' she said.

'No, I know, I've just rung his bell.'

'He's in hospital.'

'In hospital! Why?'

'Beaten up,' she said, leaning over to me and whispering: 'in a public lavatory.'

She nodded knowingly and watched my expression.

'You know what people get beaten up in lavatories for?' she smirked.

'Look, can I just leave this by his door?' I asked, ignoring her question.

'Sex,' she said. 'You'd never believe it, a young lad like that. And no, you can't clutter up the hallway with that thing. There's no knowing how long it'll be before your friend comes back to move it.'

'How about if I leave it with you, then? You can pass it on to him.'

She looked at the rug and felt the corner of it.

'Oh alright, go on,' she said.

She lugged the rug inside whilst I thanked her.

'Poor sod,' she said under her breath. 'I dunno what makes them do it.'

Mat was in the District Hospital. I drove straight over and went to his ward – a clinically clean and depressingly bright place, institutional and overwhelmingly impersonal. On entering I saw him immediately. He was with his mother and his sister, who sat in resigned silence at his bedside; a bunch of flowers on his table, along with a bowl of fruit. There was something absolutely the same about all the people in here. They all had the air of having relinquished all responsibility for themselves.

I hesitated in the doorway and he looked over my way. His head was bandaged and he turned to say something to his sister, who stood up and came over to me.

'Hello Peter,' she said, taking me by the arm and walking out with me into the corridor.

'How is he?' I asked.

'Okay. Not badly hurt. It's shock mostly, and a cut just

126

above the eye. He was lucky not to lose it. They're keeping him under observation overnight. He should be out tomorrow, then mum's taking him home for a few days.'

I nodded, feeling shy.

'Can I go in and say hello?'

'I don't think he wants to see you, Peter.'

'What, not even to say hello?'

'No, not even that I'm afraid. He asked me to ask you to go.'

She gave me a sad but friendly smile, squeezed my elbow, then left me there in the corridor. I was horrified that Mat wouldn't see me. The brilliance of the corridor's lighting seemed falsely cheerful, and I felt suddenly and crushingly responsible for what had happened to him. He'd been to a toilet and had got himself queerbashed. He'd gone because I'd turned him down. I couldn't imagine him going to a place like that in search of sex, so it seemed a logical assumption that he'd done it because of me.

It was Martin's nightmare that he would be queerbashed, and I'd always laughed at him for it. But now it had happened to someone I knew – a friend who now refused to see me.

Martin wasn't in when I got back. Only Jerome. He helped me in with my things, but I wanted to talk to Martin.

'He's down at the Union bar,' Jerome told me. 'You could go and look for him. I'll come with you if you like.'

'No,' I said. 'I'll stay here.'

Jerome lit some incense – one of the seemingly ubiquitous symbols of my new life – and sat on the floor whilst I made us both coffee.

'Sit down here,' he said when I handed him his mug. 'Sit in front of me and relax. Look at me.'

He looked straight at me and I felt disarmed.

'Tell me what's the matter,' he said.

'It's Mat, a friend of ours,' I told him. 'He's been queerbashed and I feel responsible.'

127

'You feel responsible? Why? Did you do the queerbashing?'

'No, but it wouldn't have happened if it wasn't for me.'

'This sounds strange. Why should you feel responsible?'

'Because I didn't give in to him.'

It sounded quite logical to me, but Jerome couldn't see it. I tried several times to explain, but he still didn't understand.

'Of course it's not your fault,' he said. 'We all effect each other. What you did might have effected Mat, but you can't be held responsible for his actions. And what makes you think he wouldn't have gone to that toilet anyway?'

'Because it's a bit, well... sordid, isn't it?'

'Is it. Why?' He laughed. 'You've lost me there. Why should it be sordid?'

'I don't know,' I said, feeling annoyed that Jerome couldn't see my point of view.

'Look,' he said, 'just don't blame yourself, okay?'

'But why did Mat refuse to see me in the hospital?'

Jerome shrugged.

'Perhaps he's just not ready to forgive you for rejecting him.'

'See,' I said, 'it is my fault.'

'Right,' Jerome said, 'we're going to have to do something about this. You're being irrational.'

He took a last gulp of coffee and stood up.

'Okay,' he said, taking the cushions from the settee and laying them end to end on the floor. 'Lie face down on these. Take your shirt off.'

'Why?' I asked.

'Just do it.'

He left the room whilst I did as he'd asked. He came back with a bottle of oil and sat beside me.

'Okay, rest your chin on your hands, elbows out.'

He poured some cool oil onto my back, then began to smooth it over my skin in long movements, starting at the base of my spine and working upwards and outwards. It smelt of lavender and the firmness of his hands seemed to be pressing my muscles into submission.

'Just relax,' he told me. 'Let your feelings of guilt leave you. You're far too tense, I can feel your stress from here. Let it go. Let it be smoothed away by my hands.'

He ran his fingers along my arms, right to the finger tips.

'Feel me getting rid of your stress,' he said. 'Feel me drawing it out along your arms. Feel it spraying out from your fingers into nothingness. Feel calmness instead. Let your body sink into calmness.'

It was working. It was the most extraordinary feeling. Jerome went on massaging my back for some time, then he stopped.

'This isn't the right place to do a full massage,' he said, 'and that's what you need. Come with me.'

We went into his bedroom and he spread a huge oily towel on the bed.

'Take your trousers off, and socks. Lie on the bed in just your underwear.'

I did as he said, and lay on my back, almost in a doze, as he continued.

'Now,' he said, 'there's tension here across your shoulders and up your neck. Just let yourself go. Let your muscles unclench, and as they unclench, your worries will ease as well.'

He pulled at my shoulders, heaving them up and round in a circular motion. And gradually I felt them relax and become heavy in his hands.

'Good,' he said. 'Good.'

He smoothed more oil down over my front and on down my legs. I could feel the hairs there dragging slightly against his palm, and suddenly it felt sexual. This man was touching me in an intimate and sensual way. I couldn't help but feel sexual. He must have noticed my erection, but ignored it and kneaded my shins and thighs with his firm fingers.

'Good,' he said. 'Just relax. Let go. Let yourself go.'

I kept my eyes closed as he ran his fingers up the inside of my thigh and over the bulge of my erection. With a deft movement, he slipped his hand into my undershorts.

'I don't think you'd better do that,' I whispered.

'Why not?'

'I don't want you to.'

'Just relax,' Jerome told me. 'Just relax and listen to me.'

He eased my shorts down slightly and held my penis in his oily hand, stroking it as he talked.

'Just relax, Peter, it's okay. Just relax. Now, you said you feel guilty about Mat, yes? Well, hasn't it occurred to you that the reason you feel guilty is because you wanted to give in to him. You wanted to, but you couldn't bring yourself to. The reason why you feel guilty is because you wish you had given in to him. You wish that you'd taken the opportunity to make love to him. You wanted to know what it was like, but you were afraid of what it might mean if you enjoyed it. But it doesn't matter what it means. If it feels right, then it is right. That's all there is to it. That's all that matters.'

Still stroking me, he leant gradually forward towards me.

'Don't think about it, Peter,' he said. 'Just let it happen.'

And he kissed me, a long gentle kiss that was a perfect kiss coming as it did whilst I was so completely relaxed. He just sat beside me, fully clothed, and slowly kissed me, slowly wanked me in long strokes. And when I clenched, when the muscles in my thighs became taut, he continued to whisper to me.

'It's okay, it's okay.'

And it was okay, that final moment. I was calm, reassured, enveloped in Jerome's assurance and free to take this experience as it happened – to go with the flow as Jerome would have said. After I'd come, he leant over for some tissues and wiped me clean. I started to sit up, but he pushed me down.

'No,' he said, 'I haven't finished.'

He pulled my shorts back into place, then resumed the massage.

'Let it go,' he said. 'Let all feeling go, and be left with calmness and peace. Feel that I am sending you love through my fingers. Not sex, but love. We are close, and I'm pouring calm energy and peace and love into you through my hands, through my touch.'

He went on like this for some time, his touch getting lighter and lighter until, finally, he stopped altogether. He sat beside me in silence for a short time, then got up.

'Lie there for a couple of minutes,' he said. 'I'll go and run a bath for you.'

I lay and felt relaxed, relieved and somewhere deep inside astonished that the big event that I had wanted and dreaded for so long had happened to me at last. Jerome had made it all so easy. He had talked me through it. I had lain there and he had done the rest.

It was only when I was in the bath that I began to feel the panic. What had I done! What about Martin – Martin and Jerome? What about Coll? What about Mat? What about me?

Jerome knocked on the door.

'Can I come in?' he asked.

'It's locked,' I told him.

'Well unlock it.'

I stood up in the bath and leant over to undo the catch. I felt suddenly very, very young. I'm only nineteen, I wanted to tell Jerome. Please, I'm only nineteen.

He came in with two glasses of wine and, handing me one, leant over and kissed me on the mouth, then sat on the edge of the bath.

'I can guess what you're thinking,' he said. 'You're wondering what this means for the future. You're wondering about me and Martin, and you're thinking that I've got a nerve to seduce you like that.'

'Something like that,' I said. 'Though I don't think you're to blame for seducing me. I suppose I wanted it to happen.'

Jerome nodded.

'But you are worried about me and Martin.'

'Yes,' I said.

'Don't worry. We're not having a relationship,' he said. 'We've just made love a few times, that's all. That doesn't make us an item.'

'I feel like I've opened the wrong door,' I said, 'or turned

131

down the wrong street. It's unfamiliar, and I don't know whether that's going to be good or bad.'

'You're very young,' he said. 'It would be terrible if you had all the answers at your age. I'm thirty-eight and I don't have all the answers. Thank God. The only thing I have learned is to go with the flow. Life is beautiful, Peter, really, really beautiful. And it's too short to foul it up with stupid things like guilt and inhibition.'

I knew it was the truth, but I did feel guilty. I couldn't suddenly not feel guilty just by wanting it. And I felt inhibited by his age. He was exactly twice my age – old enough to be my father. That meant something.

FIFTEEN

By the time I took the train back to Leeds the next night I
had rationalised what had happened between Jerome and
I. It had been hardly anything, not proper sex at all. He had
tossed me off. I hadn't seen his body, his penis... it might
just as easily have been a woman's hand tossing me off. It
didn't prove anything. It wasn't conclusive. When I got
back to the flat I would tell him that I'd enjoyed myself, but
that I wanted to leave it at that. He would understand.

I could hear the noise from two streets away and didn't
associate it with where I was living. I turned the corner
into Millers Road, saw that builders were putting
scaffolding up round the house. They'd obviously been
there all day and were inside the house ripping out fittings,
skirting boards and making a general din. The door to our
flat was intact, but they'd already ripped up the carpet
from the stairs. When I got in, Jerome and Martin were
there, trying to do some work. It was only then that I
remembered that Jerome's eviction order had come up that
day. I had been too preoccupied to think of it.

'What's happened?' I asked, sticking my head round
Martin's door.

'Jerome lost his case,' he said. 'But he's got the right to
appeal, so they can't get us out of here until that's gone
through. But it will go through, of course.'

'So why are they putting up scaffolding outside if we
don't have to leave?'

'There's nothing to stop them making a start on the rest
of the building.'

'Oh.'

'The foreman came up and offered Jerome eight hundred
quid in cash to leave.'

'And what did he say?'

'Told him to fuck off. For a gentle loving person, he can

133

be incredibly aggressive. I was impressed. But the foreman wasn't exactly conciliatory. I think there's going to be trouble.'

'So how long have we got?'

'A month at least, maybe six weeks. Maybe even longer. But I don't know that I can put up with this noise. They're doing it deliberately.'

So within days of settling into my little room, the peace was shattered. The workmen stayed until gone eight, and then left. The quiet was almost audible. Martin looked put out by it, but Jerome seemed pleased. He had the light of conflict in his eyes, and was clearly determined to stick this one out. He seemed to be painting more intensely than ever, only taking time off to eat, sleep and go for walks when Martin was around to keep an eye on the builders.

At the weekend I sat for them both again. It had been a strange week of hard work at the museum, and easy conversation in the evenings. It was great to be living in the same flat as Martin. It reaffirmed my friendship with him, and I enjoyed being in his company. Jerome hadn't said anything about what had happened between us. He seemed to have given up, at least for the time being, on any social contact with either of us and spent all his time working in his room. It suited me, but I could tell that Martin was disappointed.

'Do you remember the year before last,' he asked me one evening, 'when we went up to the Highlands with my family?'

'Of course,' I said. 'It was the best holiday I've ever had.'

'I was thinking of going up there again this summer. Do you fancy coming with me?'

'Brilliant idea.'

Last time I'd gone to the Highlands, my trip had coincided with one of my mother's trips to France. I'd had to put Emily into kennels. Thinking of this now gave me another of my regular pangs of loss.

'Maybe Jerome would like to come.'

'If he can be inspired by a mere bush, just think what a mountain would do for him.'

134

Martin laughed.

'Be overwhelmed I should think.'

We were in the sitting room drinking beer. The window was splashed with cement from where the workmen had been doing some repairs to the roof.

'You know,' said Martin, 'I've been a bit obsessed lately. With sex partly, and with my work. It's Jerome that has sparked me off. I've never worked so hard on my paintings before. He's been a great inspiration. I'll feel awful when we all have to leave this place and move on.'

'Maybe we could get somewhere else for the three of us.'

'No,' said Martin. 'I'm leaving when the course finishes, and Jerome's getting itchy feet. You must have noticed. He'll be off as soon as he's thrown out of here. He's not the kind of person who could ever cope with being settled.'

'But I want to be settled somewhere.'

'Me too. But not Jerome. He can't take it. I liked that at first, but once I started feeling involved with him, it seemed like he was rejecting me by not reciprocating my feelings.'

'But he's the warmest, most loving person I've ever met.'

'That's just it,' said Martin. 'He loves everyone. It was no different once we were lovers. He was exactly the same. He gave no more, nothing personal or exclusive to me. He didn't make any effort to spend extra time with me, to be particularly affectionate to me, to show me that I was important to him.'

'He's too old for you anyway,' I pointed out. 'And you could never have a lasting relationship with a man like that. Enjoy it for what it is. Enjoy it whilst it lasts.'

'That's exactly what Jerome would say.'

'And he'd be right.'

I hadn't seen Coll for some time when she appeared the following Wednesday. I had deliberately not gone round to see her after disturbing her with Eddy the previous time. Besides, she knew where I lived and it was close enough. I'd decided to leave it up to her to get in touch.

'God,' she said. 'How can you live here with all this

135

noise and mess? I had to climb over a pile of planks in the hall.'

'It's a point of principle,' I told her. 'Jerome has a right to live here, and we're not going to give in to harassment.'

'Okay,' she said. 'That's up to you. I wouldn't put up with it. I'd move out.'

I shrugged. She looked like she'd made an extra effort tonight, with two shades of colour on her lips – bright red with a dark line edging it – and deep, dark eyeshadow. She was also subdued, but not in a depressed way. She seemed coiled, sprung inside with explosive energy. She had come round for sex, I could tell. Not for company – for sex. It annoyed me slightly, whilst at the same time reassuring me, sexually. She dragged me away from Martin almost immediately and we went into the bedroom. She brought with her the two sticks of incense that Martin had lit, and he looked at me, annoyed, when she picked them up.

Once in the bedroom, she asked me to take her clothes off. It was something I did without much enthusiasm, without much thought. I was not particularly in the mood for this. She'd disturbed a good conversation, and I was resentful that she could impose herself on me in this way. It also annoyed me that I hadn't got the assertiveness to tell her to either sit with us and talk or go away. Perhaps she sensed this in me, because as we were performing the mechanics, and as I was – finally – becoming lost in the sensations of sex, she jabbed the two burning sticks of incense that she was still holding, hard against my skin; one on my back and the other against my side just below my armpit.

I yelled with pain. She laughed, but I pushed her away. It wasn't funny, and pain of that kind was far from erotic. I glared at her and rolled over as she continued to laugh.

'Fuck, that hurts,' I swore.

'You take everything so seriously,' she said. 'What's a bit of pain, for God's sake? Don't be such a baby.'

'You're weird,' I told her. 'You like to hurt people. I should have realised when I saw you hurting your parents. I should have known that before long you'd want to hurt

136

me.'

'It's nothing,' she said. 'Don't take it so seriously. I'm sorry if I hurt you.'

'No you're not,' I said, getting up and starting to dress. Once I'd put my jeans on, I stopped to look at the burn under my arm. There was a small pink dot where the skin had been broken. It was weeping slightly, and was more painful than its size would ever suggest.

'I can't believe you did that,' I said, amazed.

She looked at my expression and laughed again.

'You look so funny when you're angry,' she said.

'Jesus,' I whispered, incredulous, 'I can't believe this.'

'Don't be so melodramatic,' she said. 'It's not as if I've actually damaged you.'

'Oh no? What do you do when you actually damage people then? Chop a leg off, perhaps, or disembowel them?'

'You know,' she said, 'you've got quite a sense of humour.'

'Get out of here, Coll. This is ridiculous.'

She pulled on her dress and I zipped it up perfunctorily.

'I guess I've really overstepped the mark, haven't I?' she said, looking at me carefully.

'Yes,' I agreed.

She adjusted the strap of her dress, seemingly unconcerned. I got the feeling that – as far as she was concerned – things were going according to plan.

'So that's it, then?' she said. 'You don't want to see me again?'

I shook my head, not so much to say no as to express my disbelief at what she had done.

She nodded as though I'd given her the correct answer to a mathematical problem.

'Never mind,' she said. 'It was interesting anyway.'

Carrying my shirt, I saw her out of the flat. Martin came out into the small hallway as I closed the door.

'What were you two doing!' he asked, worried. 'You sounded as though you were being stabbed to death with knives.'

137

'Incense sticks, actually,' I told him, showing him the two burns.

'Wow,' he breathed. 'I knew she was strange, but that's in the ultra-strange category.'

'I don't know why she did it.'

'She's on some hate kick,' he told me. 'First with her parents and now with her lovers. I think she was terribly unhappy as a child.'

'I wasn't exactly in bliss all my life,' I said, 'but I've never wanted to jab people with incense sticks whilst making love to them.'

Martin shrugged.

'Have another beer,' he smiled.

The auction of my father's work crept up on me so silently and so unheralded that I hardly thought about it. I got a letter from my mother asking if I wanted to go down to London with her for the sale, but I telephoned and declined. I didn't feel any differently about it now that time had passed. I still felt unable to witness the final breaking up of that unique collection that had hung on the walls of my old home.

'I can understand why you don't want to go,' Martin told me. 'But I wish I could be there. I'd love to see your father's work taken seriously at last.'

'But only as merchandise.'

'That's one thing you can't get away from in art,' Martin told me. 'But at least some of the paintings will be bought by serious collectors.'

'I hope so.'

'Of course they will. I'd love to see if some of them go to public galleries.'

But, as it closed in on me, May 17th loomed up all the same. In the last few days I felt breathless every time I thought of it.

'I know he was a Scottish painter,' Maggie said, 'but there is a connection with York. It would be nice if the city could buy one of his pictures. Do you know if that's a possibility?'

'I don't know,' I said. 'I haven't kept up with what's happening.' 'I'd like to see one in the gallery here,' she said. 'It would seem right.'

I agreed with her. I'd be able to go and look at it for a start. I tried not to think about it.

One thing I discovered was that Bratt's had published a catalogue for the auction. All thirty-four paintings were beautifully reproduced in full colour. The catalogue cost £30, but was worth it. I bought two copies, just in case one was damaged or lost. Martin managed to persuade his parents to buy a catalogue too, to give to him. He seemed much more excited about it than I was. But then, he was an artist.

The day of the auction came and went without a word. On Sunday Martin came running through to my bedroom just after eleven, carrying an armful of Sunday papers.

'Mum and dad phoned a little while ago to tell me to go out and get the papers,' he said. 'And look, the auction's in the Sunday Times, and The Observer! The big canvas from your old hallway – it sold for £36,000!'

I sat up and looked at the paper that Martin was shoving under my nose.

'Okay, okay,' I groaned.

'Come on, Peter, show some enthusiasm. £36,000. That's over twice the previous best price for a Paul Ellis!'

I scanned the short column about the auction. Prices had ranged from £14,500 up to the record figure of £36,000. The paintings had been sold for a total of £843,000.

'Who'd have thought it!' Martin gasped. 'It's amazing! Come on, get up and come through for some coffee.'

When I went through, Martin was beside himself with excitement.

'I can't resist telling you,' he said. 'I still can't believe it myself.'

'Sit down, Martin,' I told him, a little irritated. 'Sit down and tell me whatever it is.'

'Dad's bought one.'

He sighed with adolescent rapture.

139

'Dad bought an original Paul Ellis at last week's auction.'

Now it was my turn to be amazed.

'Why didn't you tell me before?'

'Because I didn't know before. They didn't say that they were thinking of buying one, because they knew how disappointed I'd be if they ended up not being able to afford it.'

'But how much did they pay for it?'

'£23,500!'

'I didn't know they had that sort of money.'

'Nor did I really. It was a bit of a stretch for them, I think. But they're thrilled.'

I sighed at the thought.

'I'm so pleased,' I said. 'I'm so pleased that one of them at least has gone to people who will appreciate it. That's been my biggest fear... '

'You'll have to come over and see it sometime soon. That's what they asked me to tell you.'

'Okay,' I said. 'I'd like that.'

It wasn't until Tuesday, when my mother got back from London, that I heard anything more. She phoned me up at the museum and asked me out to lunch.

Well, that was a first in itself. It was a warm late-spring morning, and I walked to Betty's feeling strangely calm. It was all over at last. Everything had been completed. All that was still to come were the last details of where they had gone, and for how much. It made me feel good to think that one of them had been bought by the Armstrongs. All had not been completely lost for me.

My mother was the nearest I've ever seen to being excited. She looked absolutely calm, but there was a sparkle to her eyes that was new. Of course, I thought, she's rich now.

It was difficult to take it all in. First of all, Edinburgh City had bought two of his paintings; fourteen had gone to Europe and seven to America – mostly to anonymous private buyers. Ten had gone to galleries – four in the U.K

140

and six abroad. My mother gave me a printed sheet with the details. I noticed that Mr and Mrs Armstrong were not mentioned on the list, so I said nothing about my own and Martin's pleasure on that score.

Secondly, and even more surprisingly, I was handed a medium-sized portfolio. It was torn and dusty.

'This is a folio of your father's work,' my mother told me. 'I found it when I was clearing out the attic rooms for the builders. I want you to have it.'

I was moved almost to tears as I took the folio from her. I was astonished at the gift.

'But why are you giving these to me?' I asked. 'I thought you didn't want me to have any of his work. You were so annoyed when I bought the marble statuette.'

'I was annoyed because of the unnecessary expense you went to,' she told me. 'All you had to do was ask, Peter, and I would have given it to you.'

I closed my eyes briefly and counted to three. It would be of no use to contradict her.

'Never mind,' I said.

'I thought you'd like to have it, that's all,' she told me, indicating the portfolio. 'I just want it to be appreciated.'

I gasped at this. What was all this magnanimity all of a sudden? The only reason why she'd sent them to auction was to make money. Had they been of no monetary value, she would probably have scrapped them.

'Tell me,' I said, asking a question that had begun to bug me lately. 'Why did you wait so long before selling the paintings? If you never liked them, why didn't you get rid of them years ago?'

'I don't know,' she replied. 'Maybe it's like wallpaper. You get used to it, and then you stop wondering whether you like it or not. I had got so used to your father's work that I'd stopped seeing it any more. When I was told that I'd have to spend £35,000 getting number fourteen sorted out, I realised that I had all this stuff on the walls that would be much better off elsewhere. Besides, it's far better for his work to hang in galleries and houses where it'll be enjoyed.'

141

I knew she didn't give a toss whether it was enjoyed or not. Her hypocrisy was galling and I couldn't understand it. Then it suddenly clicked. Of course! It would have been the auctioneers and art lovers in London who had done it. They'd have told her what a great service she was doing to the art world by making my father's work available; what a great opportunity she was giving to collectors; what a splendid and generous woman she was. It made me feel sick.

'There are one or two financial matters that have to be sorted out,' she said. 'First of all, Bratt's strongly suggest that you insure the work in the folio. I know they'll only be drawings and so on, but even so... That means living somewhere that has a burglar alarm for a start, otherwise you'd never be able to afford the premiums. I'm having one fitted to the house right now, so maybe it would be better for me to hang on to the folio for the time being.'

'Okay,' I said. 'But I don't suppose I'll be able to find somewhere to live that's got an alarm. It's not the sort of thing that rented accommodation has.'

'No, I know,' she said. 'I was thinking of buying some more property in York. To rent out mostly – to tourists perhaps. That's far easier in the long run. I could get you a place too. I wouldn't charge you any rent, of course. But still, property would be a safe investment for my money. I've got to find something to do with it... '

I thought of Jerome being evicted in Leeds, and realised with absolute certainty that if ever she got into that situation, my mother would do the same. She wouldn't think twice about evicting tenants – throwing them out onto the streets. She'd done it before with people who'd fallen behind with their rent at Bernard Terrace. Only she did it in a quiet uninvolved way, getting other people to do it for her so that she never had to confront the reality of what she was doing. I felt angry against her, angry and helpless. After all, she was offering me something I couldn't bring myself to refuse.

'That would be great,' I said.

'Well say it as though you mean it,' she told me.

I bumped into Dave Boothe on the way back to the museum. He seemed to spend his whole life hanging round Skeldergate Bridge these days. He came over as I walked along the river.

'Don't try and nail your filthy crimes on me,' he hissed.

'Not mine,' I told him. 'You were the one who murdered my dog.'

'Who says?'

'I saw you, Dave,' I said. 'You were at Bernard Terrace that evening. You can't deny it.'

'Yes he can,' Paul interjected. 'He was with me and some mates.'

Dave smiled in complicity, but I refused to rise to his bait. This young man wasn't even worth my contempt.

'Oh,' I said, 'you faked an alibi. Surprise, surprise.'

And with that I walked off, shrugging to myself at the intransigent patterns of futility that seemed to show in life, like the hollow rib-cage of some decomposing corpse.

SIXTEEN

I was doing an early evening sitting for Martin when I told him about the lunch I'd had with my mother.

He called me an ungrateful sod.

'She's buying you a flat!' he cried. 'You can't get much luckier than that.'

'I'm much more pleased about the portfolio.'

'There's another thing. You're getting a flat out of this – and a valuable collection of artwork.'

He shook his head in undisguised envy.

'What's it like?'

'I don't know. I handed them back to my mother to look after. I wasn't prepared to look through them in front of her. I feel too private about them for that.'

He nodded.

'I can see that.'

I know I should have been grateful, and I was in a way. But not to my mother. She was rolling in money, and her gifts to me were not prompted by generosity or kindness.

'If all this is generosity,' I said, 'why has she never been generous before? It's strange that this altruism has suddenly come upon her when it's terribly easy for her to make a gesture.'

'Cynic,' said Martin.

But I was right.

I didn't rub things in by telling him that she'd given me a cheque for £2,500 to repay the money I'd spent buying the marble statuette... (And, I thought, that's another thing I'll have to get insured.)

Being promised somewhere to live in maybe two or three months time was great as far as it went, but Jerome's appeal was due to be heard in two days and we knew he'd lose it. Martin had been to the housing officer at the council and had been assured that we wouldn't be asked to leave

144

that day. We'd be given a couple of weeks at least. But then what? I refused to think about it.

'I'm getting ready for my end of year exhibition,' Martin sighed. 'I could do without being made homeless right now.'

'How's that going?' I asked.

'Oh, you know. It's hard.'

I'd sat for both Martin and Jerome several times now. Martin would get so far with a drawing or painting – until he was sure of the proportions and the lighting, and then he'd take it into college to work on it there. The result of this was that I hadn't yet seen any of his finished work. Martin was very protective about his space at college and had never invited me down to look at it, though I had made hints several times. I was interested and intrigued to see his final show.

As the light faded, the doorbell rang. I went and opened the door to a stranger.

'Good evening,' he said. 'You're Martin?'

'No, I'm Peter,' I said. 'Martin's inside. Do you want him?'

'No, no,' he said, 'don't bother. I wanted to talk to one of you.' 'What about?'

'About moving out of here.'

'Well, you'd better talk to Jerome about it rather than us,' I told him. 'We're staying here as his guests for a short while.'

'I'm afraid Jerome is unavailable at the moment. He tried to take his life today.'

'What?' said Martin, who had come up behind me.

'He's been admitted to a private mental hospital near Harrogate,' the man said. 'I'm told it's very good. He's been there before,' he added, seeing Martin's expression.

'How do you know?' I asked, suspicious now of this eager man.

'I'm his brother.'

'His brother!'

'Yes. Can I come in for a moment?'

I let him in and we went through to the front room.

145

Martin came through as well and we asked for an explanation.

'When Jerome came back to England, he naturally wanted somewhere to stay,' the man told us. 'I had a flat vacant, so naturally I let him move in... '

'You're his landlord!' I couldn't believe it.

'So you're evicting your own brother?' Martin asked. 'Bastard,' he murmured.

'We agreed that he'd only take the flat for a while. Until I could get planning permission sorted out on the building. I even offered to rehouse him, but he refused to leave.'

'Oh, you offered to rehouse him?' Martin sneered. 'Where?'

'In a bedsit near Quarry Hill... '

'No wonder he refused to leave,' said Martin.

'That's not the point,' said the man, 'the point is that Jerome has been admitted to Brearton Hall, a private mental hospital near Harrogate. He will be there for at least twenty-one days observation, and probably longer. Which means that he is no longer resident here.'

'I see,' said Martin, 'no need for getting the heavies round to clear him out. How convenient.'

'I can't believe Jerome would try to commit suicide,' I said.

'He's tried before,' the man said. 'Several times. Twice before he went out to the States, and at least once whilst he was there.'

'He mentioned it to me,' Martin told me quietly. 'But he said that it was all in the past. All over with.'

'But,' I said, 'he was so full of life. He must be the sanest, alivest person I've ever met.'

I remembered the massage he'd given me; the way he'd spoken to me about going with the flow, about doing things because they were right – about appreciating life. It was inconceivable that he could have tried to kill himself.

'How did he do it?' I asked.

'Sleeping tablets,' the man said. 'I came round here this morning to talk to him and we had a bit of an argument. I suspected that he might do something stupid, so I came back after lunch... '

He looked at us briefly, one after the other.

'It's okay, don't worry about him. He'll be alright. He goes through phases, that's all.'

Phases, I thought, phases! It sounded like he was talking about lunar cycles or something; as though Jerome's attempted suicide was no more serious than a recurrence of indigestion.

'I want to see him,' I said.

'Of course you can see him. I'll give you the address.' He took some paper from his filofax and wrote it out.

'Phone them first to make sure he can receive visitors,' he said, handing the paper to me. 'I'm sure he'd like to see you.'

'Ah,' said Martin, realising something important, 'where does that leave us?'

'Well,' said the man, 'you're not actually tenants here. You have no tenancy agreement, so you have no rights at all. Technically I could have you removed from the premises right now. But I won't do that. You need some time to get your things together. I thought maybe twenty-four hours?'

We ended up at Steph's. We fitted four car loads of belongings into her sitting room, and two stolen single mattresses. It was all piled high against one of the walls and made the small room look smaller. Ian, Steph's flatmate, looked more and more annoyed as we brought the stuff in.

'I've told him it's only for a few days,' she whispered, 'but I don't think he's very pleased.'

'I'm sorry if we're causing you trouble,' Martin whispered back.

'I'm not,' she smiled. 'He's a miserable sod. The inconvenience will do him good.'

On the last journey I bought a three litre wine box and considered my considerable naivety. I had imagined a relaxed summer in the company of two people that I felt close to. I hadn't imagined a time when this would come to

147

an end. Of course, this was ridiculous. Martin only had three weeks before the end of his foundation course. There was no point in him looking for somewhere else to live in Leeds. He'd be moving home for the summer so soon. He had a couple of interviews coming up, and I had no doubt that he would be moving down to start on a degree course in London, as he hoped, in September.

He had always been a permanence in my life, like my father's paintings, and it was strange and sad to think that all this had changed. And now that Jerome was gone, it suddenly struck me that I didn't have to pretend about my feelings for him any more. I didn't have to kid myself that I didn't enjoy that brief sexual encounter – that I didn't want a more complete consummation. Whilst he was around, I was bridled by my inhibitions. But now that I wouldn't be forced to translate my wishes into actions, I realised I wanted to repeat that one physically intimate moment between us. He had made it so easy for me to give in to him. He had given me such an overwhelming gift – and not just sexually. He had given me something of his passionate appreciation of life. He had infected me with something of his need to lap life up as completely as possible. And I had given him so little in return – except to see him, I now realised, as some kind of idealised father figure.

It struck me then that over these last few weeks, for the first time, I had been genuinely happy. I had been happy and I hadn't even realised it. And now that time was over.

'Don't worry, Peter,' said Steph, noticing my expression, 'you'll be alright.'

'Will I?' I said. I had meant it to sound flippant: a joke. But it came out laden with self-pity and I felt myself flush with embarrassment at this unwitting confession of my sadness. Steph came over and sat beside me on the settee. She put her arm round my shoulder and sat with me in silence. Martin poured us all some more wine.

'I think we'd better go and get Jerome's stuff from the flat,' he said. 'I know there's not much room here, but if there's nowhere else to take it, we could get hold of a van

148

and take it up to my parents place at the weekend.'

'Maybe his brother will take it,' I said.

'That's what worries me,' said Martin.

We took a train to Harrogate on Saturday. Two short bus journeys left us a mile from the hospital. We were both overdressed, having left when it was cloudy. Now the sun was hot and I walked with my jacket and sweater over my arm. The country here was richly green, undulating, well-treed and, I thought, rather bland. Martin was still subdued after his clash with Jerome's brother the day before.

I had been at work when Martin and Steph went over to get Jerome's things. It seemed that when they'd got to the flat, it had been cleared already. Workmen had made an early start and smashed out the rotting window frames, pulled up the carpets and torn out everything in the kitchen. Jerome's clothes had been in a pile in the hall, the books were boxed and ready to be taken away. Everything else was a pile of crumbling ash in the courtyard. They'd burned the lot. Papers, magazines, paintings... Nothing could be salvaged. The brother, who was supervising the clear out, had merely shrugged when confronted.

The gateposts of Brearton Hall, when we came to them, were neo-classical moulded concrete. The long drive was tree lined.

'I don't get this,' I said as we started up the drive. 'If Jerome's brother can afford to put him in an expensive place like this, why couldn't he have found him a decent place to stay?'

Martin shook his head.

'It would have been far cheaper too,' he said.

'But then,' I suggested, 'maybe it's not his brother that's paying.'

Brearton Hall was a smallish country house with modern excrescences. People were out in the grounds enjoying the sun. It all looked very normal. We asked for Jerome at the reception, and were taken to the day room by a male nurse. Jerome was the only person there.

'Jerome?' the nurse called as we came into the room. 'Visitors.'

He was sitting by the window in a deep, comfortable chair. He slowly levered himself up as we approached, placing his hands on our shoulders and kissing us on the cheek.

'Come and sit with me,' he said. 'It's lovely here.'

We pulled up two chairs and sat on either side of him.

'The nurses are very good here. I like it. I suppose Alex told you that I've been here before?'

'If Alex is your brother, then yes,' I said. 'Are you alright?'

'Yes, fine,' he said. 'I just feel sleepy all the time. It's the drugs they're giving me. I feel sleepy and numb. And old.'

Martin glanced at me. We had decided to say nothing about the paintings.

'Do you fancy going for a walk?' Martin asked. 'It's warm outside.'

'No,' he said. 'I'd rather stay here. Do you want some tea?'

I nodded.

'Please,' said Martin.

'There's a machine in the reception area... '

'I'll get it,' I said, and left them together in that large, bright room.

I felt numbed too. Jerome was like a shell. He seemed to have been drained of everything that had made him special. It was creepy – like looking at an animated corpse. Some people, I realised, as I balanced three teas on a cardboard tray, feel too much; they feel too intensely – burn too hard.

When I came into the day room, Martin was holding both of Jerome's hands in his. I gave them their tea.

'Thanks,' said Jerome. We fell into silence.

What had I expected? I don't know.

A girl walked past the window and looked in. She waved at Jerome and smiled a wide, intensely happy smile before walking on.

'How old do you think she is?' Jerome asked.

150

'I don't know,' I said. 'Twelve? Thirteen?'

'Eighteen,' he said. 'She's got anorexia. Stopped growing years ago. She's never had a period.'

He gazed out of the window for a short while.

'She was here last time I was in. Maybe she's been here all the time in-between. Doesn't look a day older than when I last saw her two years ago. That nurse who showed you in, he was here before. I asked him once if he was gay and he laughed. I think they think it's a part of my disorder, but if you ask me, it's the only thing about me that's sane at the moment.'

Martin and I sipped our tea and felt uncomfortable.

'I thought you were in New York two years ago,' Martin said.

'I was,' Jerome agreed, 'but I came back for treatment.'

'How long are you going to be in here?' Martin asked.

'I don't know,' he said. 'For as long as it takes, I guess. Until I've had a rest. Until I'm better.'

He shook his head a little, as though to clear his head.

'No,' he said, 'not until I'm better. I'll never be better. Just until I'm in control again.'

'Then what are you going to do? Come back to Leeds?'

Jerome didn't answer immediately. He drank some of his tea as if he hadn't heard Martin. He stared blankly for a while, then looked at us both in turn.

'Sorry,' he said quietly. 'I'm sorry. I guess I've really let you down.'

'You've done too much,' I said, 'for us to ever feel that you'd let us down.'

'Don't worry,' said Martin. 'We're okay.'

'Feel love for me,' he said. 'When you leave here, feel love for me. I think I need it.'

'You don't have to ask for that,' said Martin. 'You've already got it.'

On the way back to Leeds, I was haunted by Jerome's empty face. Every time I thought of it I shivered. Martin, it seemed, was even more upset than me.

'God,' he said as we sat on the train. 'It's terrible. I

aspired to be like Jerome. Still do, in a way. I aspire to be like him as he was when I first moved in with him. Lively, thoughtful, passionate about everything. Towards the end he began to shut himself away. I thought it was because he wanted to work hard – because he was inspired. If only I'd realised... '

'You couldn't have realised,' I told him. 'You didn't know what signs to look for.'

'How could his brother burn all those paintings... I know they weren't masterpieces, but they had something going for them. I would have wanted one. I would have paid for one.'

SEVENTEEN

On Sunday morning, Martin's parents drove over to Leeds to collect his effects. They came over in a Range Rover and a Ford Escort, fitting everything in at a squeeze. Martin went with them. There was no room for me.

'But you'll have to come soon, to see our new masterpiece,' Mrs Armstrong told me. 'We haven't got it at the moment. We're having it reframed.'

'I'll be back this evening,' Martin told me. 'We can finish off that wine box if you like.'

They drove off and, after they'd gone, Steph helped me move my things – which had accounted for less than half of what we'd brought from Jerome's flat – into her room.

'It doesn't bother me if it's cluttered,' she said. 'I only sleep here.'

Back in the sitting room we put the two mattresses on top of each other, then leant them against the wall behind the door and threw a bedspread over them.

'There,' she said. 'Ian can't complain now. It looks fine.'

She stood looking at the tidy room.

'Now what shall we do? Fancy a walk?'

'No,' I said. 'My mother always goes out on a Sunday morning. I'll take the train over to York. I can't resist having a look at that portfolio. I can sneak into the house, have a look at it, and then sneak out again.'

'Can I come?'

'Of course, if you want to.'

'Good. We'll take the car.'

We got to York shortly after twelve. The whole house was in disarray. Dust sheets were everywhere and the carpets were covered with thick canvas. Builders' materials littered the hall. The whole place was being redecorated. The ceilings had been given a first coat of paint, and the wallpaper was being stripped.

I couldn't find the portfolio at first, but eventually discovered it in the cupboard under the stairs. We took it into the dining room. The chord tying it was perished and dusty.

'It hasn't been opened,' said Steph as I tried to gently undo the knot. 'I'm surprised your mother wasn't interested in the contents.'

'I'm not,' I said. 'She doesn't want to have anything to do with my father. She didn't pass this on to me to be kind. She passed it on to get rid of it.'

'I don't suppose it matters why she's given it to you. The main thing is that she has.'

I fumbled slightly with the knot as it came loose, feeling suddenly nervous. The folio opened with a dusty crackle and revealed a sheaf of high quality drawing paper, maybe twenty or thirty different sized sheets.

The top sheet was a self-portrait in charcoal – a simple, signed sketch dated 1969.

'This is incredible!' Steph breathed, taking it gently and holding it up for a closer look.

The next drawing was another figure drawing, but not of my father. It was of a young man asleep on a chair. There was something tense, but flowing about the lines. There followed a series of sketches of figures, landscapes and abstract designs; then several watercolours, two of which were practice colour sketches for paintings that had just been auctioned. I felt tight inside with excitement. This was mine! It was genuinely competent work, not the doodles or notes that I had feared. All these pieces would look good framed and hung on a wall.

After the watercolours, there came a series of drawings of naked youths, either standing, sitting, or in action – laughing and wrestling. The subtle eroticism was unmistakable. It wasn't lost on Steph either and she glanced at me with interest as I stared down at the drawings. The next one was a sketched bathing scene. Two naked youths were splashing each other in a calm sea. It had that outwardly innocent sexuality so common in Victorian pictures of female nudes. This prudish quality had obviously not been lost on my father. It was titled "Youthful Eros" and there was a cartoon cupid, top right, drawing his bow at the boy on the left. Underneath the title there was a caption. "Martha waited by the beach huts for her young love. But fate had other plans... " And underneath, faintly, in someone else's handwriting: "Martha was a dyke anyway."

The final drawing was a stylised picture of two naked men wrestling.

'That's a copy of a Gaudier-Brzeska,' Steph said. 'I've seen the original in Martin's book.'

She was right, I realised, and I made a mental note to compare it with the lines on the sculpture later.

Steph was arranging the drawings on the table.

'I didn't know your father was gay,' she said.

I didn't reply. I nearly said "he wasn't", but it would have been pointless. These pictures proved nothing, but they suggested a great deal. It made me wonder why I had never suspected this before. If he had been gay, then that would explain a great deal about my mother's attitude towards him now.

'I'm taking these away with me,' I said. 'If my mother sees them, she'll destroy them.'

Steph nodded.

I was desperate to tell Martin and seethed all afternoon, impatient to show him the pictures. I whiled away the afternoon trying to trace the lines from my sculpture. It took a long time, but when I finally deciphered the lines, I found that they represented one of two figures from the Gaudier-Brzeska original. Martin had taken his book home, so I had no way of corroborating what the picture actually was, but I had no doubt that this was the Gaudier-Brzeska that Mr Munro had talked about. The drawing in my father's portfolio was a kind of key. I pinned my tracing up on the wall and looked forward to showing it to Mr Munro.

In the end, when Martin came back, it was an anticlimax. He arrived at nine and, although he was as excited as me about the quality of the drawings, he didn't seem surprised

155

at all.

'I suspected that he was gay all along,' he said.

'You never said,' I replied.

'I didn't want to tell you A, because there wasn't any proof, and B, because you would have accused me of wishful thinking.'

'What made you suspect, then?' I asked.

'All these figures he painted. All these dark paintings. In everything he did the figures were always male.'

'That's not very conclusive,' said Steph.

'No, I know, but there was something about the way in which he painted them. There's a subtle undertone of homo-eroticism.'

'I didn't see it,' Steph murmured.

'That's because you have no eye for male eroticism,' he said.

'I'm sure I would have picked up on it if it was there.'

'Call it intuition, then,' he said. 'But I knew.'

'There's only one way to find out for sure.'

'What's that?' Martin asked.

'I'll go and ask my mother.'

'Are you sure that's wise?' Steph asked.

'I don't care if it's wise,' I said.

'She'll only deny it,' said Martin.

'But I'll know if she's lying, I always do.'

'I'll drive you over,' Steph said.

'No, it's okay, I'd rather talk to her on my own.'

'Don't worry, we'll both stay outside in the car – or in the pub if you'd prefer.'

'Oh, I see,' I said, 'Martin's coming too now is he?'

'You can't leave us in suspense,' said Martin. 'Besides, you'll need support.'

So we drove over to York for the second time that day. As we approached on the A64 I could see the tower of the Minster and it was like returning to a city I hadn't been to for years. The racecourse was empty except for a few dog-walkers, and the flat expanse of grass was a reminder of my past. It was only weeks since I'd brought Emily here, one moist Saturday of diffused light.

156

My mother was in, as usual, watching television. She turned in surprise as I walked into the room – annoyed, I think, at being disturbed.

'Hello, Peter. I didn't expect to see you this evening.'

'I came round to ask you a question.'

'Oh?'

'Yes. I wondered if you could tell me whether my father was homosexual?'

My mother gave an involuntary jerk as I said this, as if she been surprised by a loud noise. It was all that was necessary to convince me. She paused to turn the sound down, then turned to me.

'Of course he wasn't,' she said, with such a natural authority that I paused for a moment.

'Look, it's alright mother,' I said, 'I don't mind.'

'You don't mind what? You don't mind being told that Paul was the victim of filthy rumours, or you don't mind being told that he was homosexual?'

She spat the word homosexual at me as if it might cause me physical injury.

'No, I mean I don't mind you telling me, because I know it's true. He was gay, wasn't he?'

'If you're so sure about it,' she said, 'why ask me?'

'Okay,' I replied, 'but I'm ninety per cent sure. At least.'

'And who told you this? Martin?'

'No, no one told me. I worked it out for myself.'

'Ah,' she sighed. 'You've been to see Alasdair Munro again, haven't you? You said you would.'

'I expect I am going to see him at some point,' I said. 'But I haven't yet.'

'What was it then – did you get a letter from him? A telephone call?'

'No, it was nothing like that.'

'He was always a man who sneered at other people, who lied about them.'

'You can't say that,' I said. 'I've met him and I know he isn't like that.'

'Oh I see, you haven't been to see him and you're suddenly an expert on his character.'

157

'I went to see him once, to collect the statue.'

'And you know all about what sort of man he is?'

'I don't think he's a liar,' I said simply.

'So he told you that Paul was homosexual? What else did he tell you? I suppose he told you that he and Paul were... '

She stopped, quite suddenly, appalled at what she had been about to say. Instead I finished off her sentence for her.

'Lovers,' I said. 'Of course... '

We sat in The Bishop and talked. The place was the same, the clientele were the same – it must have been me who was different. Martin was as lively as I've ever seen him.

'I've got to meet this Mr Munro,' he said. 'There's so much we can ask him... so much he can tell us.'

'I suppose I'll have to go over and see him,' I said.

'You don't sound very enthusiastic,' said Steph.

'I'm not really,' I told her. 'Or rather, I'm nervous. Why didn't Mr Munro tell me all this himself when I first met him?'

'He wouldn't have wanted to upset you,' Steph said. 'How could he know what prejudices you did or didn't have?'

'I just can't understand why my father married my mother?'

'Let's go and ask Mr Munro,' Martin suggested.

'Maybe he was bi-sexual,' said Steph.

'Yes, maybe,' said Martin. 'Look, you can phone him up tonight and arrange something.'

'It's nearly half past ten,' I pointed out. 'It'll probably be half past eleven by the time we get back to Leeds.'

'Phone him tomorrow.'

'Okay,' I agreed. 'I'll try and arrange to go over and see him next weekend.'

'Next weekend!' Martin exclaimed. 'I can't wait that long. Arrange to see him as soon as possible. Whatever day it is I'll phone the museum and tell them you're sick.'

'What makes you think I want you to come along?'

'What makes you think you can stop me,' he said. 'I've got as much right to see Mr Munro as you have. Your father's been a mystery to me for more than ten years. We've always wondered about him. You can't go on your own.'

'No,' I said, 'I suppose not.'

Why was I suddenly feeling so reticent? Surely this was my big chance to answer all those lingering questions? And Martin would be much better at asking them than me. I'd probably end up getting tongue tied if I was on my own – or, worse still, I'd run away like last time.

Back at Steph's we drank another glass of wine, then laid the mattresses out. Steph went straight to bed, but Martin and I stayed up for some time, talking about my father; about the pictures in the portfolio; about getting them framed. We talked about many things, but we didn't talk about the future. Change was too close and too definitive for me to want to disturb the present with talk of parting.

At around midnight I made us coffee which we drank in our respective beds. We fell silent and I lay there feeling close to Martin, close to my father. As Martin finished his coffee he sighed.

'You know,' he said. 'I really miss Jerome.'

I nodded.

I thought of him, drugged until he'd become lifeless. What did the future hold for him? Intense emotion followed by collapse, over and over again as the years passed? I wondered if this was what happened to everyone who immersed themselves in life so completely, so passionately.

'He changed me,' said Martin. 'In so short a time. Perhaps I ought to go and tell him how grateful I am.'

'Maybe,' I said.

He'd changed me too, but I couldn't tell Martin. He'd made me unsure again – of myself; of what and who I wanted for the future. But he'd settled me too, in a way that I couldn't describe. He'd touched some infertile corner of my being and made it grow. Did he know? I'm sure he did at the time.

I felt tired when I went to work the next day. Underslept. I'd dreamed all night, vague worrying dreams about nothing in particular. It was only when I phoned Mr Munro at lunch time that I began to feel better. He wasn't surprised to hear from me and arranged a meeting for the following evening. I didn't tell him what I wanted to see him about, but he sounded as though he'd guessed.

So, I'd set this thing in motion. I was going to meet my father's lover. It intrigued me and frightened me at the same time. Perhaps if they'd loved each other, then that would humanise my father at last – or make him into even more of a stranger...

I thought of the Death Letters and my childhood fantasy of my father being loved, lost and mourned – not some blank space that might as well never have existed. Mr Munro was one blank space that was now filled, but there were others and I now wanted Martin there to help me fill them.

I hired a car again. There was something incompatible about public transport and experiences like these. Besides, the journey would have been tedious by train and bus. I had expected Martin to be lively and talkative, but he wasn't. He was introspective and thoughtful. We hardly spoke at all except when we came to Sheffield and he map-read me to Dore. I realised suddenly that he was nervous. Nervous! I'd never seen him like this before. It made me understand that I wasn't the only one who had some kind of emotional account to settle here. Martin was an artist, a friend and a fellow investigator.

I had brought the portfolio, along with the tracing I'd made of the statuette and Mr Munro's book on Scottish painting.

Mr Munro, when he answered the door, smiled broadly at us both.

'I've brought a friend,' I told him.

160

'Come in,' he said, 'and welcome.'

He showed us into the hall, then opened the door to the sitting room. We stood in the entrance for a moment.

'Yes,' he said. 'I bought one. I couldn't resist it. It was probably my last chance to afford one.'

On the opposite wall to the bright abstracted landscapes, there hung one of my father's larger and darker works.

'It used to hang in one of the upstairs bedrooms,' I told him, going over to look more closely. 'I'm pleased you bought it.'

'So am I,' Mr Munro assured me. 'I'm having to sell a fair few other pieces to afford it, but it was high time I had a clear out. There's a lot of stuff in this house that I don't particularly care for. Now come in and sit down.'

Martin was awestruck by the room. He just stood and stared.

'Martin's at art college,' I explained. Mr Munro smiled.

'I'll give you a tour later,' he said. 'Would you like a drink? I usually have a whisky at around this time.'

'Please,' said Martin.

'Not if I'm driving,' I said.

'Coffee?'

'Thanks.'

Mr Munro went to the door, opened it and called out.

'Graham, any chance of a coffee in here?'

There was a murmur of assent from the next room, then Mr Munro closed the door.

'Now,' he said as he poured two whiskies. 'What can I do for you both?'

'At last,' I said, 'I've plucked up the courage to come back and ask everything that I didn't ask last time I came.'

'Fine,' he said.

'And I wanted to be here to listen,' Martin added. 'I'm as curious as Peter.'

'Okay, start asking.'

'First,' I said, 'we've discovered that you and my father were lovers.'

'Ah,' he said, pausing briefly to hand Martin his glass. 'How did you find that out?'

161

'From my mother,' I told him.

'Your mother!'

'Yes, it was a slip of the tongue really.'

'So fragile a thing, then, your finding out.'

'I'd already discovered that he was gay,' I said. 'It was this work of his. My mother gave it to me without even looking at it.'

I picked the portfolio up and opened it on the coffee table. Mr Munro leant forward and began to go through the work. At the second picture – of a young man asleep in a chair – he laughed.

'This is me,' he said. 'Paul drew it around the end of 1970. I assumed it had been destroyed. Or lost.'

He continued to look through the work.

'There's some really interesting stuff here,' he said. 'I expect you're pleased to have got hold of it.'

'Very,' I told him.

When he came to the drawing titled "Young Eros", he laughed again.

'I remember this one too,' he said. 'Look, this is my handwriting.'

He pointed to the caption that said "Martha was a Dyke anyway" and shook his head. The door opened and a man came in. He was taller than Mr Munro and blond. Younger too, perhaps thirty-seven or eight, moustached also, and cheerful. He handed me a mug of coffee. Martin gave me a knowing look as he glanced at Graham and Mr Munro.

'This is Graham. Graham, this is Martin and Peter.' He handed Graham the drawing. 'Look. This is something Paul did years ago.'

Graham smiled as he looked at it.

'I recognise your handwriting,' he said.

'Whisky?' Mr Munro asked.

'Yup.'

Graham sat down on the settee beside me.

'So you're Peter Ellis?'

'Yes,' I replied.

'Your father was a very talented man,' he told me. 'Alasdair tells me that you know very little about him.'

'That's true,' I said. 'Which is why Martin and I came this evening. To find out more.'

'One thing I want to know,' said Martin, 'is why you didn't tell Peter about your relationship with his father when he first came to see you.'

'But he was so serious. How could I say anything when he was so nervous! Anyway,' Mr Munro added, turning to me, 'questions like that are up to you to ask, not for me to anticipate. What would have happened if you didn't want to hear what I had to tell?'

There was nothing I could say to that, so I remained silent. Mr Munro picked up the Gaudier-Brzeska drawing.

'Ah,' he said, 'I see you've deciphered the sculpture.'

EIGHTEEN

We ended up staying for dinner – something we hadn't planned to do, but Mr Munro made it so easy for us to accept his invitation. He had an easy grace about him and an informality that made it impossible not to relax. Martin was clearly smitten, by both Mr Munro and Graham, who spoke with casual familiarity and was obviously pleased to have guests.

The table in the dining room was laid with linen and china, and antique glass in various shapes and sizes.

'My passion,' Graham told us. 'Alasdair has his painting, and I have my glass.'

I found myself drinking from a plain Tudor goblet of slightly uneven soda glass. Its preciousness was exhilarating, but frightening, and I worried that I might drop and break it.

'I've often imagined this happening,' Mr Munro told me as we drank a brightly clear consommé. 'Meeting Paul Ellis' son. I didn't really think I ever would. It's been strange meeting you, because you're so much of a real person. I mean, then you were just a problem.'

'I can believe that,' I said.

'But in what way was he a problem?' Martin wanted to know.

Mr Munro shrugged.

'It was a long time ago,' he said.

'I'm sorry, Mr Munro... ' I said.

'Alasdair, please,' he told me. 'I hate to be Mr Munro to anyone, least of all you.'

'Okay,' I agreed. 'Alasdair. I know this must seem like prying, especially when it comes so long after the event. But it's important to me, and it's not idle curiosity.'

'I know,' he replied, 'and I'm not reticent to talk about it. I'm trying to remember, that's all.'

He drank his soup and thought for a few moments.

'Your existence,' he told me, 'tied Paul to your mother. He was concerned with doing the right thing, even if it was difficult or painful for himself. Quite what he felt about your mother I don't know, but he would have done almost anything not to hurt her, in spite of knowing their marriage could never really work.'

He put his soup spoon down and played with the stem of his glass.

'But why did he marry her?' Graham asked.

'Social pressure, probably,' Alasdair shrugged.

Graham shook his head sadly.

'Paul found it so difficult to love Helen – physically,' Alasdair went on. 'That was a problem he only fully understood after he was married; which was when I met him. He was very unhappy, but working hard. And what Paintings! He'd left behind his bright little abstract pictures and was developing an original and disturbing style all his own. Helen hated the new pictures and wanted him to get back to his earlier and more immediately commercial style.'

'But artists have to go with what they feel, or they go under,' said Martin.

'Exactly,' said Alasdair. He took a sip of his wine before continuing.

'Your mother was quite a lot older than Paul,' he said. 'Eleven years, I think – and fifteen years older than me. When I met her I was twenty-one and she was thirty-six. It seemed like a huge age difference and on the few occasions that I met her, I couldn't relate to her, either as a person or as Paul's wife.

'She sort of caught Paul, or at least that's how I saw it. I'm not impartial, I know, so maybe I'm being harsh. Helen's father was a landlord in Edinburgh. He had property across the city, and Paul was one of his tenants. Helen liked his bright abstractions – they were easy to like, so bright and simple and meaningless. Paul was very young for his age. Shy and introverted. She, I think, felt she'd done nothing with her life and it amused her to

165

fraternise with a real live painter. Paul, of course, was flattered by her attention.

'She gave him money, which was a godsend to Paul, who couldn't otherwise have worked full time on his painting; and when she suggested marriage, it didn't seem too bad a compromise. At least he'd still be able to work. For a man who was so sensitive, it was an astonishing mistake to make. But he saw it as a way to keep on painting. The marriage was a bit of a sham, but I think they both knew that it would be to an extent.'

'I can't understand people who compromise in their relationships,' said Graham, 'when they're the fundamental basis of your life.'

'But maybe people want to lead precarious existences,' Alasdair said. 'Maybe artists need that to function creatively.'

'And that was how my father was when you first met him?'

'I didn't get to know him for some time after our first meeting, which was a pretty unauspicious affair. I'd got a degree in art history which led to a job in an Edinburgh gallery, just off Princes Street. I'd only been working there for a short time. We had several of your father's paintings for sale so, as you can imagine, it was a thrill to meet him.

'I think he came to see someone, and I had to show him through to their office. That was all. But I was struck by him at once. Not because he was good looking, but because he was exactly what I reckoned an artist should look like. He wasn't very well dressed and he looked as though his thoughts were somewhere else. I was intrigued by him right from the start.

'The second time I met him was at an informal gathering at the gallery. Several artists whom the gallery represented were there for drinks. I was bored because everyone thought I was too young to be taken seriously. Paul was bored because he was on his own and had nothing in common with the other artists present – painters of skill but little merit.

'I got talking to him because he remembered me from

166

our previous meeting. Very soon we realised that we shared the same taste in art. We both admired the Abstract Expressionists and post-war American art. People like Rothko, Pollock, Lichtenstein and Warhol who were being ridiculed by those I worked with. They were angry and jealous that these people were so successful and so new. But Paul was different. He admired them too. We were the youngest people there by some years and it gave me a great feeling of clandestine brotherhood to be in opposition as-it-were.'

'God, it sounds exciting,' said Martin. 'I wish I could be submerged in that kind of atmosphere with other artists. To me it's such a solitary business.'

'Art always is,' said Alasdair. 'Always.'

'Maybe,' I suggested, 'it's the in-between bits that need to be less solitary. The times when you're not painting... '

'Yes,' Alasdair agreed. 'But sometimes the in-between bits can be the worst, if things aren't going well. Sometimes artists need to be pushed into getting on with work. Paul was like that right from the beginning. Once he was going he would work incredibly hard. It was difficult to get him started, that's all.'

'And how did he manage that?' Martin asked.

'I commissioned him once,' Alasdair told us, 'when I still hardly knew him. That gave him inspiration. I had a bit of money put aside at the time, so, shortly after our initial conversation, I got in touch with him and asked if I could commission a couple of paintings. I was living at home and had nowhere to hang them, but I realised that if I didn't act then, there would come a time when I wouldn't be able to afford it. He accepted my offer and we organised a price, which I thought breathtaking at the time, but which seems more like an insult now. I think he was glad to accept the offer because he was under a lot of pressure to produce more and more of the same sort of work – work that he'd left behind. I put no restrictions on his subject matter, stipulating only the size of canvas.

'In the end, he painted me three for the price of two. Those ones on the wall next door.'

167

'That was certainly one of the best commissions you gave,' said Graham.

'The best.'

'What did you do about the third canvas?' I asked.

'I was overwhelmed, of course, and offered to pay for it, but he wouldn't let me. So, I took him out to dinner instead... and that's what started it all off.'

Alasdair paused to look at me.

'You make it sound very romantic,' Graham said.

'It was romantic,' Alasdair replied.

'And did my mother know?' I asked.

'Your mother knew about it almost immediately,' he told me. 'It was impossible to hide, I guess. The first time we met she treated me with polite indifference; the second time with open hostility. She was very persuasive with Paul too. She forbade him to see me and threatened to cut off his money. Really! As though he were her son. Threats. Emotional blackmail. I don't think it was his infidelity that got to her – it was the fact that I was a man. She even threatened to involve the police.'

'Don't forget,' said Graham, 'that homosexuality wasn't legalised in Scotland until 1981.'

'Yes,' Alasdair agreed. 'Not that the police spent much time prosecuting people like me and Paul. But Helen could have made trouble for us if she'd wanted. Paul hated to make a scene and it was all too much for him. He told me we had to stop seeing each other and he immediately went off to the continent for a month with Helen.'

'Not very nice,' said Graham. 'I bet you felt naff about that.'

'I was expecting it,' said Alasdair. 'You see, Paul had a great weakness, and that was his inability to do what he wanted to do. He always chose the path that caused the least ructions, and I was certainly a ruction in the smooth running of his life. So it wasn't a surprise when he stopped seeing me. But it was no less painful for being anticipated. We'd only been seeing each other for four months, so I couldn't tell whether I was important to him or not. Whatever he felt, he threw himself into the role of the happily married man with a vengeance, and disappeared.'

'Leaving you abandoned, as-it-were,' I said over a mouthful of carrot.

'For a time. I next saw him about three months later. It was sad, then, even though I'd lost a lot of my respect for him, to see him so restless and worn out by his failure to play the conscientious husband. We decided that we'd have to meet secretly again and it made me take the plunge and move away from home into a bedsit in the Grassmarket. It was rather seedy, but at least it was private – and cheap.'

'Loss of respect is a difficult one,' Graham murmured. 'How did you get that back?'

'Maybe I never did fully,' Alasdair said. 'It was a difficult time. Paul was up and down a lot. His moods were difficult to cope with. He'd be sullen and quiet one moment, and then recklessly, hysterically cheerful the next. I tried to calm him down, but he was only happy when work was going well. Those were great times, times that I felt I really loved him; saw the person he might be if only he'd leave Helen and move in with me. Occasionally he'd tell Helen that he had to go down to London and then we'd spend a couple of days together in my bedsit, afraid to go out in case he was seen. He was calm and happy then, and I knew that one day, sooner or later, he would have to leave her.

'He always said he'd do it as soon as he was earning enough money to support himself. I was content with that because we both knew that we wouldn't have to wait long.

'It was then that Helen told Paul of her pregnancy. We were all surprised. Even her, I think – and especially me. I had never even considered the possibility that this might happen because I knew of Paul's reticence to even touch her. However, it seems it all happened during that month abroad.'

'Paul fucked it up, then,' said Graham, 'literally.'

'I was horrified by the news,' Alasdair continued, 'and knew it would change everything. Paul would never leave Helen now because she was to be the mother of his child. I

169

really cursed that child, I can tell you! I would probably have wished it dead if my wishes could have borne fruit. It seemed to drive a wedge between us in a way that Helen could never have done. Paul disappeared again and I wouldn't see him for weeks on end. But he always turned up again, eventually. Sometimes he was excited at the prospect of fatherhood, and sometimes tired, empty, with his tail between his legs because he couldn't quite cope. Life with Helen was one long, slow drain on his emotional resources and he needed me to help him keep going. I needed to be needed too and was prepared to stay in the background in the hope that things would change.'

Graham poured out more wine, and I put my hand over my glass in refusal.

'And they did change. After you were born, Paul soon realised that he would never make a doting father. He was an artist and he could only sustain a fanatical interest in something for as long as it took to create it. And, by now, you were well and truly created.

'Although he never stopped loving you, after a while you ceased to be the hold on him that you had been. Helen knew this. She also knew that Paul was seeing me again, and hated me for getting in the way. But I didn't really get in the way. If it hadn't been me it would have been someone else, and if it hadn't been someone else, he would have had a breakdown – perhaps even have committed suicide. I know he had it in him. But I think I helped him stay stable. I could give him love – and I did love him. It was something he never got from Helen... He loved me too, but was appallingly bad at expressing it. If he ever admitted his love for me, it only made his life seem that much more of a mess. So, he kept it to himself and never verbalised it, though it was always there – in the way he looked at me sometimes; the way we were happy just to be in each other's company; the way we made love...

'There was a lot of beauty and happiness at that time. But it was also painful. Paul got a good commission and an exhibition in London. It was the break he'd been after. He wasn't going to make a fortune – not even a modest one –

170

but it was a start. Helen was furious about it all. She had grown to hate his new style and she wanted to pressurise him into going back to the kind of work he'd been doing when they first met. Which goes to show that she didn't understand anything about Paul. Or art for that matter.

'But he still didn't leave her. I'd known him for eighteen months by now and I was getting to the point where I needed some sort of resolution. It was all very well being a secret lover, a secret source of inspiration, and a secret source of strength. But there comes a point when secrecy is no longer enough. I couldn't take his indecision any more and I was beginning to hate Helen, which shocked me. I hadn't realised that I was capable of hating anyone.'

'I am,' said Martin, quietly, looking at his plate.

'The main thing,' said Alasdair, 'was that I felt it was worth it. I felt that the months of frustration and pain were worth it for a lifetime with Paul. We were both young. It was only a matter of time before Paul came to me. I knew that and it gave me strength.

'When he died in that stupid, stupid way – and it wasn't suicide by the way. Drinking all that whisky was typical of his hysterical recklessness. When he died, I had this irrational idea that Helen had murdered him. I don't mean poisoning his whisky or anything. I mean, I felt that she had driven him to this, which I reckoned was as good as murder. I felt that she'd drained him so much that he'd just stopped living. I was out of my mind, really. I kept thinking that if he had to die then, then Helen had robbed us of eighteen months of happiness.

'I went to pieces completely. After worrying about Paul having a breakdown, it was me that fell apart. I nearly lost my job, and then to top it off, I had a dreadful scene with Helen in Princes Street Gardens. I saw her walking across the grass, pushing her pram which was stacked with bags and boxes at the back end. She looked perfectly happy. I could have coped if she'd been downcast, but she wasn't. She'd been on a shopping spree in Forsyth's and looked on top of the world. I went for her, I'm afraid. I couldn't take it.'

Alasdair paused for a few seconds. He was looking at me in that same analytical way that he'd done the first time we met, and I realised quite suddenly what he was doing. He was looking for signs of Paul in me.

'I still feel ashamed of what I did,' he said. 'Everything came out, then. My hatred, frustration, grief... it all needed to come out, but it was terrible that it should have to come out in public, and in front of Helen. I stood there and shouted, accused, cried... a man knocked me to the ground and the police were called. I was charged with assault, though I didn't actually touch her.'

He looked at me frankly, honestly.

'I've never told that to anyone. Not all of it. Not even Graham.'

He looked at Graham with a slight smile.

'Somehow,' he said, 'it seemed inappropriate to tell the man I love about another man I loved. Then, I was young and idealistic, so it seemed that much more profound – Love, Art and Death. It seemed like tragic fate, when in fact it was just a tragic mess.'

'I'm glad you told us,' said Graham. 'I've always wanted to know the details.'

Alasdair looked down.

'It's just that in these things there is no comparison,' he said. We sat in silence as Graham gathered our plates and went to get the dessert.

'You must have really missed him,' I said. 'I'm sorry it worked out like that.'

He shook his head.

'No, don't be sorry. I found happiness, beauty, love and pain with your father. Some people find only pain.'

He stood up and picked up the bottle in front of him.

'More wine?' he asked.

Martin nodded and Alasdair filled his glass. Graham came back in with a dark mousse, put it on the table, then stood behind Alasdair and gently massaged his shoulders, stooping to kiss the top of his head.

'Anyway,' Alasdair went on, 'who's to say we would have been happy together if he hadn't died. Life is never

172

simple and painting is often an unhappy profession to choose if you're an honest painter. I don't regret the past, and apart from a period of loneliness after Paul's death, I've had a very happy life. So, as I see it, I'm a very lucky man.'

'I can't say I'd see myself as being lucky after all that,' said Martin.

'I didn't at the time.'

Graham patted Alasdair's shoulders, then went and sat down.

'Did you know that Helen sold everything after Paul died,' Alasdair told me. 'At least, all the work she could get her hands on. The paintings she sold last month at auction were in London when Paul died, so she didn't get them until later. I was surprised to hear that she'd hung them on her walls.'

'They were there from before I can remember,' I said.

'Maybe she used them as status symbols after Peter's father was out of the way,' Martin suggested.

'Maybe,' said Alasdair.

'I wonder why she moved to York,' said Martin.

'That,' said Alasdair, 'I can't tell you. It was after my time.'

'It was after her father died,' I said. 'She upped and left when I was two. I don't remember Edinburgh at all.'

'A shame,' said Alasdair. 'It's a beautiful city.'

After dinner, and some talk of art, travel and other things, we went through to the front room for coffee. Martin squeezed my shoulder as we left the dining room. He looked refreshed, excited. Pleased.

When we were sitting down, Alasdair went over to the mantelpiece.

'Do you have many photos of your father?' he asked.

'No,' I said, 'almost none. The magazines that have articles about him always seem to print the same picture.'

He picked up a photo from beside a small ornamental pot and handed it to me. My father was standing beside a very young-looking Alasdair who had his arm round my father's shoulder. They both looked happy and relaxed. On

173

the back it said "Kettle's Yard, 1972."

'That's the name of the gallery where we first saw the work of Gaudier-Brzeska,' Alasdair told me.

I looked again at the photograph. My father was grinning mischievously into the camera. He was wearing extremely baggy, light coloured trousers, plimsolls and a plain shirt open at the neck. Alasdair was dressed similarly. They looked absolutely timeless. Apart from the fact that it was in colour, it could have been a picture from the Thirties as easily as the Seventies. There was something incredibly alive about my father. He looked young and carefree – not a husband with a young child. I could feel his presence, almost hear his laughter. It was a sunny day in the photo, like the sunshine from earlier on today. It was just that time had intervened – got between us somehow.

'Paul was twenty-eight when that was taken,' Alasdair told me. 'I was twenty-two.'

'It's a great photo,' I said, handing it to Martin.

'Keep it,' he said.

'No, really... '

'I've got others,' he told me.

'Incidentally,' he added, 'I've got something of a confession to make.'

'Oh?'

'Yes,' Alasdair said. 'There is something I should have told you last time you were here, but I didn't. About the marble statuette.'

Martin looked interested at this and glanced at me. He handed the photo to Graham.

'Actually,' Alasdair said, 'I knew all along which Gaudier-Brzeska it was that your father used for his sculpture. It was a copy of a plaster relief called "Lutteurs". It was made in 1914 in a series of six. Look, I've got a photo of the one in the Pompidou Centre in Paris.'

He leant over and picked up a small framed post card and handed it to me. There were the two wrestlers, arms interlocked, in a stylised hold that resembled an embrace.

'What I didn't tell you at the time,' he said, 'is that there are two.'

174

'Two sculptures!'

'Yes,' he said. 'I have the other one. I'll go and get it.'

He left us and Martin gestured to me in realisation.

'Of course!' he said. 'If your sculpture depicts only the first of the wrestlers, we should have realised there would be another one depicting the second.'

I nodded.

'Except that I'd have thought Alasdair would have told me about it before.'

'But don't forget,' said Graham, 'that this is an especially private and personal thing for Alasdair. He didn't know anything about you when you first met.'

Alasdair came into the room with the second sculpture. It looked identical to mine. He gave it to me and I looked at it carefully. Now, in my hands, I could discern that the lines were different, as was the lustre, and markings of the marble.

'You see,' said Alasdair, 'this was a kind of secret between me and Paul. We had always thought of the Lutteurs relief as looking more like lovers than wrestlers. We joked that it was a representation of the two of us. Each one was one half of an embrace – useless when apart. Lutteurs was the key with which to decipher the secret. On the base of each one was the clue. The inscription on yours is LUTT. G. P.E. 70. It's the first half of the word Lutteurs, plus the first initial of Gaudier-Brzeska's name, then Paul's initials, followed by the date. Mine has the rest.'

I turned it over and there it was: EURS. B. A.M.

Slotted together, I realised, the inscription would read: LUTTEURS, G.B. P.E. A.M. 70.

'A.M. for Alasdair Munro,' I said.

'I want you to have it,' said Alasdair.

'I couldn't,' I said.

'Why not?'

'It must be worth a small fortune, for a start,' I said.

'Together they might be worth a small fortune,' he said. 'Apart, they're merely curiosities.'

'In which case, I should give mine to you. You're the one it was made for.'

'No,' said Alasdair, 'I'd be pleased if you'd take it. It would make me happy to feel that you had it. Take it as a reminder that your father was once in love.'

'Okay,' I said slowly. 'I'll take it. What can I give you in return?'

'Nothing,' Alasdair laughed, 'I don't want anything. A gift is a blessing on the giver.'

I paused to look at the sculpture.

'At least take these two drawings,' I said, indicating the portfolio. 'There's the portrait of you sleeping, and the one you wrote on.'

Alasdair looked down at the table and smiled.

'Yes, good,' he said. 'I'd like that very much.'

NINETEEN

When we got back to Steph's it was gone one o'clock and she was in bed. Martin and I crept through and made ourselves some coffee, then poured ourselves two half glasses of wine to finish off the wine box. I had Alasdair's sculpture with me and, together with its twin, I put it on the mantelpiece.

'Now that's something really special,' said Martin looking at them both.

The release of pressure that I felt after talking to Alasdair was so great that I felt as though I was expanding to fill the room after being squeezed into a tiny space. Knowing about my father was a truly wonderful experience. I know he had been a preoccupation with me for as long as I could remember, but there was something even more basic than that – there is something debilitating, I realised, about people who are complete blanks. My father had remained a dark secret in my life, and I had always feared that he might one day be revealed as a monster of some kind – a man with some vile secret.

But my father's secret had been love, no less, and it made me smile to think of it.

What an extraordinary man, Alasdair. So generous and so honest.

'I liked his boyfriend,' Martin commented.

We had stayed on in Sheffield for several hours and talked about things other than my father. Martin and Alasdair had talked about art, we had talked about going on holiday to the Highlands, about travel in general – about anything that came to us.

When we'd left, I realised that I was already feeling some kind of blood-relationship bond to him, as though he was my uncle, or someone closer still.

'That was one of the best evenings ever,' Martin said to

me as he reclined in an armchair and sipped his coffee. 'Just think, that'll never happen again. Ever.'

'What?'

'Finding out about your father. It's happened. You've done it, after all these years of wondering.'

I nodded, feeling suddenly utterly exhausted.

'I don't know how I'm going to get to bed,' I said. 'I feel too tired to move.'

Martin crossed to the settee and sat down beside me. He put one arm round my shoulder and rested his head against my chest. He didn't say or do anything. Just rested his head against me as if he was sleeping. I nearly did fall asleep, too, we stayed like that for so long. But eventually, I dragged myself up and got undressed for bed.

When Martin lay down beside me on my mattress, it didn't seem strange, or wrong, or unwanted. It didn't even feel sexual. Just close. He nestled against me and fell asleep almost immediately. I lay there for some time, too tired to sleep, and felt Martin's gentle breathing against my neck. I wondered briefly if this had been inevitable, and decided that perhaps, if we're lucky, these things happen when it is right for them to happen and not before.

In the morning, when Steph came through, she didn't register any surprise at seeing us in bed together. She didn't even say "just as I thought". She made us coffee and asked us how it had gone with Alasdair.

The fact that she'd seen us together like this somehow confirmed absolutely the fact that things had changed between us. Even if I'd wanted to, which I didn't think I did, there was no way that I could deny this – no way that I could make Steph somehow not see us like this.

I knew that Steph would assume that something had happened between us – that sex had happened between us – and that was reasonable enough. But the fact was that nothing had happened. We hadn't even kissed.

Martin, it seemed, was even more unsure than I was. When we had breakfast he was almost painfully polite and considerate. It occurred to me that he wasn't sure whether I was pleased or offended by what had happened. I smiled at him as we told Steph about Alasdair, but that only made him look less sure still. This surprised me, and as I was the first to leave, I had to go without resolving anything.

And that was it. I left to get the train for York wondering what, if anything, had happened.

At work I felt disorientated. I was surrounded by people whose lives were settled. They had spent ordered years of stability eating, sleeping, having sex, watching television, going out for drinks or to see friends... They were the same, but I had been changed. I felt overwhelmed by all the things that had happened to me, overwhelmed and different. I looked at the fading pink scar on my hand where Dave Boothe had cut me, and I wondered what had happened to him. I wondered about Mat and Jerome. I wondered about Martin.

'Are you alright?' Maggie asked me mid-morning.

'Yes, sorry,' I said. 'I'm a bit preoccupied today.'

She nodded briefly.

'Found anywhere else to live yet?'

'No,' I told her. 'I'm still on Steph's floor in Leeds.'

'That sort of thing is very preoccupying,' she commiserated.

But I wasn't preoccupied with finding somewhere to live. That was no problem. When Martin left college in ten days time, I'd look for a room somewhere – probably in York – until I got somewhere more permanent sorted out. If my mother came up with something, good. If she didn't, well, I'd survive.

Martin turned up at half past twelve wearing a dripping cagoule. Perhaps I should have been surprised to see him. But I wasn't. He was agitated and I noticed Maggie watching us with her "what now?" look.

'I've got to talk to you,' he said.

'Let's go somewhere for lunch.'

'It's pissing down outside.'

'The museum snack bar's alright,' I said. 'Let's have something there. I'll be finished here in a couple of minutes and I'll follow you down.'

As I gathered my papers together, Maggie smiled at me

179

and gestured towards where Martin had stood.

'Really, Peter,' she said, 'you do seem to have the most complicated lifestyle.'

I blushed and she laughed.

'Complicated and intriguing.'

I usually ate in the snack bar twice a week and today I ordered my usual. Three eggs on brown bread toast with a large mug of fresh decaffeinated coffee. Martin had the same.

'I couldn't work,' he said. 'Last night kept on getting in the way.'

'Why, what's the matter about last night?' I asked.

'You tell me,' he said. 'You're the one I'm worried about.'

'Why? I'm not worried about you.'

'You seemed so cool this morning,' he said.

'No I wasn't,' I disagreed. 'I was being careful because Steph was there.'

'Is that true?'

'Yes.'

'That's okay then, isn't it?'

'I suppose so.'

He looked at me so intensely that I felt uncomfortable. Martin was my best friend. He was the only person I felt I knew really well. But I didn't know how to react to him. I didn't know what to say. By sleeping on the same mattress as me he had changed everything.

But then, he hadn't just slept on my mattress, he had held me like a lover. That was what had changed things. I didn't feel like his lover, but I certainly no longer felt that I was just his friend.

'Come on,' I said once we'd finished eating, 'you've never seen around this place, have you, not properly.'

'I came years ago with mum.'

'Exactly.'

We went out into the main hall. There were only two people there, looking at the sombre pictures that were hanging above the dark wood-panelled walls.

'What can you hear?' I asked.

'Nothing,' he said.

'No, not nothing.' I stood behind him and put my hands over his eyes. 'Try again.'

He listened for a while.

'Okay,' he said. 'I can hear distant traffic, birdsong... and clocks.'

'How many clocks?'

'I don't know.'

'Try and count them.'

'One, two, three, at least three, maybe more.'

'Eleven on this floor,' I said. 'This museum is a place of clocks. You can't get away from the ticking. I like it.'

We went into the next room, a bright room with a pale parquet floor and tall glass cabinets. There was a collection of musical instruments here, as well as three clocks. A large wall clock, a small pendulum clock, and a great musical-chime clock in the middle of the floor. There were two paintings of a man and his wife above the great sandstone fireplace. We were the only ones there.

'Okay,' I said. 'Look around the room as though you're going to be tested on what's in here. Memorise it.'

Martin looked carefully round him, smiling slightly.

'Now,' I said. 'Close your eyes. Think. This isn't a museum at all, it's an old private house. The paintings above the fireplace are of the owner and his wife. The ticking clocks signify the past. We are alone in this room waiting for the owner to come in with his wife. Any minute now the clocks are going to chime and then they're going to come into the room. The young lady of the house is going to come in and start to play the harpsichord in the window. The butler is going to offer us tea.'

I stopped speaking and we stood there in silence, Martin with his eyes still closed, a vague smile hovering. Then the first clock started to chime one o'clock. We waited as, over the minutes, clock after clock throughout the museum started to chime. Then the musical-clock only feet away started whirring, chimed, and played "I dream of Jeannie with the light brown hair." It sounded nothing like a harpsichord, but I could see that Martin was enjoying it.

'So,' he said opening his eyes, 'who are the owners?'

181

'I'm surprised you don't know,' I replied. 'They were notorious at the time. They ran one of the biggest brothels in Yorkshire, and they sold their daughter, Martha, into virtual slavery as a whore. Being very beautiful, she made them lots of money. But her heart wasn't in it... '

'Because Martha was a dyke anyway!' Martin laughed. 'Very good. Now let's go for another coffee.'

'There's lots more to see.'

'Another time,' he said.

In the snack bar we laughed together about nothing in particular and I felt at ease again.

'You know,' he said, 'you really brought that to life in there. I've never felt that in a museum before.'

I shrugged modestly.

'I think it's important to be able to make these places feel like they're not mortuaries for dead people's possessions.'

'It's like art galleries,' Martin said. 'They're dead too, mostly. Paintings should hang in homes, not on great impersonal walls in empty rooms.'

He sipped his coffee.

'Please, please, please let me get into St Martin's,' he said to the ceiling.

He had an interview the next day, in London, for St Martin's School of Art. I had little doubt that he'd get in, but Martin was nervous about it. After that it was his end of year exhibition. I wanted to see Steph's work as well, and Coll's. I had only seen one or two of the things that Steph had worked on back at the flat, and I hadn't seen anything of Coll's at all.

Martin and I went out for a drink together that evening. Steph diplomatically stayed out of our way, though it wasn't necessary. We had a good time and didn't talk about things like relationships. I didn't want to tie anything down with words, pigeonhole what was happening to us, talk about it until it became something else.

I felt on the edge of Martin's life. I was up in York starting a career here. Getting settled. Martin's future was elsewhere, where probably nothing would ever be settled.

182

But our friendship was a great deepness and it was something that we wallowed in without the future casting us ashore.

I wanted to get drunk, I wanted to do this so that I could do what I knew I wanted to do. I wanted to make love to Martin without hesitance – and I needed to be drunk to do it. I needed to fold back years of keeping him at arms length. I needed to cull my absurd desire not to be attracted to him.

I thought of Jerome, still at Brearton Hall, and thanked my memory of him for what he'd given me – the first beginnings of the ability to go with the flow.

Back at Steph's Ian was sulking in his room as usual. Steph was still out. Martin closed the door and we looked at each other, motionless, for the tiniest fraction of a second, then we fell into an embrace, as from a great height, and kissed so hard that our teeth connected with a painful jolt, leaving me with a cracked lip and a blood-smeared smile.

'Lie down,' Martin told me and went off to get some toilet paper.

I lay and felt the cut with my tongue and smiled again, feeling suddenly sober.

'Okay,' Martin said when he came back, 'let's have a look.'

He kissed me first and came away with a blood smear on his lips and chin.

'You look like a vampire,' I told him.

'You look like a vampire's victim.'

He wiped the blood away, then I did the same to him. I could feel my lip swelling, and when we kissed again it gave me a sensation of unreality, as though I'd just come from the dentist. I licked the slight stubble of his chin and tasted the iron tang of my own blood there.

He held me. He held me so hard that I gasped for breath and struggled to get free, but he hung on, so I returned his grasp and clutched him as tight as I could, lying rigidly against him. He laughed, then hiccupped, and we released each other.

183

'Quick,' he gasped and began to tear off his shirt. I followed suit, my clothes suddenly in the way, and I dragged my jeans off in one long, desperate sweep. Then we were back together, breathless still, and straining to hold, kiss and touch.

Martin stopped so suddenly that I hesitated. He looked down between us and he shook his head.

'You've still got your socks on,' he said, leaning down to pull them off. When he had done so, he traced his finger down the sole of my foot, making me squirm, then kissed my toes one by one.

'I bet no one's ever kissed your toes before,' he said.

'No,' I agreed. 'No one's kissed my toes. Until now.'

I felt released from that taut energy of moments before and a languid warmth started to submerge me as I lay back in the strange newness of someone so familiar.

In the morning Martin and I walked to the station together. He was carrying his portfolio and looked young and vibrant, I thought, in the sharp sunlight. I felt boring to be going back to work.

We said goodbye on the platform and it was as though we'd only just met. The question that I would have expected to ask at this moment was "when will I see you again?" But we were sharing a room and I didn't have to ask.

'See you later,' I said instead and smiled at his smile.

He touched my lip with his forefinger, on the small, dark cut.

'See you,' he said.

TWENTY

The three of us got dressed up for the exhibition.

'Although exhibition is far too grand a word for what's actually on show,' Steph said.

'Rubbish,' Martin disagreed. 'It's brilliant. At least, some of it is.'

Martin put on his tails. Steph wore a sheer black dress with sequins. I wore all white except for a yellow bow tie. We took a bottle of wine each and set off. Martin seemed nervous. I suppose it was nerve wracking to think that it was all on view now, the sum total of his year's work. But Steph seemed odd too, as though they had a secret that they were sharing, from which I was excluded.

When we arrived, Martin became curiously shifty and started to make me feel nervous too.

'What's the matter?' I asked. 'It can't be that bad.'

'Oh, can't it?' he said mysteriously as we went in.

The art school was on one floor of a block and virtually every space available had been used for the exhibitions. The grey lino floors were swept, but spattered with dried paint and glue. There were marks on the walls from where things had been pinned, stapled and blu-tacked in the past. The whole place was shabby, bright and inspiring. Before starting, we took some plastic cups from the temporary bar and opened my bottle of wine. I poured out most of the bottle, filling our cups to the brim. We went through Studio 1, where Coll and Steph had their work. Steph's was made up of expansive, colourful designs and ideas for sets and costumes. There was a video to accompany it of three short performance art pieces. The video screen was beside the work and was set up on continuous play. We stopped and watched the dance-orientated pieces for a while before moving on.

'I'll come back to look at these properly later,' I said.

Coll had done a bit of everything. Photography, screen-printing, ceramics. She had done a set of 3-D pieces in chicken wire and plaster that I couldn't work out, but which had some kind of organic look about them. Martin made no secret of the fact that he thought they were dreadful.

Studio 2 was where Martin had his work. It was set up at the far end of the studio and was instantly recognisable. To me, at least. I had sat for him three times at Jerome's flat, and these three canvasses were all there. But what had he done to them!

Each one had been embellished so that they had become quite different – not simple life paintings at all. All had some kind of sexual theme. The first, in which I was reclining in a seat wearing only my jeans, had been arranged so that my jeans were undone and half way down my legs. A figure was kneeling down in front of me and... and what? Sucking me off? Tossing me off? It was impossible to tell. But there was something disgusting about it. Not about the fact that it depicted sex, but because my body had been hi-jacked in this way. In the picture my expression remained the same as when Martin had originally painted it – relaxed, almost asleep. It made the painting into some kind of erotic fantasy. Was the person in the chair imagining what was going on? Was the dark figure in front of him real?

The second painting was of me lying, full length, on the settee and looking down at the floor. Martin had painted it so that a man – again a mysteriously vague man – was pushing his erect penis into my mouth.

The third, in which I was leaning against a window frame and looking out, had been converted into a buggery scene. This time the person looking out of the window – I can't bring myself to say 'I' because this person was no longer me – was being fucked by someone who, although viewed from behind, could easily have been Martin. I now realised why he had been so nervous about me coming here with him tonight.

I turned to him to ask for an explanation, but he had

186

slipped away. Instead Steph took my arm and leant against me.

'Well?' she asked.

'Well what?'

'What do you think of them?'

'I think they're disgusting,' I said.

'Surely not,' she said. 'Maybe you're just embarrassed.'

'It's not that,' I said.

'I think they show such a lot of potential,' she went on. 'Look at the sureness of the way he's painted them. They caused a sensation whilst he was doing them. Even the principal came to discuss them. There was some talk about not putting them on show because they had penises in them, but that would have been absurd. He's impressed a lot of people with these – not always favourably. But he'll walk into any art school in the country with talent like this.'

'I can't believe that he could do this,' I said. 'It's dishonest of him to twist these things round.'

'You can't stipulate what Martin should or shouldn't do with his work,' she told me. 'You agreed to sit for him. It was up to him what he did with his material.'

'I'm not arguing,' I said. 'I agree with all that. I still think they're disgusting.'

'But why!'

'Because he's taken my body and, without my consent, he's violated it on canvas. I feel as though I've been raped.'

'Oh, come on Peter,' she said, 'you're being over-dramatic.'

'No, I'm not,' I shook my head. 'Don't you see, Steph, it's all a lie? This kind of impersonality? Look here,' I pointed at the one of the young man on the settee, 'he's lying there with someone else shoving a prick into his mouth. There's nothing mutual about it at all.'

'But sex is like that sometimes.'

'I'm sure it is,' I agreed. 'But not for Martin. I thought that was the whole point, that artists should be true to themselves. I don't care if it's true for everyone else. For Martin it's a lie, and that's what matters.'

He had lied to himself, and somehow, to me.

'Anyway,' I said, 'where is he? Why's he slunk off like he's the one who's embarrassed?'

'He was worried that you'd be upset by them.'

'He was right,' I said. 'And now I'm going to go and tell him so.'

I left feeling choked, thinking: how could he do this, how could he? I finished off my wine, then emptied the last inch from the bottle into my cup and left the bottle on the floor. Martin didn't seem to be in any of the studios. It occurred to me that he had painted these before we had slept together, which made it worse, somehow. It ruined the spontaneity that I had felt the other night. It made me feel that I had been used.

I bumped into Coll as I came through Studio 1.

'Hi,' she said. 'I didn't expect to see you here.'

'Why not?'

'Because of those twee pictures of you that Martin's done.'

'They may be many things,' I said, 'but they're not twee.'

'Don't you think so?'

'No, I don't.'

'I can see that you don't like them.'

'You're right, I don't.'

'I'm not surprised. I'd be insulted if I was you.'

'Why?'

'They're so obviously wet dreams about you, Peter. I bet he sits and wanks over them whenever he feels randy.'

'Now it's you who's being insulting.'

'Maybe,' she sighed, smiling. 'Maybe. A little more wine?'

I nodded and she took a bottle of red wine from her table and filled my cup.

'So, I've finished here at last,' she said. 'It's been a long year, and I'm glad it's over.'

'What are you going to do now?'

'I'm moving in with Eddy. He's got a house-share with three other people, over by the market.'

'And what about next year?'

'I'm not going on to do a degree,' she said. 'It's all such a load of crap in the end, sitting around and analysing your arseholes to see if something will come out. You've got to get on with life, and to do that, you've got to be out there living it.'

'Everyone has to find their own way,' I said.

'Cheers to that!'

And we drank.

I wandered round again, but still there was no sign of Martin. I was drunk and unhappy, and angry with him. Steph poured me some more wine and I drank too quickly. She could see I was upset, but there was nothing she could do in the glare of Martin's absence. I ended up standing in front of his work. There were other pieces as well as the three that I'd been so offended by. There were drawings, watercolours, photos and a series of six etchings of different faces. These I thought excellent and wondered if, once I'd got through my anger with him, he might give me one. I was looking at them when he put his hand on my shoulder.

'I'm back,' he said.

'Where have you been?' I asked, my voice neutral.

'Upstairs,' he said, 'with my tutors. I've been given a special commendation. They want to keep a couple of my pieces for the school, to go in next year's prospectus.'

'Which ones?' I asked, feeling suddenly cold.

'Not the paintings,' he said with the slightest smile. 'Something from the rest.'

He had the sparkle of success and achievement in his eyes and this made him look indulgently attractive. But this, in it's turn, made me feel even more upset and angry.

'How could you do it?' I asked, wanting to sound assertive, but sounding merely petulant.

'What do you mean?'

'These pictures. They're such a lie. What were you trying to achieve?'

'I wasn't trying to achieve anything,' he replied, 'except to express myself.'

'And what have you expressed? A pathetic distortion of

what I thought was between us. You've dragged us both into some kind of shitty crudeness.'

'Don't be childish,' he told me. 'Sex isn't a distortion.'

'This sex is,' I argued, 'because it's a lie.'

'What are you trying to say?' he asked, exasperated.

'I know everyone thinks your work is wonderful,' I said, 'and I know you'll think I'm upset because it's me in the pictures. But it's not that. You've lied to yourself, and you know it. This isn't you. It's cynical and world weary and it's demeaning. To you as well as me.'

He didn't say anything for a moment. Just looked at me, his eyes emptying of all the joy in his achievement. I suddenly wanted to shout, I didn't mean it, please, I didn't mean it, just so that he wouldn't look so empty. But I did mean it. That was the thing.

'You've spilt some wine down your shirt,' he said.

I looked down. There was a diffused red streak, about four inches long, down my chest.

'Yes,' I said. 'I know, I'm drunk. That's what you're saying, isn't it? I'm drunk and I'm saying stupid things that I don't mean.'

'I'm saying you've spilt some wine down your shirt.'

'God, Martin,' I said. 'Why did you bring me here?'

'Because I thought you had a right to see my work. I thought you'd like it.'

'Oh yes,' I said. 'Why were you so fidgety when we came here tonight, then?'

He shrugged, looking away from me.

'I'm going home,' I said. 'I can't stand any more of this.'

'Wait,' he said. 'I'll come with you, but I can't leave for ten minutes or so. I've got to talk to someone.'

'No,' I said. 'I'm off.'

I turned to go and he grabbed my arm.

'So you're the only one who's got feelings here?' he cried. 'You think I've deliberately tried to offend you? Don't be so crass Peter. Don't be so fucking selfish!'

'Selfish?' I couldn't believe it. 'Selfish! It's you who's been doing all this, it's you who painted the pictures... '

'And it's you who's deliberately not trying to see my

190

side of it.'

'I'm sorry Martin,' I said, 'I can't. I just can't.'

I walked home alone. It was warm out of the wind, but in the open there was a strong breeze that blustered my hair and made me feel even more isolated. I was being pressed upon by everything around me. I felt sick and over-tired. My anger gone completely, I felt that Martin had redefined our terms into a language I couldn't understand. He was back there at college being celebrated. He was the rising star, the big fish in their pond. Perhaps he would be a big fish in anyone's pond. And I was out here, away from him, wanting him, envying him.

Perhaps that was it – I was jealous of him. Of his talent. Of other people admiring him. Maybe it was narrow-minded of me to be offended. Perhaps I had shown up some great insurmountable gap between us, some fundamental lack of understanding of him. Perhaps, through the briefest of sexual relationships, I had cancelled out ten years of friendship...

Back at the flat I felt truly homeless for the first time. Here I was, dossing on someone's sitting room floor. I had no plans, didn't know what my mother's plans for me were, had done nothing to look for somewhere else to live. I realised that I hadn't done anything because I didn't want to have to accept that any move I made would be a move away from Martin.

Only a few hours separated my present insecurity from a sensation of peace and stability. I'd had no idea what a fragile thing that evenness had been, or how easily it could be shattered.

Steph came back at around eleven. I was too sunk in on myself to properly respond to her greeting. She disappeared into the kitchen, coming out a few minutes later with two coffees. She handed me one.

'You look as though you've murdered someone and regret it,' she said.

'Thanks.'

'This isn't the end,' she told me. 'You've got to have your differences, you and Martin. If you felt the same about

191

everything, then there wouldn't be a relationship – you'd be the same person.'

'I don't know what I feel,' I said.

'You look depressed.'

'Okay, that's something I feel. Depressed.'

'Love is never easy,' she said.

'Is that what this is, then?' I asked her.

'You're asking me?' she laughed, incredulous. 'No wonder you're depressed.'

I tried to smile at her and failed.

'Let's see what's on telly,' she said, leaning over and switching on. There was a soap, a documentary on Eastern Europe, an American comedy show, and a Jane Fonda movie.

'Great,' she said. 'I love Jane Fonda.'

I lay there and watched the screen, but didn't really take it in. Jane Fonda was playing some kind of glamorous cowboy/girl. It was all dust and aggression and macho and it washed over me like some pointless anaesthetic for the two hours that it lasted. When it finished, Steph switched off, made me another cup of coffee, and sat with me in silence.

At a quarter past one, Martin came back. He was paralytic, and had been crying.

'Now,' she said, as he came in, 'I'll leave you to it.'

She got up and squeezed my shoulder for a moment, applying a gentle, sure pressure for perhaps half a second before leaving the room.

'Where've you been?' I asked.

'At college,' he slurred.

I thought I'd been drunk, but Martin could hardly stand up. He came over and collapsed against me.

'You're right!' he wailed, 'you're right about my paintings and I didn't even see it.'

He started to cry again.

'Everyone kept on telling me how good they were,' he sniffed, 'or how interesting, or shocking, and all I could think of was what you said – about them being untrue to me – and all I could think of was that you were right, that they weren't good because they were lies.'

'It's okay,' I said and stroked his hair.

'So I took them out and burned them,' he said. 'Look.'

He had black smears of ash on his hands.

'You didn't have to do that,' I said.

'Yes I did,' he said, 'to show you I'm sorry.'

'You don't have to apologise.'

'Yes I do.'

'You didn't set out to do anything other than express yourself. You don't have to apologise for that.'

'Don't be so fucking understanding,' he said. 'Be angry.'

'I'm not angry anymore.'

'God,' he said, and kissed me.

He lay there, his forehead against my cheek, and breathed shallow breaths. Now, I thought, now was the time to ask the question I'd been wanting to ask for weeks.

'When I last saw Mat,' I said, 'he said that you were in love with me when we were at school.'

Martin sat up and looked at me, almost sober for a moment.

'God, Peter, you are so blind,' he said, then threw up down my shirt.

TWENTY ONE

The following Saturday I received a letter from Alasdair:

Dear Peter,
Each year Graham and I take a cottage on Tiree for a
fortnight. It occurred to us that seeing as you may be
going up to the Highlands, you might like to come and
visit us on this Hebridean island. Our dates are July 5th
– 20th. Do come, both of you, if you can make it.
All the best.
Alasdair.

'Well?' I asked Martin, handing him the letter at
breakfast.
'Well, what?' he said. 'Let's go, of course.'
'Okay.'
It was only ten days away, but I'd have no trouble in
taking time off because there was nothing I was doing at
the museum that couldn't wait.
'I'll get my tent from home,' Martin said. 'We can spend
a week up in the mountains, and another on Tiree.'
'Good,' I nodded.
I was going to spend the weekend with Martin at his
parent's house, then on Monday, Martin would stay at
home whilst I took up residence in a shared house in York.
It was a terraced house a little down from Bootham Bar
and I'd heard of it through Maggie. I didn't know anyone
there, but even if it was awful, at least it was only
temporary. My mother had informed me that she was
already drawing up the contracts on a flat by Goodramgate
and, if I liked it, I could stay there. We'd had lunch together
in Betty's the previous Wednesday, and my father hadn't
been mentioned. She'd acted as though she'd forgotten
about our contretemps concerning his sexuality. And, who

knows, perhaps she had.

I worried about how much I was going to see of Martin once we'd both moved out of Steph's, but he laughed at me and told me that it had taken him ten years to discover that I was a born worrier. He told me that there would be no problem. I could stay weekends at their house and he could come and see me during the week.

'But what about the rest of the people I share with?'

'What about them?'

'They might disapprove.'

'So what? What are they going to do, throw you out?'

He had a point. I wasn't going to be there long.

'Okay,' I said. 'We'll see how it goes.'

The last few days had been the most settled days I could remember. Having recovered from our hangovers after the exhibition, we found that it had somehow cleared things between us. I was able to be close to him in a way that felt right to me. There was no talking about it – we got on with it.

After breakfast we took a train to York and then on to Knaresborough, where Mrs Armstrong met us in the car.

'Hello you two,' she said.

'Hello mum,' Martin replied jumping into the front of the car.

'Hi,' I said, getting into the back more slowly.

'How was the exhibition?'

Martin looked round at me and grinned.

'Memorable,' he said.

'Memorably good or memorably bad?'

'Memorable for the hangover the next day,' he told her.

'Ah.'

Mrs Armstrong drove us out to the house, a converted farmhouse near Staveley village.

'Caz is here for the weekend,' she said. 'She breaks up in a fortnight.'

'I haven't seen her for ages,' I said. 'Nearly a year.'

'That's what she said. The last time you stayed was when you and Martin went off with your tent for a week on the moors.'

195

I remembered that week, a week of long walks and poor weather. A week of great friendship, conversation and moderate alcohol. A week before sex had arisen between us.

The house was the same. The rich, red brick covered by wisteria; the small formal garden at the front with its cropped yew tree and rose garden. It made me feel as though I was back at school, and brought back that sense of time here being precious. I'd felt that weekends here had been stolen from the dull routine of life with my mother and had looked forward to them with an intensity that had highlighted the emptiness of the rest of my life.

Caz came out as she heard the car arrive.

'Hi, Pete,' she smiled.

'My name's Peter,' I corrected her.

'Oh yeah, Peter,' she said.

It was our perennial greeting, an affectionately personal thing between us. It made me feel that I'd come home. Caz had just turned eighteen and was taking 'A' levels this year. She was twenty-one months younger than Martin, but they could have passed for the same age. She had the arrogant surety of a school prefect – the brash confidence that life would treat her well.

'Coffee?' she asked.

'Do some for us all,' her mother said, taking my weekend bag from the boot.

'You two go in,' she said as Caz disappeared into the house, 'I'll take Peter's bag up to the spare room.'

'No, mum,' Martin said. 'Peter's going to sleep in my room.'

I felt a flush of embarrassment course through me at this. It hadn't occurred to me that Martin was going to be so open about what was happening between us. I was reminded suddenly of past conversations that I'd had with Mrs Armstrong about girlfriends.

She looked at me and saw me blush, smiled briefly, then nodded.

'Okay,' she said.

When we got inside Martin squeezed my elbow.

196

'You've gone purple,' he told me.

'Of course I have,' I said.

'It's okay, mum doesn't mind.'

At least I knew this was true. The Armstrongs had been very supportive to Martin and had met at least one of his previous boyfriends. But I was still embarrassed. It wasn't as if I was a stranger here – I was virtually part of the family. To be seen to be Martin's boyfriend was something I should have prepared for. But I hadn't.

We went upstairs almost immediately and, as soon as we were in Martin's room, he pushed me onto the bed, then lay beside me.

'You're going to have to get used to this eventually,' he said, kissing me. 'You'll be spending a lot of time here over the summer. There's no point in pretending... '

'I know,' I told him. 'I hadn't thought about it, that's all.'

He traced the line of my jaw with the point of his tongue.

'Don't worry,' he said, getting up. 'Now come on down and don't be shy.'

He stood in the doorway and smiled at me, and as I passed he whispered 'I love you,' so quietly that I couldn't be absolutely sure that he'd said it. I turned to ask what he'd said, but he kissed me again and ushered me downstairs.

'Come into the sitting room and see the painting,' he said.

It was one of the pictures that had hung on my bedroom wall. It was so familiar, yet seeing it like this on another wall made it seem new.

'I remember it from the mantelpiece in your bedroom,' Martin said. 'I don't know how many sticks of incense I've burned in front of it... I thought it might have a scent from them, but it doesn't.'

He stroked the heavy, plain black frame with his finger.

'I don't know why they reframed it,' he said. 'This one is the same as the first one – just bigger.'

'It gives it an extra sense of importance,' I said.

'Maybe,' he said, unconvinced.

197

'At least it's somewhere where I can get to see it.'

Martin nodded and turned to leave, glancing back at the painting with a nostalgic look.

In the kitchen, Caz had obviously been told about the change in my circumstances with Martin. She looked amused and smiled at me broadly.

'Well,' she said, and shook her head. 'Well!'

'Don't look so smug,' Martin told her as he took a loaf out of the bread bin.

'Just wait till I tell Anna that you and Peter are having a thing,' she said.

'Whatever a thing is,' said Martin.

Anna was in Caz's year at school, although as far as I knew they weren't close friends.

'I don't know that that's wise,' said Mrs Armstrong, who was sitting at the table flicking through a magazine.

'Why not,' said Caz, 'if it's true?'

'Anna's not quite as open-minded as we are,' she said, 'and she's got a different perspective on it.'

'What do you think, Peter?' Caz asked.

'I think I'd rather not think about it,' I said.

Caz laughed.

'To think I nearly made a pass at you a couple of years ago,' she said.

'Why didn't you?' Martin asked.

'Because he's been around too long,' she said. 'He's too familiar. It would only have been out of desperation to lose my virginity.'

'Thanks!' I said.

'Losing your virginity's a terribly important thing,' she said seriously. 'You've got to do it with the right person.'

'And did you do it with the right person?' I asked.

'No,' she said. 'And neither did Anna.'

'Okay, okay,' said Martin. 'Let's talk about something else.'

'Fine,' she said and crossed to where Martin was making some toast. 'Well done, darling brother.' She put her arms round him. 'I knew you would get in.'

She kissed his cheek.

198

'Can I come and visit you in London?'

'Of course.'

'We've got a bottle of champagne in the fridge,' Mrs Armstrong said. 'We'll have it at dinner, to celebrate.'

Martin looked at me and winked.

Dinner was excellent. We had baked sea bass with a herb sauce, new potatoes and lightly steamed green vegetables. There was plenty of wine that Mr Armstrong provided from the cellar and, before the dessert, champagne.

'Here's to an excellent future,' said Mr Armstrong, raising his glass. 'For us all.'

'Hear, hear,' said Caz. 'Here's to Martin being as successful as Peter's father.'

'Depends in which way you mean,' Martin laughed.

'I mean, I hope your paintings sell for £24,000 each before too long.'

'So do I,' he said.

'You know the Paul Ellis in the front room?' his father asked, leaning forward slightly as he spoke. 'It'll go to you one day.'

'Oh dad,' Martin sighed, 'that's not for ages. Thirty years at least.'

'Yes, okay,' he said. 'But it'll happen one day.'

'It should be passed on to you, your children and your children's children,' Caz said.

She looked at me.

'That's the trouble with homosexuals,' she said, 'they make life so complicated.'

'They don't make life complicated,' Martin told her, 'life is already complicated.'

We all fell silent as Mrs Armstrong served the chocolate mousse.

'Anyway,' Caz said out of nowhere. 'I can't believe you haven't invited me up to the Highlands with you. You know I'm dying to go.'

'That's not fair,' said her father. 'Putting it like that.'

'I want to go with Peter,' said Martin. 'On our own.'

'Lovers!' Caz breathed. 'So boring. They always want to

199

be alone together.'

'You've really got a thing about me and Peter, haven't you?' Martin said.

'I think it's amusing, that's all.'

'Why?'

'Oh, you wouldn't understand.'

'Try me.'

'No.'

Martin smiled.

'Would you like to come up to the Highlands with us?' he asked.

'Is that an invitation?'

Martin glanced at me. I shrugged.

'Yes it is,' he said.

'No thank you,' she told him. 'You should have asked without prompting.'

'What difference does that make? I'm asking now.'

'No, it's okay.'

She took a mouthful of mousse.

'I didn't want to go anyway.'

'Why did you say that you did?' Martin asked.

'I just wanted to have the pleasure of turning you down,' she told him.

It was a strange weekend. I found that I was being treated with extra deference by Mr and Mrs Armstrong. I also thought I detected a wry amusement, but I may have been mistaken.

On Sunday evening, before I left for York, Mrs Armstrong took me aside.

'Peter,' she said. 'John and I wanted to tell you how pleased we are about what's happened. We've been worried about Martin, especially with Aids and everything, and now it's so nice to see you together like this. You both seem so much happier... '

The other two in the house in York were Jill, a twenty-seven year old nurse, and Dave, a teacher. They had a lightly off-beat manner and seemed to accept my presence

200

without particular interest or concern. Jill, it turned out, was single, and Dave had a girlfriend in Wetherby.

When Martin came over on Monday night and I introduced him to them, they seemed politely interested to discover that I had a lover, but the gender seemed to be of no importance. I was pleasantly surprised by this lack of concern, having expected at least some raised eyebrows. Actually, I was a little disappointed. I had a sensation that what was happening to me was something quite extraordinary, and it was a little deflating to have it regarded as perfectly normal.

'It's only because you feel that you're breaking some kind of taboo by loving me,' Martin said. 'You'll get over it.'

The first night I spent in my new digs with Martin turned out to be an unsatisfactory affair. The bed was far too narrow for us to sleep together in comfort and it let out the most graphic grating when we started to make love. The floor was the only place for discretion, and we ended up pulling the mattress onto the carpet and sprawling together, half on, half off, in semi-unconsciousness. Waking up at eight was unsatisfactory too. I left Martin to sleep on whilst I swallowed a bowl of cereal and a mug of coffee and left in a desultory haze for the museum.

TWENTY TWO

'It's mine,' I said as I opened the door of my six year old Volkswagen to let Martin in.

'How come?' he asked.

'I bought it.'

'Where did you get the money?'

'It was the £2,500 that my mother returned to me. I've insured the car for both of us.'

'That solves our transport problem, then,' he said, getting in and stroking the faded fabric of his seat with mock reverence. 'Why didn't you tell me you were going to do this?'

'Because I didn't know whether I'd find something I wanted.'

We had initially arranged that we'd take the train to the Kyle of Lochalsh with our bikes, then go from there in the hope of making it down to Oban within a week. But my bicycle was getting old and I hadn't been for a long cycle ride in years. A car was a much better idea.

'Where do you want to go?' I asked as I put the car into gear.

'How about some shady lane where we can make love. Strangely, I've never done it in a car before. It would make a good start to the holiday.'

I didn't think he was serious at first, but he was. We drove out towards Castle Howard and turned off by some woods. A short way up a narrow lane there was a gate into a field which was bordered by the wood. I drove in feeling lightly clandestine and parked in the shadows.

When we pushed the front seats forward as far as they could go, there still wasn't much room in the back. In fact it was very uncomfortable, for both of us. I couldn't stretch my legs, and Martin ended up with his knees jammed against the back of the driver's seat. I was also absurdly frightened that someone would discover us, and kept on looking out of the windows to check. We didn't take our clothes off. Martin pulled his trousers down and opened his shirt. I didn't even do that. We clung to each other in a constricted embrace that inhibited movement, and made us short of breath.

Afterwards we lay together in a grotesque embrace, my arm stretched out between the front seats, and Martin crushed into embryonic submission beneath me. Martin smiled and struggled to stretch.

'I'll never do that again,' he said, 'I feel like I've broken my back.'

I disentangled myself from him so that I could zip up my flies.

'Still,' I said, 'at least we can say that we've done it.'

He nodded.

'Though I'm not sure who I'd want to tell.'

Once in the front again, I looked back and noticed a fine streak of semen across one of the back seats.

'Would you lean over and wipe that up,' I said as I started the car.

'No, leave it,' said Martin. 'It can be a touching memento – a car seat forever stained by love.'

The drive up north the next day took us thirteen hours. I had been stuck in York for too long, and the first sight of mountains made me feel that the provincial flatness of the Vale of York had somehow flattened my own view of the world. Up here the landscape was uncluttered and refreshing.

'I don't know why I've never made the effort to come up here again,' I said to Martin as we left Crainlarich.

Martin shrugged and continued driving.

'I think I'm on a two year time-fuse,' he said. 'If I leave it too long, I get home-sick for the mountains.'

The mountains of Torridon were not spectacular for their scale, but for their ancient wildness. We camped behind the youth hostel there and felt miniaturised by the landscape.

Martin was full of stories about the area. There was an

203

ancient open-air church, Am Ploc, that he took me to one rainy afternoon. It was a place where the rain seemed to echo a spirit of community with the earth, where the rows of rough-hewn stone seats waited in silence for a sermon that would never now be preached. I felt open here, and cleansed by the cold July rain.

Martin looked so at home, unshaven, standing by a cairn at the summit of Beinn Alligin or Liathatch, whilst I looked out at the view, breathtaken, footsore and painfully happy. It rained moderately, which is to say two days of heavy rain, three days of intermittent rain and two days of warm sunshine.

On the last day we took the long walk up to Choire Mhic Fearchair at the back of Beinn Eighe. It was a place that we had meant to visit the last time I'd come to the Highlands, but bad weather had prevented it. This time the day encouraged us with bright sunshine. I set out in old training shoes and jeans; Martin in his stout walking boots and designer outdoor wear. We both wore dark glasses and I at least felt that this day was a day of grace, a gift of light to us both.

The Choire itself rested on a shelf in the crook of the mountain. Scooped by an ancient glacier it still had an ice-age feel about it. It was a large bowl-shaped recess, perhaps half a mile across, with a clear, dark lake in the shallow base of its crucible. A waterfall spattered from a wide lip at the near end. Beyond rose three quartz buttresses, each a thousand feet high. The rocks were shabby with lichen, and the heathered rocks were spongy with moss.

I sat and stared, and shivered at the still beauty. Martin sat beside me and put his arm round my shoulder.

'There's a crashed plane at the far end,' he told me. 'From World War Two. Someone's made a shelter out of part of the wreckage. We'll go and have a look in a minute.'

I could see the path, a fine line that scratched its way round the base of the buttresses to the screes at the end.

'We can climb up this way to the summit, if you've got the energy.' 'It's our last day,' I said. 'There are no mountains on Tiree and I can put up with aching legs. I don't know when I'll next have the chance to come here.'

The little shelter was sadly evocative of the inhospitality of the surroundings. It was more of a windbreak than an actual shelter, as it had no roof. One side was made up of a large strip of torn aluminium, and the other of piled stones. We were here on a bright, warm day. I couldn't imagine what it would be like to be caught here after dark in bad weather.

Climbing scree was exhausting. Twice the effort of walking on solid ground because you kept on slipping back. We had to climb three or four hundred feet like this before we came to a ledge between two peaks. It was eighteen inches wide. On the side we'd come up there was a four hundred foot drop and, on the other, six hundred.

'Neat, huh?' said Martin.

'Scary.'

And that word applies to so many things, I thought. Scary. My sense of vertigo was heightened by my tiredness, and the intoxication I felt with my surroundings; with Martin's presence. Three deer were visible in the distance at the head of a long scree slope, and peak after peak slipped away into the haze.

The summit was flatter, more obscure and more remote than the other two I'd looked from over the past week. Sitting down, I looked out at the view.

'Isn't the world huge,' I said.

It took us six hours to drive to Oban from Torridon. Then a four-and-a-half hour crossing to Tiree, restful whilst we cruised up the Sound of Mull and out into the open sea past the islands of Muck and Eigg. The landscape passed so slowly that it seemed permanent, yet looking up after twenty minutes or so, all the angles had changed.

'Over there,' said Martin, consulting his map. 'Those islands there, they're called the Treshnish Isles. That middle one is called The Dutchman's Cap.'

'Very appropriate,' I said, 'considering its shape.'

'Yes,' he said, looking out at the islands and behind at

the distant peak of Ben More. 'We'll be there soon. Let's go up front and see if it's in view.'

Tiree was clearly visible – a flat island rucked across the horizon like a ruffled carpet. Over the next forty minutes it gradually expanded to fill our horizon. The pier, neatly spiking into the bay from the middle of the island, was a fragile strand of connection and focus. There was quite a crowd waiting for the boat, and pens full of sheep awaiting transportation. As we approached, Alasdair and Graham could be seen on the far right of those waiting. They were both wearing jeans and dark windcheaters; calm and still, waiting slightly separate to everyone else so that they stood silhouetted against the sand behind them.

As Alasdair picked us out amongst the other passengers leaning over the railings, he raised his hand and smiled. Graham made no move at all. We both waved back and went down to get our bags.

'I'm nervous,' said Martin as we took our place in the crush of people waiting to get off.

'Me too,' I agreed.

The tide was up and the gang plank steep. We edged down onto the pier and into the breeze, sun casting crisp shadows across the concrete.

Alasdair held out his hand and, as we greeted each other, he took my bag. Graham patted me on the shoulder in a more casual manner.

'Only twenty-five minutes late,' he said. 'Not bad.'

'Did you park your car okay?' Alasdair asked.

'Yes, by the station in Oban,' I said. 'No problem.'

'Good. Let's go.'

We started off towards his car which was parked on the slope down to the pier.

'Brought swimming things?' Alasdair asked.

'Of course,' Martin said, 'as requested.'

'Excellent.'

Graham drove us down to the south end of the island, to the long curve of Balephuil Bay. Here we took our first swim of the week in the clear, breath shatteringly cold sea; great rolling breakers tumbling us over the sand. This was followed by a picnic of wholemeal bread, exotic herb pate, bottled asparagus, dried preserved tomatoes, olives, dates, cold wine and hot coffee.

'We bought most of this food in Edinburgh on the way up,' Alasdair told us, 'to supplement what we can get in the little Co-Op by the harbour.'

Out of the wind it was warm and we lay on towels to sunbathe as we ate. We talked of our journey, of the weather and of the island.

'I'll take you up to Ceinn a' Mhara after this,' Alasdair told us. 'Up past the ruined chapel.'

'You should be honoured,' Graham told us. 'Alasdair is very selfish about Tiree. He wants to keep it all to himself. It's quite something for him to let others see his secret places.'

'You've seen all my secret places,' Martin whispered to me as he leant his chin on my bare shoulder.

'We'll leave all this lot here,' Alasdair said, 'and open the second thermos of coffee when we come back.'

Walking along the beach I looked out at the sea and thought: this was so easy. All I had done was get in a car and drive up here. It was as simple as that. I had left so many things behind that I thought were intrinsic parts of myself, but which turned out to be simply excess baggage. I'd left behind my worries about time and routine; my preoccupation with finding somewhere to live and with framing and surrounding myself with my father's work – with worrying about what would happen to us when Martin went to London...

Here we were instead, walking through the sensual undulations of grassed-over dunes, the insistent breeze echoing the hissing sound of distant waves. I was basking in the simple landscape; in the touch of Martin's hand, and the casual openness with which Alasdair and Graham had given their hospitality.

That first day was like the rest of the week. Lots of food, sun, walking, conversation, swimming and the pleasure of being with people who knew the island. We were shown the tiny ruined chapel, the dramatic turbulent waves of the deep cleft at Ceinn 'a Mhara – pronounced Kenavara – the strange stone on the middle of the north side that rang with a musical note when struck. We explored the ancient fortifications – the Brochs and Duns. We had long dinners; long arguments about life and politics.

But it wasn't perfect. Very soon after we arrived – on the second day perhaps – I noticed that there was something wrong with Martin. He was unusually subdued; saddened by things I couldn't name. I felt that he was withdrawing from me, and though we still held each other at night, there was something absent about him. I couldn't talk to him about it, because I couldn't be sure it wasn't my imagination. But it began to make me feel introspective too, and as the week wore on our conversations became more wistful and more about the nature of beauty and creation. Several times we talked about death and suicide, as though it was a subject of intimate concern.

On the last day we all split up and each went to our favourite place of the past week. Martin went back to Ceinn 'a Mhara, Alasdair to the long, wild beach by Ben Hough, Graham to Loch 'a Phuil. I went to Hynish, the southern tip of the island, with its steep inclines and intricately worn rocks. It was like being surrounded by sculptures. The sea had worn the rock into twists, indentations filled with clear water, tall columns perforated with eye-like holes. We had arranged to meet at five on the beach on the north side of Ceinn 'a Mhara for tea.

There was something memorable about the solitary way that I was utterly happy with my own company, utterly unpreoccupied and refreshingly free from a sense of loneliness or isolation. I even managed to sing to myself once in a while – something I never do in public because my singing voice is so embarrassingly flat.

As I came over the rise of Ceinn 'a Mhara, I could see Graham's car being driven carefully through the dunes towards the beach where we were to meet. Further away, perhaps a little over a mile, I could see two figures walking towards me. Although it was impossible to tell, I was sure that it was Martin and Alasdair, and I was suddenly absolutely sure that they were talking about me.

TWENTY THREE

At dinner we drank Co-Op white wine, and afterwards Alasdair produced a bottle of port.

'Saved for this evening,' he told us, arranging four small glass tumblers.

'Look,' said Martin, 'I think I'll have mine later if that's okay.'

He got up and went to the door.

'Where are you going?' I asked.

'Out for some air,' he told me, and left.

I pushed my chair back, ready to get up and follow him, but Alasdair gave me an intense look that said "let him go". He calmly poured three glasses of port.

'What's going on?' I asked. 'Why is Martin being like this?'

'Don't you know?' Alasdair asked in return.

'No,' I said. 'I don't.'

Alasdair shrugged.

'I know he's been talking to you,' I said.

Alasdair nodded.

'So tell me what's the matter.'

'Well,' he said. 'I don't know where to begin.'

'Maybe I should go out for a walk too,' said Graham.

'No, it's okay,' Alasdair told him.

I looked at Alasdair and laughed.

'Oh, I see,' I smiled. 'He's asked you to give me a talking to.'

'I wouldn't put it like that.'

'But that's more or less it.'

Alasdair shrugged.

'Okay, what have I done wrong?'

'Nothing wrong,' he said.

'No,' Graham agreed, handing me a tumbler of port. 'And anyway, what is wrong?'

'I feel like a schoolboy,' I said. 'I feel as if I've been called into the masters' common room for a telling off.'

Alasdair looked upset by this. Graham laughed.

'All this has nothing to do with us, Peter,' he said. 'It's between you and Martin. We're not here to tell you anything.'

'Except,' said Alasdair, 'that Martin asked me to explain his feelings.'

'Why couldn't he have done it himself?'

'Have you ever done it to him?' Alasdair asked. 'Have you ever told him how you feel about him.'

'Of course,' I said. 'It's obvious what I feel for him.'

'But have you actually told him, in words?'

'Told him what? That I love him?'

'Yes.'

'No, I don't think so. Not in words.'

'It's a strange business,' said Graham, 'relationships. They need to be constantly reaffirmed. People are so insecure about themselves that they need to have the obvious stated over and over again. If you care for someone, you've got to tell them. Every day.'

'I'm not that demonstrative,' I said. 'I can't go up to Martin and throw my arms round him and tell him that I love him.'

'Why not?' Graham asked.

'I don't know, I just can't.'

'You're going to have to do something,' said Graham. 'You've got to reassure Martin. You've got to give him some indication of what you feel for him. He deserves it.'

'Sex is something that has just happened to you,' Alasdair told me. 'Love is something that people have had to thrust upon you, and you simply let it happen.'

He looked straight into my eyes and held my gaze until I looked away. I felt absolutely powerless in the face of his strength of will.

'I've seen this before,' he went on, 'in your father. You're the same, and all I can say is do something Peter, because if you sit back and wait for life to play into your hands, then it will slip through your fingers and leave you with

211

nothing. Take control for once. Do what you want, not what others have pushed you into. Why does Martin always have to make the first move?'

I couldn't answer that. I felt childish in front of Graham and Alasdair, foolish. I stood up slowly.

'Okay,' I said. 'I'll go and look for Martin.'

He was up by the tiny sandy cove round from the north point. I knew I'd find him there, because this was where we'd come stargazing on the second night; where we'd made love on the beach and felt close. He was sitting on a rock in the gathering dusk and looking out to sea. I sat beside him and he didn't look at me; just continued to stare out to sea.

'Everyone,' I said slowly, 'everyone that I've been to bed with has seduced me. I've never instigated anything. Even Anna was the one to make the first move. I'd never thought about it until now – that I'm a person that lets things happen rather than makes things happen. Because I couldn't see this about myself, I didn't understand it as a problem. I thought it was because I'm shy, because I'm undemonstrative. I thought that people would intuitively know what I wanted. I especially thought that you would know what I feel, because you've known me so long.'

I stopped talking and looked at Martin. Everything was quiet. Even the unruffled sea was silent.

'It's my birthday tomorrow,' said Martin. 'I'm going to be twenty.'

'I know,' I said.

Martin leaned down, scooped up a handful of sand and threw it as far as he could. It shushed across the surface, leaving dull streaks that stretched down through the clear water.

'I'm sorry I'm so undemonstrative,' I told him. 'But you must know how I feel about you.'

'Why should I know that?' he asked.

'Because we've been so close.'

Martin leant back and looked up at the sky.

'I should have talked to you before,' he said.

'I thought things happened between people without the

need to talk about it,' I said. 'I suppose I never said anything to you about how I feel because I was afraid to make a commitment to the future.'

'I don't want a commitment to the future,' he said. 'I want a commitment to the present.'

I looked carefully at his face.

'I love you so much that it frightens me,' I said.

In that moment I realised that this was true. I was afraid of failing with Martin, and so I'd never really begun with him.

'Come on,' he said, 'let's go for a swim.'

He stood up and began to take off his clothes. I followed suit in the cool evening air. We waded out and gasped at the cold. When I took the plunge, I kept my eyes open in the darkening water.